Elizabeth Bennet's Excellent Adventure

A Pride and Prejudice Vagary

by Regina Jeffers

Regency Solutions

Copyright © 2015 by Regina Jeffers
Cover Design by Sarah Callaham
Interior Text Design by Sarah Callaham
All Rights Reserved.

All rights Reserved under International and Pan-American Copyright Conventions. No part of this book may be used or reproduced, transmitted, downloaded, decompiled, reverse engineered, or stored in or introduced into any information storage and retrieval system, in any form or by any means whether electronic or mechanical, including photocopying, recording, etc., now known or hereinafter invented without the written permission from the author and copyright owner except in the case of brief quotation embodied in critical articles and reviews.

This is a work of fiction. Names, characters, places and incidents either are the product of the author's imagination or are used fictitiously, and any resemblance to any actual persons, living or dead, events, business establishments, or locales is entirely coincidental.

Elizabeth Bennet's Excellent Adventure

A Pride and Prejudice Vagary

Regency Solutions

Chapter 1

I KNEW YOU BUT A MONTH before I felt that you were the last man in the world whom I could ever be prevailed on to marry.

Darcy closed the door behind him; Elizabeth Bennet's rebuke rang in his mind as he walked the quarter mile to Rosing Park and entered the manor through the servants' quarters. On this evening, he would not return to his Aunt Catherine's drawing room. Darcy was not fit for company.

Closing his eyes to the reality of Miss Elizabeth's rejection, Darcy leaned his head against the wood panel. It took all his well-honed discipline not to slam the demme thing upon his entrance. It would do his temper well to rattle every edifice in this wing of Rosings, but Darcy wanted no one to know of his return to the manor until he could bring his emotions under control.

"As if that will ever occur," he groaned in frustration as he pushed off from the door.

He ripped his cravat free and tossed the cloth across the back of the nearest chair.

"How can the chit be so ill advised?" Darcy fumed. "She is more concerned with Mr. Wickham's supposed 'misfortunes' than the brilliance of a connection to my esteemed family."

Darcy spit the word "misfortunes," the taste of the word

not suiting his tongue.

"I credited the lady with more insight than what she displayed."

Collapsing across the bed, Darcy covered his face with one of the bed's pillows, attempting to block out the image of Elizabeth Bennet's perfect countenance, but a pair of fine eyes and a crooked smile of anticipation claimed his mind. Images of kissing Elizabeth's soft lips easily invaded.

Tossing the pillow away, Darcy sat up abruptly.

"How am I to be rid of her? How does a man rip out his heart and toss it aside?"

He stood to pour himself a stiff drink, tossed if off, and filled the glass a second time.

"I permitted the lady her say," Darcy reasoned aloud, "and her unpredicted response stole my reason. I did not counter well."

Darcy made a circuit of his room while he sipped the brandy, praying the activity and the drink would calm his heart and numb his mind.

"What would Miss Elizabeth do if I told her that in the short time I held her acquaintance proved to me we were meant for each other? Or that I will relive forever every interaction we held and the joy I experienced at bringing an elusive smile to her lips?"

Darcy paused in mid stride: The image of Elizabeth Bennet filled him with deep regret for opportunities lost.

"Why did I not say as such to the lady?" he wondered aloud. "Did Miss Elizabeth not deserve to be wooed?" Darcy groaned in self-chastisement. "What did I say to bring forth the lady's censure?"

Darcy sat heavily in the nearest chair. Leaning his head against the back's cushion, he closed his eyes to relive those few minutes that changed his life for the worse.

Miss Elizabeth did not discourage him after Darcy confessed his regard for her, and he took her silence as permission to continue. He thought he spoke well of his feelings.

"Did I err in expressing my initial disdain for the lady's

family obstacles?"

He shook off the idea as quickly as it arrived.

"Certainly Miss Elizabeth must understand the need to speak the truth of our joining. Most assuredly many would offer Miss Elizabeth their disdain, labeling her with most unkind words. I meant only to warn her of the obstacles we would encounter."

He set the drink glass down hard upon the table.

"What is there to do but depart Rosings and place the woman behind you?" he told the empty room.

Darcy stood in dejection to wrestle his jacket from his shoulders and to remove his waistcoat, but he could not shake the idea that he had something yet to say to Elizabeth Bennet.

"A farewell letter," he whispered the possibility. "One that addresses the lady's assertions of Mr. Wickham and one that has Miss Elizabeth cursing her inability to recognize how she wasted the opportunity to save her family from the entailment hanging over them like the sword of Damocles.

"Writing such will permit me the release I require to start again," Darcy reasoned. "To place at Miss Elizabeth's feet the blame of her rashness."

Recognizing the exercise for what it truly was–an opportunity to assuage his anger and his pride, Darcy sat at the desk to put pen to paper. He would hold nothing in check, not his anger at Elizabeth Bennet's misguided defense of George Wickham, or Darcy's deep passion for the woman.

"Be rid of my demons," he murmured as he wrote the salutation "Miss Bennet."

Over the next hour Darcy filled several sheets of foolscap. He permitted himself the pleasure of describing George Wickham in the crudest terms available in Darcy's vocabulary for almost as quickly as he decided to write to Elizabeth, Darcy knew he would never present the letter to her. Darcy had no intention of ever seeing the woman again; therefore, he claimed the freedom of saying what he never could have of his former friend.

Afterwards, Darcy tossed those pages to the side and began

his "love" letter anew.

> *My dear Miss Bennet,*
> *It grieves me to know I brought despair to your lovely countenance. It grieves me that all I said and did was for naught, for I wished nothing more than to claim your heart. It grieves me that the shadow of a man, not truly your equal, claims the regard I desire. I parted from you with a heavy heart–with the knowledge that you think I am proud and stern and highhanded when, in truth, I wish only to protect and cherish you. Even after our words of disparagement, there is one thing I can never give you: I cannot promise never to love you.*

Some time later, his reason returned, Darcy downed another drink before stretching out his long frame upon the bed. Thinking he might sleep a few hours before it was necessary to explain his early departure from Rosings to Lady Catherine, he closed his eyes. Yet, no relief was to be had. His exercise in exorcism proved fruitless.

"What am I to do?"

True his heartbeat had slowed to normal, but Darcy's chest still ached from disappointed hopes.

"I cannot permit Miss Elizabeth to execute a connection to Mr. Wickham. It would kill me to think of her heavy with Mr. Wickham's child. I could accept her happiness with another, but not with my father's godson. Moreover, I owe the lady a proper explanation for my interference in Bingley's life. I must sever the ties properly; I cannot permit our connection to end in such bitterness."

Resolved to act with honor, Darcy rose to return to the desk. He caught the pages where he spoke of Wickham's baser actions, and tossed them upon the dying embers before tossing another log upon the fire.

Before beginning anew, he folded the pages where he spoke

of his devotion to Elizabeth and sealed them with a wax wafer. With a sigh of inevitability, Darcy took up the pen a second time. He never thought one of his duties would be to release the woman he loved to another, but Fate possessed a bizarre sense of humor. With a freshly sharpened point to the quill, he scratched out the necessary apology.

> *Be not alarmed, madam, on receiving this letter, but the apprehension of its containing any repetition of those sentiments, or renewal of those offers, which were last night so disgusting to you. I write without any intention of paining your, or humbling myself, by dwelling on wishes which, for the happiness of both, cannot be too soon forgotten: and the effort which the formation and the perusal of this letter must occasion should have been spared, had not my character required it to be written and read. You must therefore pardon the freedom with which I demand your attention; your feelings, I know, will bestow it unwillingly, but I demand it of your justice.*

Darcy read back over this first paragraph and frowned.

"Not what I wish to say to the lady," he grumbled, "but it is more aligned to Miss Elizabeth's sensibilities."

He returned the pen to the cradle.

"It would be bloody more pleasurable simply to kiss the chit into submission."

With a sad chuckle of resignation, Darcy resumed his cautionary tale to the woman who owned his heart.

Elizabeth wished she could rise from the bed and pace the floor, but as she shared the room at Hunsford Cottage with Maria Lucas, all Elizabeth could do was to stare at the draperies and relive her confrontation with Mr. Darcy.

The gentleman's proposal left Elizabeth beyond expression.

Dumbfounded, she did not initially react. In silence, she cursed her inaction. Mr. Darcy's words incensed her. There was no affection in his recitation upon his heart and his pride or in his sense of her inferiority, of its being a degradation, or of the family obstacles, which judgment opposed in inclination.

In spite of Elizabeth's deeply rooted dislike of the gentleman, she could not be insensible to the compliment of such a man's attentions, and she was at first sorry for the pain Mr. Darcy received; till, roused to resentment by his subsequent language, Elizabeth lost all compassion in her anger.

Despite her frustration with the Mr. Darcy, Elizabeth attempted to compose herself to answer him with patience. Yet, her reason deserted her when the gentleman concluded his speech by representing to her the strength of that attachment, which, in spite of all his endeavors, he found impossible to conquer, and with expressing his hope that it would be rewarded by her acceptance of his hand.

The gentleman held no doubt of a favorable response, she thought. *Did Mr. Darcy truly know so little of my nature? Mr. Darcy spoke of apprehension and anxiety, but his countenance expressed real security.*

The realization exasperated Elizabeth's fragile control. A rush of heat climbed up her neck, claiming her cheeks. She was well and truly caught in a maelstrom of emotions. She recalled how, in instinct, Elizabeth squared her jaw and set her resolve to deliver her sally.

Mr. Darcy leaned against the mantelpiece with his eyes fixed on her face. He seemed to catch her remarks about how his regard would know an easy death with no less resentment than surprise. His complexion paled with anger, and the disturbance of his mind was visible in every feature. The gentleman struggle for the appearance of control, and he refused to open his lips until he believed himself to have attained it. Elizabeth found the pause deuced frustrating.

When Mr. Darcy spoke again it was with forced calmness, a control Elizabeth both admired and despised.

She made her accusations regarding Bingley and Jane, confirming her suspicions from her earlier conversation with Colonel Fitzwilliam. Elizabeth thought Mr. Darcy wholly unmoved by any feeling of remorse. The dratted man even looked at her with a smile of affected incredulity. How did one argue with someone who displayed no emotions beyond a lift of his eyebrow?

"Can you deny that you have done it?" she demanded.

With assumed tranquility Mr. Darcy replied: *"I have no wish of denying that I did everything in my power to separate my friend from your sister, or that I rejoice in my success. Toward him I have been kinder than toward myself."*

Elizabeth disdained the appearance of this civil reflection, but its meaning did not escape her, nor did it offer her any conciliation. In retribution, she assaulted Mr. Darcy with Mr. Wickham's repeated tales of neglect.

Elizabeth held no idea why she chose Mr. Wickham to defend. The officer quickly abandoned her when those in the neighborhood learned of Miss King's fortune. Perhaps it was because Mr. Wickham's desertion still stung her pride, and indirectly Mr. Darcy's negligent behavior toward the gentleman's esteemed father's godson kept Mr. Wickham from considering Elizabeth more than a mild flirtation. Perhaps it was because Mr. Darcy's initial snub hurt more than Elizabeth would ever admit, and she meant to even the field. Perhaps it was because Mr. Darcy's observations regarding her family found the target.

Whatever her reasons, Elizabeth knew from the manner in which Mr. Darcy kept secrets regarding Mr. Wickham that her defense of the man would ruffle Mr. Darcy's feathers as the gentleman did hers.

"But disguise of every sort is my abhorrence," Mr. Darcy declared.

Despite her best efforts, Elizabeth had to concede that point: Mr. Darcy was cruelly honest.

An errant thought demanded her attention: *If Mr. Darcy is as honest as you believe, was it necessary to question the depth of the man's affections?*

Such was a prospect upon which Elizabeth refused to spend time in contemplation for the idea frightened her more than she could express.

Even so, when Elizabeth permitted it, the thought she might accept Mr. Darcy if she knew nothing of his involvement with Jane's separation from Bingley took root.

And as to Wickham, she was not foolish enough not to recognize Mr. Wickham spoke too freely of his claims of abuse at Mr. Darcy's hands. Although Elizabeth appreciated Mr. Wickham's singling her out, she knew something of the way of the world, and as incensed as she was at Mr. Wickham's misfortunes, Jane's caution regarding the esteem with which Society held Mr. Darcy did not slip Elizabeth's notice.

The tumult of Elizabeth's mind remained painfully great. With Mr. Darcy's exit, she knew not how to support herself, and, from actual weakness, sat down and cried for half an hour. Her astonishment, as she reflected on what passed, increased by every review of it. That she should receive an offer of marriage from Mr. Darcy, that he should be in love with her for so many months; so much in love as to wish to marry her in spite of all the objections which made him prevent his friend's marrying her sister, and which must appear at least with equal force in his own case was almost incredible!

It was gratifying to inspire unconsciously so strong an affection. But his pride, Mr. Darcy's abominable pride, his shameless avowal of what he did with respect to Jane, his unpardonable assurance in acknowledging though he could not justify it, and the unfeeling manner in which he mentioned Mr. Wickham, his cruelty toward whom he did not attempt to deny, soon overcame the pity which the consideration of his attachment had for a moment excited.

And still the memories invaded her sleep. She relived the events again and again, praying each time would be the last. *How was she to face Mr. Darcy? Did his cousin know of the gentleman's intentions? Would the colonel shun hr? How was Elizabeth to explain the change in the tenor of her relationship with Mr. Darcy? Was there a means to sweep the incident from Mr. Collins' threshold? And what would Lady Catherine and Mr. Collins do if they gleaned a hint of Elizabeth's daring to entice Mr. Darcy?*

Darcy had less than three hours sleep, but he meant to encounter Miss Elizabeth in the parkland before he set a course for London. He would deliver his explanation into her hands and then disappear from the lady's life.

"I wish to depart for London after breaking my fast," Darcy instructed his valet as Sheffield tied a perfect cravat on the first attempt.

"Everything will be as you wish, Sir," Sheffield responded crisply.

"Do you know whether Colonel Fitzwilliam summoned his man of yet?" he inquired.

"He has not, Sir."

Darcy brushed Sheffield's hands away.

"You may attend the dust upon my person after my morning walk in the park," Darcy ordered. "I mean to speak to my cousin regarding my departure and then claim a bit of exercise in the plantation."

Darcy dabbed at a nick on his chin with a clean cloth. Distracted by the image of Elizabeth Bennet, he cut the tip of his chin when he insisted upon shaving himself over Sheffield's objections. He strained to see the small opening that seeped blood.

"What of your letters, Sir?" Sheffield asked.

Darcy leaned closer to the small mirror.

"Place the thicker one inside my coat pocket and the other in my trunk," he murmured.

Assured the cut would not stain his cravat, Darcy permitted Sheffield to assist him into his greatcoat.

"I shan't be long," he assured before disappearing into the

bowels of Rosings Park.

Elizabeth awoke the next morning to the same thoughts and meditations, which had at length closed her eyes. She could not yet recover from the surprise of what happened; it was impossible to think of anything else, and, totally indisposed for employment, she resolved soon after breakfast to indulge herself in air and exercise.

She was proceeding directly to her favorite walk, when the recollection of Mr. Darcy's sometimes coming there stopped her, and instead of entering the park, she turned up the lane that led her farther from the turnpike road. The park paling was still the boundary on one side, and she soon passed one of the gates into the ground.

After walking two or three times along that part of the lane, the pleasantness of the morning tempted her to stop at the gates and look into the park. The five weeks she passed in Kent made a great difference in the country, and every day added to the verdure of the early trees. She was on the point of continuing her walk, when she caught a glimpse of a gentleman within the sort of grove that edged the park; he was moving her way; and fearful of its being Mr. Darcy, Elizabeth directly retreated. But the person who advanced was now near enough to see her, and stepping forward with eagerness, pronounced her name.

Elizabeth turned away, but on hearing herself called, though in a voice which proved it to be Mr. Darcy, she moved again towards the gate.

He had by that time reached it also, and holding out a letter, which she instinctively took, said with a look of haughty composure, "I have been walking in the grove some time in the hope of meeting you. Will you do me the honor of reading that letter?"

And then, with a slight bow, he turned again into the plantation and was soon from sight.

With no expectation of pleasure, but with the strongest curiosity, Elizabeth opened the letter, and, to her still increasing wonder, perceived an envelope containing several sheets of letter paper, written quite through in a very close hand. Pursuing her way along the lane, she began her reading.

It was all Darcy could do to walk away from Elizabeth Bennet. All his hopes of knowing happiness rested in the woman. Certainly he would claim another to wife for Darcy owed his family name an heir for Pemberley, but another would never claim more than his name. As he took his chosen mate to bed to beget a son, Darcy would close his eyes and imagine Elizabeth beneath him. His actions would not speak well of him, and Darcy would regret them, but he knew it would be so.

In emotional disturbance, he stumbled upon the path, and for a moment Darcy thought to seek Miss Elizabeth out and beg her to reconsider. He lifted his eyes to the new day, but it would not prove fair for him. Darcy would return to the loneliness that haunted him for years. The blood still rushed through his veins, but no life sprung from his chest. Darcy thought Elizabeth a treasure to cherish, but he erred.

The realization was more than he could bear. Darcy wished to rail at the world. To cry for his loss. To pray for a different outcome. Yet, as a man of many responsibilities, such luxury of self-indulgence was not afforded to his ilk.

If Elizabeth, when Mr. Darcy gave her the letter, did not expect it to contain a renewal of his offers, she formed no expectation at all of its contents. But such as they were, it may well be supposed how eagerly she went through the missive, and what a contrariety of emotions the man's words excited. Her feelings as she read were scarcely to be defined.

"How dare he?" Elizabeth murmured more than once.

She read with an unexplained eagerness, which hardly left her power of comprehension; and, from impatience of knowing what the next sentence might bring; she was incapable of attending to the sense of the one before her eyes. Mr. Darcy expressed no regret for what he did to Jane and Mr. Bingley, and his words smacked of pride and insolence; yet, Elizabeth's feelings remained more acutely painful and more difficult to define. Astonishment. Apprehension. Wonder. And even horror. She wished to discredit Mr. Darcy's words entirely, but a part of her claimed his recital as worthy.

Flustered by the honesty with which the gentleman spoke, Elizabeth placed the letter in a pocket.

"I shan't look upon it again," she declared. "I will not regard it. When the opportunity arrives, I shall burn it."

In a perturbed state of mind, with thoughts that could rest on nothing, Elizabeth walked on, but it would not do. In half a minute, she retrieved the letter from its hiding place. Collecting herself as well as she could, she read Mr. Darcy's letter again.

Elizabeth was struck by the impropriety of what the letter held in regards to her appraisal of Mr. Darcy and Mr. Wickham. Elizabeth wondered how the feelings of both men escaped her previously. She noted the indelicacy of putting himself forward as Mr. Darcy did–of the means by which the gentleman described the anguish of the betrayal in which she unconsciously participated. The inconsistencies of the conduct of all concerned screamed her name.

That as proud and repulsive as were Mr. Darcy's manners, Elizabeth never in the whole course of their acquaintance–an acquaintance which latterly brought them much together and which gave her a sort of intimacy with his ways–saw anything that betrayed Mr. Darcy to be unprincipled or unjust–that among his connections he was esteemed and valued.

Although Mr. Darcy's letter shocked her, Elizabeth could not help but to place the blame of the gentleman's despair upon her shoulders.

After wandering along the lane for two hours, giving way to every variety of thought, reconsidering events, determining probabilities, and reconciling herself, as well as she could, to a change of sudden and so important, fatigue and a recollection of her long absence made Elizabeth, at length, return to Hunsford Cottage.

She entered the house with the wish of appearing cheerful as usual and the resolution of repressing such reflections as must make her unfit for conversation.

"Lizzy, I worried for you," Charlotte said in concern. "I thought to send Mr. Collins to search you out."

"Forgive me, Charlotte. I discovered a beautiful meadow filled with a variety of the most exquisite wildflowers," Elizabeth stated boldly. "I could not resist their appeal."

Elizabeth's remark was not a complete fabrication. Only last week, Mr. Darcy shared the meadow his mother once claimed as a favorite at Rosings. Elizabeth's thoughts drifted again to the enigma known as "Mr. Fitzwilliam Darcy."

"I forgot the time," she finished on a rush.

"You shall be sorry," Maria Lucas chastised, "for Mr. Darcy and Colonel Fitzwilliam called to offer their farewells."

"Farewells?"

Elizabeth found a frown of disappointment claiming her forehead. She held no desire to encounter Mr. Darcy again so soon, but Elizabeth could not shove away the feeling of regret creeping into her chest.

"I did not know the gentlemen meant to depart so soon."

Charlotte took up her sister's tale.

"Mr. Darcy remained only for a few minutes before he took his leave, but the colonel tarried for nearly an hour, hoping for your return."

"The colonel expressed a desire to walk after you," Maria said in awe. "Imagine engendering the attentions of an earl's son."

Elizabeth's thoughts were not of Lord Matlock's son, but rather his nephew.

"I am sorry to miss them," she declared, and despite her dread of another meeting with Mr. Darcy, Elizabeth meant her words.

Elizabeth possessed no idea of how she could look Mr. Darcy in the eye after reading his letter; yet, she did not like the idea of never knowing the gentleman again.

"If you will pardon me, I shall place my cloak in my room and then rejoin you so we might continue the sampler Charlotte wishes to send to Lady Lucas," Elizabeth said with practiced courtesy.

"Why do you not leave your cloak on the peg by the door?" Maria observed.

"Because I mean to brush the dust from the hem once the morning dew dries," Elizabeth countered.

She hurried away before Maria could lodge another objection.

Inside the small bedroom, Elizabeth fished Mr. Darcy's letter from where she concealed it beneath her arm. Her cloak hid all traces of the cream-colored paper against her brown day dress. She slid Mr. Darcy's missive between layers of her unmentionables. She would make an excuse to return to the room later to secure the letter and perhaps read it again. The wonder of it all mortified her while making Elizabeth quite giddy.

Chapter 2

THE MOMENT ELIZABETH OPENED THE DOOR to the room and spotted the pale countenance of Maria Lucas, she knew her world tilted upon its points. Maria held Mr. Darcy's letter in her hands.

"What are you about?" she demanded as she attempted to conjure up an appropriate excuse for the letter's presence in her belongings.

Maria jumped in surprise. A flush of color spread across the girl's cheeks.

"Oh, Lizzy, I am so sorry. I searched for the green ribbon you borrowed two nights prior."

The letter fluttered in the air as Maria gestured to the dresser they shared. As foolish as it would sound to others, Elizabeth prayed Maria's handling of the letter did not damage it.

"I did not mean to intrude," the girl pleaded.

Elizabeth closed the door behind her.

"Yet, you did intrude on my privacy."

Maria glanced to the still open drawer containing Elizabeth's intimate wear.

"This letter," the girl whispered through her bewilderment. "It is from Mr. Darcy."

Elizabeth fought the urge to groan.

"It is," she said simply.

Maria lifted the pages as if to read from them.

"Who would think stuffy old Mr. Darcy could write such a letter?" Maria declared in awe.

Elizabeth crossed the short space to snatch the pages from the girl's fingers.

"Still waters carve a deep path to reach the river," she snapped.

Elizabeth had no idea why she defended the man, but she strongly disliked the idea of anyone calling Mr. Darcy "stuffy," but her.

"Mr. Darcy is in love," Maria continued as if Elizabeth offered no response.

"Perhaps," she said enigmatically as she unconsciously smoothed the pages to refold them.

"No perhaps about it," Maria protested. "Mr. Darcy is violently in love with..."

Maria gasped for air, and Elizabeth braced her shoulders against the accusation. She had not had time enough to analyze Mr. Darcy's professions of affections.

"In love with...Miss Bennet. With your sister Jane. Did Mr. Darcy ask you to serve as courier? Is that the reason you always disclaim the gentleman's worth?"

The girl's words stunned Elizabeth, and it took several elongated seconds before she drew her wits about her.

"I assure you, Maria, that Mr. Darcy does not speak of Jane," she said evenly.

"But the letter is addressed to *Miss Bennet*, and it speaks of another man not your sister's equal. Surely Mr. Darcy speaks of Mr. Bingley's connections to trade," Maria reasoned. "I never thought of Mr. Bingley's wealth still being a detriment to his attentions to Miss Bennet, but now I understand Mr. Bingley's quick withdrawal from Netherfield after his ball."

Elizabeth shook her head in the negative before sighing

heavily in resignation.

"While in Kent, I am *Miss Bennet* to Lady Catherine and her household," Elizabeth argued. "Without doubt, you heard Her Ladyship address me as such."

Maria's gaze ran over Elizabeth's dowdy appearance.

"Why would Mr. Darcy write such a passionate letter to you?"

"Ask your sister," Elizabeth said testily. "Charlotte remarked more than once of late upon the gentleman's growing regard for me."

"Which you denied," Maria said suspiciously.

"I did not recognize Mr. Darcy's regard," Elizabeth said honestly.

"What will you do about Mr. Darcy's ardor?" Maria demanded. "Unless you mean to marry him–unless there is an understanding, Mr. Darcy should not speak to you with so much familiarity."

Elizabeth replaced the letter in the drawer and closed it. She cursed herself for being so lackadaisical in regards to the letter's security.

"Is there any hope you could forget you saw the letter?" she asked cautiously.

Maria's frown lines deepened.

"It is not proper, Lizzy. A gentleman should not take such liberties. You are a gentleman's daughter, not a woman the man means to make his mistress."

Elizabeth sat on the edge of the bed.

"Would you permit me to speak to Charlotte before anyone learns of this letter, especially my cousin? Mr. Collins would take umbrage with my drawing Mr. Darcy's regard from Miss De Bourgh. This situation must be treated with discretion."

"Mr. Darcy must be made to speak an honest proposal, Lizzy," the girl asserted.

Elizabeth thought of last evening's confrontation with the gentleman.

"Trust me, Maria. Mr. Darcy did exactly that."

Two days later, over Lady Catherine's instructions that a proper young lady would not act so foolishly, Elizabeth took the public coach to London. Her Uncle Gardiner would have sent his carriage for her, but there was no time for the luxury of a private coach. Charlotte agreed that Elizabeth must speak to Mr. Darcy as quickly as possible, and so Elizabeth and her long time friend constructed a tale of Mrs. Gardiner taking ill and requiring Elizabeth's assistance.

Thankfully, Mr. Collins did not recall that Jane remained at Gracechurch Street, and Elizabeth could be spared if there were a true need for a caretaker.

"I shall write to Mama to say I mean to keep Maria with me an extra sennight," Charlotte assured. "That should provide you time to convince Mr. Darcy to renew his affections."

Elizabeth was not so certain. She provided Charlotte an abbreviated version of the gentleman's proposal, but at much as Elizabeth wished for a second opportunity to know Mr. Darcy better, she doubted the gentleman would be so inclined. Who would believe that the always-practical Elizabeth Bennet would succumb to Mr. Darcy's pretty words of devotion?

Her family welcomed her with surprised exclamations, but they readily accepted her excuse of Sir William's upcoming return to Kent as the reason for Elizabeth's early departure.

"I could not subject Charlotte to another banishment to Mr. Collins' quarters," she said with a mischievous shutter. "This way, Maria can move in with Charlotte, and Sir William may have the smaller bedroom."

"You should have sent word," her Uncle Gardiner chastised.

"I did, but we received word of a seat available on the mail coach, and I took advantage of it."

If all went as planned, her uncle would receive the hastily written post later that very day.

Jane hugged Elizabeth affectionately.

"You are always so adventurous; I wish I possessed your mettle."

Elizabeth did not feel adventurous; the possibility of another confrontation with Mr. Darcy frightened her. Yet, she knew it would be only a matter of time before Maria Lucas carried the tale of a 'lascivious' letter to the Meryton neighborhood.

Elizabeth's keeping the letter announced her complete ruin. Even so, she could not think upon the man's words without a now more familiar warmth claiming her cheeks. She knew she should curse the fates that prevented her from burying Mr. Darcy's letter before returning to Hunsford Cottage, but Elizabeth's pride at engendering such a passion in a man of Mr. Darcy's stature had her acting without reason–acting very much of the nature of her two youngest sisters.

Over supper, she laid the plan.

"I did not tell you, Jane," Elizabeth said with casual practice, "that Mr. Darcy and his cousin, Colonel Fitzwilliam, joined Lady Catherine's household perhaps a fortnight prior. The gentlemen attend to Her Ladyship's affairs at the quarter day."

"Were you much in Mr. Darcy's company?" her aunt asked more in an afterthought, rather than a question requiring a response. "I wonder if he resembles his late father."

Elizabeth's Aunt Margaret came from Lambton, a village near the Pemberley estate. Mrs. Gardiner knew something of the Darcy family.

"Her Ladyship invited Mr. Collins' household to tea quite often and to cards upon occasion," Elizabeth confided. "Periodically our paths crossed when walking the parkland."

She offered no more information as her aunt appeared content to speak at length upon the Darcys and the family's connections to the Fitzwilliam family of Matlock.

Only once did Elizabeth experience regret at her manipulations. It was when Jane made a private inquiry of Mr. Bingley. Her sister's crestfallen countenance had Elizabeth modifying her plan to contact Mr. Darcy. She would use the opportunity to foster a reunion between Jane and Mr. Bingley.

"A letter, Sir."

Darcy glanced up from his ledger to meet his butler's scowling expression.

"Did not the post arrive earlier?" Darcy inquired.

A shiver of anticipation ran up Darcy's spine. He returned to London four days prior, but the ghost of Elizabeth Bennet still haunted his days and his nights.

"This one came from a young servant at a house in Cheapside," Mr. Thacker said in distaste.

"Thank you, Thacker," Darcy murmured as he examined the flourish of his name upon the paper. It was a feminine hand that wrote his directions upon the folded over page. The realization had Darcy swallowing hard. Did his letter change the lady's mind? Did Miss Elizabeth forgive him?

Darcy wished it were not so early. If so, he would pour himself a stiff drink to bolster his resolve before he broke the wax seal.

"Fool," he grumbled. "The woman is a devious chit. Miss Elizabeth likely means to insult your pride again, saying all the things of which she wishes to accuse me."

Darcy used a penknife to cut away the wax and unfolded the single page. His eyes scanned it to know its purpose.

Mr. Darcy,

As you are likely to recognize, I rejoined my family in London yesterday. As such, it would please me to accept your call at Gracechurch Street during the customary receiving hours.

My sister Jane remains in London with our aunt and uncle. If Mr. Bingley resides at his London address, I am certain Miss Bennet would thrive under the gentleman's attentions.

E. B.

"That is all," Darcy grumbled.

He turned the page over thinking something must certainly be amiss.

"Why in bloody hell did Miss Elizabeth return to London so soon after my departure from Kent? Does she place Mr. Bingley's return to Miss Bennet's side as a contingency to our future connection? Why is Miss Elizabeth suddenly 'pleased to accept my call'? What demme foolishness does the woman practice?'

Darcy thought to ignore her summons, but when he returned to his ledger, the paper teased him from where he tossed it upon his desk. Taunted him. Coaxed him.

"I can never refuse an intriguing puzzle," he grumbled as he took up the letter again. "I must be a glutton for misery to permit the woman's manipulations."

With a sigh of resignation, Darcy rose to summon his man. He must call at the house Bingley let in Town. Darcy prayed Miss Bingley remained in the country with her older sister. It would take all of Darcy's persuasion and likely a well overdue confession to convince Bingley to take up his pursuit of the eldest Bennet daughter, but Darcy would risk losing Bingley's acquaintance if it meant he might maintain a hope of claiming Elizabeth Bennet to wife.

He did not provide Bingley a full confession for Darcy considered the possibility his friend would not accompany him to Gracechurch Street, and Darcy suspected Bingley's appearance would please both Bennet sisters. He did explain to Bingley that he and Miss Elizabeth argued over whether Bingley meant to break Miss Bennet's heart by withdrawing from Netherfield when Darcy and Elizabeth connected in Kent.

"I would never act so cruelly," Bingley protested.

"If you wish to reclaim your acquaintance, I have it on reliable information that Miss Bennet and Miss Elizabeth temporarily reside with Mrs. Bennet's brother in Cheapside. Miss

Elizabeth explained as such before I departed Rosings Park," Darcy said with false calmness.

"Then we must make our addresses," Bingley said with an energy long absent from his friend's demeanor.

Likely when Miss Bennet told Bingley of Caroline's snub when Miss Bennet called upon Miss Bingley, Darcy's friend would hold second thoughts regarding their association, but Darcy would face that dilemma when it occurred.

At length, Mrs. Gardiner's servant showed them into the parlor, and Darcy bowed before Elizabeth's aunt. Surprisingly, it was a flush of color upon Elizabeth's cheeks and the smile turning up the corners of her lips, which caught at Darcy's heart.

"Mr. Darcy. Mr. Bingley," Elizabeth said with what sounded of perfect calm, but she was anything but calm. "Please permit me to give you the acquaintance of my aunt Mrs. Gardiner. Aunt, may I present a gentleman from Derbyshire, Mr. Darcy, and Mr. Bennet's nearest neighbor in Hertfordshire, Mr. Bingley."

"Gentlemen," her aunt said graciously. "How kind of you to call upon our household. Permit me to send for refreshments."

"It is you who are kind to receive us without notice, Ma'am," Bingley said with his typical amiability. "When I learned from Darcy of Mr. Bennet's daughters being guests in your house, I insisted we renew our acquaintance. I pray you will not think us too presumptuous."

"Never so," Elizabeth added quickly. "You are most welcomed."

"Please be seated," Aunt Gardiner gestured to a grouping of chairs. It did Elizabeth well to observe how Mr. Bingley claimed the seat closest to Jane. Perhaps things would progress in that matter.

As to the other gentleman, Mr. Darcy came as she knew he would, but how was she to explain to the man that he must save her honor with another proposal.

"I would recognize you anywhere, Mr. Darcy. You have the look of your late father," her aunt remarked as Elizabeth rang for tea to be brought in.

Mr. Darcy's response spoke of the gentleman's surprise.

"You were familiar with my father, Ma'am?"

"My aunt fares from Lambton, Mr. Darcy," Elizabeth explained.

"My father was Mr. Montgomery, the surgeon," Aunt Gardiner added.

Mr. Darcy nodded his understanding.

"I am familiar with your family, Ma'am. You lost Mr. Montgomery some years past."

"Nearly five years," Aunt Gardiner replied sadly. "Along with my eldest brother. They attempted to save a family caught in the river's rising waters after a terrible storm and lost their lives."

"God moves in unexplained way, Mrs. Gardiner," Mr. Darcy said with what sounded of genuine sympathy. "I am sorry for your loss."

Her aunt bowed her head graciously.

"Let us speak of more pleasant things. Elizabeth tells me you were recently in Kent, Mr. Darcy."

And so the next half hour passed in harmonious conversation. It pleased Elizabeth to observe Mr. Bingley's tender gestures toward Jane and Mr. Darcy's genuine care of Aunt Gardiner's reminiscences. But such was not the reason Elizabeth asked the gentleman to call upon her.

"Mr. Bingley," she addressed Darcy's friend rather than the man himself. "Perhaps Jane and I might show you and Mr. Darcy Aunt Gardiner's prize roses. It is a pleasant day."

"I would enjoy the opportunity to praise Mrs. Gardiner's gardening skills," Mr. Bingley replied with a wide smile." "What of you, Darcy?"

Elizabeth was glad to hear the gentleman acquiesce.

Out in the spring sunshine, Elizabeth walked in silence beside Mr. Darcy. It did not surprise her when Mr. Bingley directed

Jane's steps toward the rose arbor.

Mr. Darcy nodded in the direction of his friend.

"If your sister still wishes the match, it is hers to claim."

"Did you explain your perfidy in Mr. Bingley's unexpected withdrawal from Netherfield?" Elizabeth asked with more sharpness than she intended.

Mr. Darcy shrugged his response.

"Not completely, but I will. Today I feared appearing on your doorstep without Mr. Bingley in tow would earn me no favor."

"And you wished my favor, Mr. Darcy?" Elizabeth asked with an arched eyebrow.

"I wished to learn of the urgency your note implied," he corrected.

Elizabeth gestured to a nearby bench. Once seated, she swallowed a deep steadying breath. She kept her eyes on her hands rather than to look upon Mr. Darcy's countenance.

"Needless to say, your letter brought me moments of unrest," she began softly.

"Unrest was not my objective," Mr. Darcy assured. "I simply wished to clarify my actions, especially as to my conduct with Mr. Wickham."

"Mr. Wickham?"

Elizabeth looked up in confusion.

"There is little in the letter that speaks of Mr. Wickham, and nothing where your former friend is specifically named."

"You must be mistaken," the gentleman insisted. "I disclosed the secret of Mr. Wickham's attempted seduction of a member of my family and the shame he delivered to her door. I pleaded for your discretion, but I thought it important for you to know the truth."

Elizabeth's irritation grew by leaps and bounds.

"Mr. Darcy, if you offered my such confidences, you can be assured that I would never abuse them; however, there is a mistake, but not on my end. I reread the letter only this morning.

It is as if we speak of two different missives."

The gentleman frowned in deep disapproval.

"Would you please describe the letter you received?" he asked in what sounded of dread.

Elizabeth could not keep the blush from claiming her neck and cheeks.

"A lady cannot repeat such promises to a gentleman," she said with a squeak in her voice.

"Please, Miss Elizabeth," Mr. Darcy pleaded.

Elizabeth looked away in embarrassment. She could not understand why Mr. Darcy meant to torment her. She shook her head in the negative as another flush of color sped across her skin.

Mr. Darcy spoke with sympathy.

"Did the letter address my desire to cherish, adore, and protect you?"

Elizabeth nodded in the affirmative this time, but she kept her eyes diverted from Mr. Darcy's.

The gentleman cleared his throat.

"I must apologize, Miss Elizabeth. I wrote more than one letter during the slow hours of the night. The first one, I burned because I spoke of Mr. Wickham in very unflattering terms. I fear my anger controlled my response. Upon second thought, I realized that particular letter was not fit for your eyes."

Mr. Darcy paused as if considering what to say next, and Elizabeth permitted herself several quick glances at his expression, but his features were unreadable.

"I must confess," he continued, "my emotions ruled my response to your refusal of my hand. I suspect the letter I presented you was my reasoning out what occurred at Hunsford Cottage. Again, the letter was never meant for anyone's eyes but mine."

Elizabeth admitted, "Many write of their anger. Mr. Bennet does so. I have witnessed my father scratching out a rant only to toss his efforts into the nearest grate."

"The letter where I offered what I hoped was a logical explanation for my involvement in Bingley's affairs and a recitation of my connection to Mr. Wickham and my turning from my former associate remains in my travel case. It grieves me that my lack of forethought exposed you to my baser side. Please forgive me."

Elizabeth looked upon him for Mr. Darcy spoke of his earnest contrition.

"I am not a wilting flower, Sir," she declared. "And although I knew shock at the familiarity with which you spoke, your words provided me a mirror to your person."

Mr. Darcy grimaced in remorse.

"Pray say the letter softened your heart on my behalf, rather than making you detest me further," he whispered.

Elizabeth was not certain she could admit the emotional turmoil his letter elicited.

"I remain uncertain, Sir. I would appreciate a more thorough explanation in the near future of our sticking points. More importantly, a giving of my heart is not the reason I summoned you to Gracechurch Street."

"Then pray tell what did," Mr. Darcy said testily.

"Whether my heart is engaged or not is irrelevant," Elizabeth declared.

She wished her words held the truth, but she suspected Mr. Darcy's passion invaded her soul.

"Miss Lucas discovered the letter where I secreted it away when I returned to Hunsford Cottage. Mrs. Collins' sister read part of the letter."

Mr. Darcy groaned in disapproval.

"Miss Lucas assumed you meant the letter for Jane and the unworthy gentleman of which you spoke was Mr. Bingley. I immediately claimed the letter as mine. I could not…"

Elizabeth broke off, but Mr. Darcy finished her thought.

"You could not bear to see your sister forced into a marriage with an ogre such as I," he said in sadness.

Elizabeth protested, "Jane could not thrive with a man of your disposition. That fact is more than obvious. My dearest Jane accepts the foibles of others more kindly than I."

Since accepting Mr. Darcy's devotion as a reality, Elizabeth did not think she could bear to observe another at the gentleman's side, but she could not give voice to those feelings. They would make her too vulnerable, and they were too new.

His lips twisted in irony.

"Yours is an understatement of the extreme."

"My temperament is not to your liking, Mr. Darcy?" Elizabeth taunted.

"Not so much your temperament, but I do not find your shrewish tongue brings me much pleasure," he admitted.

"No, I suppose not," Elizabeth agreed.

Mr. Darcy replied with a silent shrug, which left Elizabeth feeling a bit off kilter. She would prefer the gentleman would counter her assertions with words of praise. The Mr. Darcy of the letter and the one sitting beside her on the garden bench were quite in opposition.

"I am assuming," he said cautiously, "that Miss Lucas will spread news of our lack of propriety to your Longbourn neighbors."

Elizabeth surrendered to the pressing demand for a response, a response she considered for the last four days, but now that it became her time to agree, she held second thoughts.

Even so, Elizabeth kept her unwavering focus on Mr. Darcy: He was truly a handsome man in the classical sense of the word. She could imagine him as a centurion of the Roman army. Swallowing hard against the panic claiming her voice, Elizabeth inclined her head in affirmation.

"I thought…I thought since you previously proposed…"

She could not say the words. What if Mr. Darcy changed his mind? What if the gentleman refused to see the necessity in their joining? Mayhap it would be better for Uncle Gardiner to speak to Mr. Darcy's honor. Elizabeth did not tell her aunt and uncle of her dilemma for fear they would demand to read the letter and then think poorly of her.

"You thought since I previously proposed," Mr. Darcy said

in kinder tones than Elizabeth expect, "that I would agree to save your reputation with a second offering of my hand."

"It sounds so sorted when said as such," Elizabeth insisted.

"A marriage of convenience is often sorted," the gentleman observed.

"Of convenience?" Elizabeth whispered.

Shrouded in what felt of despair, her eyes looked up into Mr. Darcy's expressionless countenance.

"You do not affect me," Mr. Darcy said baldly.

"No," she murmured. "But perhaps."

His frown deepened, not that Elizabeth could blame him. Cynicism colored his response.

"I hoped for more than convenience," he explained, "but I will not desert you, Elizabeth, if you will agree to accept my hand in marriage."

Shockingly, Elizabeth wished to hear him repeat the sentiments his letter held, but she supposed her earlier refusal hardened Mr. Darcy's ardor.

Noting Bingley's return, Mr. Darcy whispered in rushed tones, "If you will permit me to escort you tomorrow, we will settled things between us then. Until that time, let us keep our counsels private."

Claiming a prior engagement with is man of business, Darcy departed before Bingley. It stung Darcy's pride to recognize the quick return of Miss Bennet's regard for Bingley. Certainly he held culpability in Bingley's withdrawal from the eldest Bennet daughter; yet, Darcy ached with the irony of the situation: He never deserted Elizabeth Bennet. Nothing or no one could convince him to do so, but although both he and Bingley would claim the women they adored, only Bingley would know his lady's affections.

"Unfair," he grumbled as he dismounted before Darcy House. Darcy tossed the reins to a waiting groom and glanced up to his Town residence.

Could he make Elizabeth Bennet the mistress of this property and of Pemberley? Could he spend a lifetime with the woman at his side and never know the perfection of her heart? Could he enjoy the lilt of Elizabeth's laugh, the sharpness of her wit, and the pleasure of her body beneath his without the love he coveted?

"Better than the alternative of taking another to wife," Darcy told his foolish heart. "Even a marriage of convenience to Elizabeth Bennet is infinitely preferable to a lifetime of wondering if she is well and happy with another. You will not possess all for which you wish, but a bit of heaven trumps the hell out of a lonely heart."

Chapter 3

DARCY STEELED HIMSELF AGAINST THE NECESSITY of the conversation.

"You considered our situation thoroughly, and it is your wish we join our lives?"

They strolled through one of the more private parks. Darcy left his curricle with his groom while he and Elizabeth sought the anonymity found among the tree-lined paths.

"I have," she said solemnly.

They walked in silence for several minutes, each lost in his thoughts.

"Although it is far from propriety's rules, I must speak honestly, Miss Elizabeth," Darcy spoke of his greatest fear in their union. "Even if ours is a marriage of necessity, I will expect you to remain loyal to our vows. I desire you by my side and in my bed. I do not wish you to think 'convenience' means we will travel separate paths."

He noted a blush claimed Elizabeth's cheeks, but she did not withdraw her hand from his arm.

"I understand."

Elizabeth's eyes remained downcast, and Darcy wondered if she held hopes of accepting his name without her wifely duties.

"You have yet to accept my proposal, Miss Elizabeth," Darcy said without the emotional upheaval streaming through his veins. "If you choose not to join our lives, I will still attempt to protect you. At a minimum a settlement to your father to secure your future to another would be in order. It was my pride which created this predicament."

This time, the lady did react to his bold assertion: Elizabeth pulled him to a halt.

"You would tempt my father with a settlement, Mr. Darcy?" she snapped. "You mean to make my claims on you disappear?"

Darcy did not respond immediately. Instead, he directed their steps along a secondary path and from earshot of the main lane. At length, recognizing the privacy he desired, he responded.

"Such is not my wish, Miss Elizabeth," he protested in a harsh whisper. "I spoke my fondest wish at Hunsford Cottage, as did you. You quite elegantly announced your disdain for me, and now, less than a sennight later, you approach me regarding the need to marry. In truth, I know not what game you play. If you wish a different course other than to be the Mistress of Pemberley, I will see you to it. Yet, if you persist in the idea of marriage, you must know the reality of our joining. I will not have you dreaming of another when you are in my embrace."

Darcy experienced a twinge of guilt for he considered acting as such with another woman if he could not claim Elizabeth to wife. He would be dreaming of kissing Elizabeth's sweet lips while siring an heir for Pemberley with another.

"I would never," Elizabeth began before swallowing her protest.

She clamped her lips together.

Darcy took pity upon her. Gently, he cupped Elizabeth's jaw to lift her chin.

"I realize my tactics are not to your liking, and it is not my purpose to laud over you. I also do not expect you never to disagree with me, though I might ask you not to speak contrary opinions before others. A man in my financial situation cannot be seen as permitting his wife too much latitude; even so, know that I will never relegate your objections to the level of foolhardiness."

Elizabeth stared deeply into his eyes, and Darcy wondered if she could view the depth of his affections for her. At length, a simple nod said she accepted Darcy's promise.

"Our situation is not ideal, but I will attempt never to disappoint you," he whispered.

Elizabeth's closeness flamed his desire for her.

"Nor I you," she murmured.

"Then will you accept my hand?"

Nervousness skittered across Elizabeth's features. Nerves and something, which Darcy prayed was not dread, claimed her stance. She licked her dry lips before responding.

"It would be my honor, Sir."

Darcy despised his selfishness...despised that part of him that demanded he claim the woman so set against him. Nevertheless, he bent his head to claim Elizabeth's lips. A gentle press. A nip of her bottom lip. A brush. And then he gathered her into his embrace to claim her mouth fully. Elizabeth leaned into him, her body warming his chest. She clutched at Darcy's jacket, and for a moment Darcy pretended the woman in his arms returned his regard...pretended that Elizabeth Bennet loved him as much as he did her.

When reality became reason, Darcy eased from her mouth, before closing his eyes to drive the desire from his veins. It did him well to have Elizabeth cling to him; perhaps in this manner, they would know contentment in their marriage.

He kissed her forehead.

"I will ride for Longbourn tomorrow to secure Mr. Bennet's permission. In that manner, the banns may be called twice before Miss Lucas returns to spread her tale. No one will consider our indiscretions from the ordinary if they learn of it."

Elizabeth's voice remained breathy, but her sensibility did not falter when she explained, "Sir William will carry news of our engagement to Kent, which will stifle Miss Lucas's immaturity, but will likely upset Lady Catherine when your aunt learns of it."

Darcy bared his teeth in the parody of a smile.

"I will address Lady Catherine's concerns when they are known."

"You will call at Gracechurch Street once you earn Mr. Bennet's permission?"

Unable to resist, Darcy again tightened his hold on Elizabeth. If they could remain as such always, they might know felicity in their marriage. It did Darcy's pride well to know she did not reject his gestures of affection.

"Nothing will keep me from you, Elizabeth," Darcy promised. "I warrant that we will deal well together."

Elizabeth's nerves were well frayed by the time Mr. Darcy called in Cheapside on the third day after their outing in the park. She could not shake the memory of the gentleman's kiss nor the manner in which her body betrayed all her Aunt Gardiner's lessons on propriety. Moreover, when Mr. Darcy did not call the previous day, Elizabeth feared the gentleman changed his mind or her father refused Mr. Darcy's request. For many months, she peppered her conversations with disparagements of her betrothed's character. Elizabeth was certain her father would know surprise at her change of heart for she knew something of the wonder of her transformation.

"I understand Mr. Bingley continues to call upon Miss Bennet," Mr. Darcy said as they sat together in her aunt's parlor. Mrs. Gardiner conspicuously placed a maid in the room as a chaperone.

Elizabeth was rarely anxious in social situations, but this new connection to Mr. Darcy had her struggling for even the simplest response.

"Yes...yes, Jane appears quite satisfied...with Mr. Bingley's attentions. I suppose he will return to Netherfield soon. For my opinion, I hope the gentleman returns before Jane and I travel to

Longbourn. I would not wish others to think my sister the type for which a man upends his life."

She noticed Mr. Darcy's frown. *Was the source of the gentleman's disapproval her opinions or his friend's return to Jane's side?*

"Needless to say you know more of Mr. Bingley's plans than do I," Elizabeth added.

Mr. Darcy shrugged off her statement.

"In truth, I spoke not to Bingley since I left him in this very parlor some four days prior."

"You did not inform Mr. Bingley of our upcoming joining?" Elizabeth asked with renewed curiosity.

She credited part of Bingley's continued presence at Jane's side as occurring with Mr. Darcy's permission. Elizabeth would need to rethink the influence Mr. Darcy held over Bingley's decisions.

"I spoke only to your father of our engagement," Mr. Darcy clarified. "Not even to my sister."

Again, Mr. Darcy took her by surprise. Elizabeth's jaw snapped shut before she could say something unwise.

"I am certain you possessed your reasons for secrecy," she said in false calm.

Another of Elizabeth's recent fears was Mr. Darcy would know shame with his connection to her.

His lips tightened, and an emotion, which appeared to be bitter grief, darkened Mr. Darcy's eyes.

"I did not wish to make the betrothal known until all arrangements were in place," he assured.

"Do you pray I shall withdraw, Mr. Darcy?" Elizabeth challenged.

It hurt her more than Elizabeth would admit to anyone that the gentleman was not proud to claim her to wife. Certainly, she was not of his social circle, but she was a gentleman's daughter.

"I pray you do not withdraw, Miss Elizabeth," he corrected. "And I would venture you said nothing to your family for if you had I should be accepting the congratulations of your sister and the Gardiners."

"I thought it best to wait until you spoke to Mr. Bennet," she confessed in resignation.

Her misplaced fears and her impetuous tongue placed another wedge between them.

Mr. Darcy shrugged philosophically.

"We are quite a pair, both accustomed to our words and our decisions being above reproach. Both fearing others will recognize our foibles. We will either thrive or destroy each other."

"What a delightful portrait you paint of our marital felicity, Sir," she retorted.

"I am nothing if not earnest," Mr. Darcy countered.

Elizabeth wished again for the return of the Mr. Darcy of the love letter rather than the ever-practical man of Society.

"Brutally earnest," she quipped. "I must keep your character in mind when I speak my opinions. Such will be my first lesson of merit in claiming the name of 'Mrs. Darcy.'"

She and Jane remained in London a little over a sennight before they returned to Longbourn. Those final days in Town were quiet busy for after Vicar Williamson called the banns, an express arrived from Mrs. Bennet with specific orders on the purchase of bride clothes for Elizabeth: Therefore, it became necessary for Elizabeth to inform her aunt and uncle and Jane of her betrothal. She remained uncertain as to the necessity to keep her news from her family. It was as if by silent agreement, she and Mr. Darcy thought not speaking of their understanding kept their situation less real.

Elizabeth sent a discreet note to Mr. Darcy of her mother's letter to warn him of the change in the status quo. Later that same day, Mr. Darcy called upon her to issue an invitation to join him for supper that very evening and a night out at the opera the following evening.

At the supper, Elizabeth took the acquaintance of Mr. Darcy's sister. With astonishment did Elizabeth see that her new acquaintance was at least as much embarrassed as she. From Mr. Wickham Elizabeth heard that Miss Darcy was exceedingly proud, but the observation of a very few minutes convinced Elizabeth that Miss Darcy was only exceedingly shy. She found it difficult to obtain even a word from the girl beyond a monosyllabic until they found a few moments of privacy prior to being summoned to the meal.

Miss Darcy was tall, and on a larger scale than Elizabeth; and, though little more than sixteen, the girl's figure was formed, and her appearance womanly and graceful. She was less handsome than her brother, but there was sense and good humor in the girl's face, and Miss Darcy's manners were perfectly unassuming and gentle. Elizabeth, who expected to discover in Miss Darcy as acute and unembarrassed an observer as ever Mr. Darcy had been, was much relieved by discerning such different feelings.

"I shall be glad to claim another sister," Elizabeth declared. "When your brother and I speak our vows, I shall leave behind four dear ones in Hertfordshire."

Miss Darcy shot a quick glance to where her brother shared a conversation with the Gardiners. Elizabeth assumed her uncle meant to ascertain Mr. Darcy's affection for her: It bothered Elizabeth that her emotional refusal of the gentleman quashed any bits of regard practiced by Mr. Darcy.

"My brother knew loneliness for too long. I shall be pleased to view William satisfied in his life," the girl said softly.

William. Elizabeth's mind registered the familiarity of his name. Why had she not called him such? He remained *Mr. Darcy*, and that particular fact grieved her.

"My brother spoke often of you in his letters from Hertfordshire, and I thought having your acquaintance would be pleasant," Miss Darcy continued. "I shall be delighted to share Pemberley with the woman Darcy esteems."

"Esteems" was not a word Elizabeth could claim either for

her emotions or for Mr. Darcy's.

"I thank you for your generous welcome," Elizabeth assured, but the girl's words cut a swath through Elizabeth's heart: She desired the return of the man who proclaimed his affections for her: The man with whom Elizabeth wished to share her blossoming regard.

When she and Jane departed London, Mr. Darcy promised to follow as quickly as was prudent.

"I must inform my family of my decision, as well as arrange for our removal to Pemberley after the exchange of our vows, but I will arrive in Hertfordshire soon. Mr. Bingley reopened Netherfield so he might continue his courtship of Miss Bennet. Despite my full confession of my perfidy in his life, Bingley claims to be worth of your sister's affections he must practice Miss Bennet's form of forgiveness. Bingley extends his hospitality for my return to Hertfordshire. I will bring Georgiana and Colonel Fitzwilliam. My cousin will stand with me as witness."

Elizabeth nodded her understanding. She prayed Mr. Darcy's long absence would not provide him the opportunity to change his mind, especially now that the world knew of their intention to wed.

"Mrs. Bennet shall be beside herself to entertain the son of an earl," Elizabeth said with common mischief.

"My cousin is not of the nobility," Mr. Darcy declared with a frown. "Only my uncle and his wife claim that distinction. Even Rowland Fitzwilliam owns only the courtesy title of Viscount Lindale. The colonel is a commoner, the same as you and I and the same as Mr. and Mrs. Bennet."

"I am well aware of the distinctions, but you most know my mother will care little beyond the colonel's parentage. It will be a feather in my mother's hostess bonnet."

As they both recognized the shortness of their time together, Mr. Darcy did not argue instead, he caught Elizabeth's hand and brought it to his lips.

"I will miss our afternoons together," he said as he brushed a kiss across Elizabeth's bare knuckles.

To her horror, she found herself leaning closer to Mr. Darcy. In the past, she often declared her dislike for the man, so how could she now find him so fascinating?

"As will I," Elizabeth admitted. "You will write?" she asked on impulse.

She hoped for a return of Mr. Darcy's expressed affections.

"I would consider it an honor, William."

The familiarity of his name upon her lips brought shock to Mr. Darcy's expression, but in a pleasant manner. The gentleman's eyes sparked, and he gathered Elizabeth into his embrace.

"Thank you, Elizabeth," he murmured as he brushed a kiss across her temple. "I long wished to hear you acknowledge me beyond the formality of our relationship."

A clearing of a masculine throat kept them from saying more. Her uncle stood under the frame of the open door.

"Mr. Bennet's coach awaits you, Lizzy. Jane is already aboard."

"Yes, Uncle."

Mr. Darcy released her from his embrace, but he kept possession of Elizabeth's hand to lead her to the waiting coach.

"Soon," he whispered as he assisted her inside. I will follow soon. Confirm a date for the ceremony with Vicar Williamson and send me word."

And then the door closed, and Mr. Bennet's coachman set the horses into motion. Elizabeth scrambled to window for a final look upon Mr. Darcy's countenance. It pleased her that the gentleman remained upon the street looking after the coach until the distance was too wide and the London traffic too heavy to maintain the contact.

She would not see him again until days before their wedding, and the prospect frightened Elizabeth more than she would admit to anyone.

Darcy addressed the salutation of the letter he wrote to Elizabeth. He would give everything he owned to possess the liberty to tell the woman on the other end of his correspondence how much he cherished her and how happy he was to claim her, but he and Elizabeth held not that type of relationship.

"Perhaps some day," he whispered. "If it is God's will, the lady will learn to love me over time."

Resigned to the situation before him, Darcy permitted his ego a bit of passion in writing, "My dearest, loveliest Elizabeth." Following the endearment, he chronicled his progress in his business by explaining the negotiations with a group looking to expand a railroad line into his part of Derbyshire.

Such expansion would provide my tenants more opportunities to sell their crops and their craft works outside the circle surrounding Pemberley. Moreover, the line would bring the world's products to our door.

My enthusiasm is only dampened by the news that the considerations will likely keep me from joining you in Hertfordshire as quickly as I would like. Please know this is not my wish, but I cannot abandon my cottagers until this business knows satisfaction. I pray you will forgive me.

In a previous letter, Elizabeth informed Darcy that the Meryton cleric would marry them on the Thursday after the third calling of the banns, and Darcy prayed his business complete by that time. He wished to remove to Pemberley after he exchanged vows with Elizabeth in hopes that his estate would soften her dislike for him and permit him time to woo Elizabeth properly. However, it could be necessary to return to Darcy House for a few days to complete the paperwork for the rail line.

Darcy would prefer not to return to London for he feared his mother's family would express their objections to the joining of the Darcy name to the Bennets and to Elizabeth. Darcy would cut ties with the Fitzwilliam faction if they persisted in their disapproval. He would know great pain in doing so, but Elizabeth would be his future whether Lady Anne Darcy's brother and sister accepted the situation or not.

Georgiana confided that Lindale questioned Darcy's sister extensively regarding Georgie's true opinion of Elizabeth. Thankfully, Darcy spent time with Georgiana beforehand in which he professed his affections for Elizabeth and in instructing Georgiana on how to thwart the Fitzwilliam family's manipulations.

Yesterday, Darcy called upon Rundell, Bridge, and Rundell to create a special ring for Elizabeth. He thought to present his betrothed with one of Lady Anne's jewels, but Darcy desired a ring to mark Elizabeth's unique femininity and to express his declaration to win Elizabeth's heart. The craftsman promised to complete the work by Monday next, in time for Darcy's departure for Hertfordshire.

"Everything will come together," Darcy pronounced as he sanded his finished letter. "I simply must bide my time until Elizabeth pronounces her vows; then I mean to earn the lady's heart. I am convinced if we are in constant company, Elizabeth's disdain will soften to my favor."

Elizabeth's jaws ached from the need for a constant smile. Another group of neighbors called upon Longbourn to learn something of Mr. Darcy's courtship.

"I thought Mr. Darcy would return to the area by this time," Mrs. Connor hinted. "When do you expect your betrothed in Meryton? We all wish to extend our felicitations."

Elizabeth understood what the woman wished to know: Had the gentleman experienced second thoughts?

Mrs. Bennet snatched away Elizabeth's response.

"Lizzy had a post from Mr. Darcy only this morning."

Her mother meant for the village gossip to know that Mr. Darcy did not abandon Elizabeth.

Elizabeth wished she knew more of Mr. Darcy's nature. Then she might determine if "this railroad business" was a convenient stall or just the unexpected claiming a bit of mayhem.

"Yes, Mr. Darcy engages in business negotiations to benefit his cottagers," she said with more enthusiasm than she felt. "I am very proud of my affianced's benevolence. His actions mark Mr. Darcy's character."

"Does he not possess a duty to the wedding?" Mrs. Connor persisted.

Again, Mrs. Bennet fended off the woman's cattiness with practiced aplomb. Elizabeth never was so thankful for her mother's ability to manage the most difficult "tabby."

"All men must do for a wedding is to stand before the altar and pronounce their vows. A wedding is a woman's domain. I assure you Mr. Darcy is quite besotted with our Lizzy. Mr. Bennet claims this is so, and you know my husband never freely speaks of what he terms feminine 'nonsense,' unless Mr. Bennet makes an earnest observation. Mr. Darcy courted Elizabeth while my daughter resided with our cousin Mr. Collins in Kent. I thought Mr. Darcy quite clever to visit with his aunt Lady Catherine De Bourgh at the same time as Lizzy's sojourn with the Collinses. We all know the only lady in the neighborhood to which Mr. Darcy presented any preference was our Elizabeth. He danced with her at the Netherfield Ball, placing Lizzy at the head of the line in a place of honor."

Elizabeth wished she possessed the same confidence in Mr. Darcy's devotion, as did her mother. Perhaps if she did not eloquently abuse the gentleman in her initial refusal, Elizabeth could believe her mother's assertions as easily as did Mrs. Connor. But Elizabeth was more practical than Mrs. Bennet. She delivered a blow to Mr. Darcy's pride, and he admitted the "love letter" was a means to purge Elizabeth from his thoughts. She could not help but wonder if Mr. Darcy succeeded in doing that very thing.

The gentleman never meant the letter for Elizabeth's eyes, and she wondered when a drop of the other shoe would occur.

On the Monday after the third calling of the banns, Elizabeth's angst increased thrice-fold with the arrival of Lady Catherine De Bourgh at Longbourn. Fearing Lady Catherine's disdain would injure Mrs. Bennet, the request from the grand Dame to follow Her Ladyship into the "little wilderness" behind the manor house gladdened Elizabeth. She expected Lady Catherine's disapproval, but if she recognized the full extent of the Her Ladyship's vehemence, Elizabeth might have clung to Mrs. Bennet's skirt tails for protection.

"You can be at no loss, Miss Bennet, to understand the reason of my journey hither. Your own heart, your own conscience, must tell you why I came."

Elizabeth pretended unaffected astonishment, but her insides trembled with trepidation. She recognized Mr. Darcy's allegiance to his family.

"Indeed you are mistaken, Madam; I am not at all able to account for the honor of seeing you here."

Lady Catherine's color increased.

"Miss Bennet, you ought to know that I am not one with whom to trifle. However insincere you choose to be, you shall not find me so. A report of a most alarming nature reached me. I was told that not only would your sister be most advantageously married, but you, Miss Elizabeth Bennet, would soon unite with my nephew Mr. Darcy. Though I know this must certainly be a falsehood, I resolved to make my sentiments known to you."

One of Mr. Darcy's letters hinted to some opposition to their betrothal, but Elizabeth did not expect Lady Catherine's highhandedness.

"If you believe the rumor impossible," Elizabeth said with well-honed patience, "I wonder why you arrived upon Mr. Bennet's doorstep."

"I mean to have the gossip contradicted," Lady Catherine declared.

"I fear you are late to the party, Your Lordship," Elizabeth snapped. "The local vicar called the banns for the third time before all in attendance at yesterday's service."

Lady Catherine gaped as if she were a fish from water.

"You speak an untruth. My nephew would not forsake the duty he owes to all his family. You drew Darcy with your arts and allurements, but it not too late for you to end this farce. I insist you abandon your promise."

"And have my name ruined?" Elizabeth said with incredulity. "The time for second thoughts is long passed. Mr. Darcy and I will not disown our commitments."

Elizabeth prayed she did not speak too boldly.

Lady Catherine pulled herself up tall.

"Let me be rightly understood. This match to which you aspire will never take place. Mr. Darcy holds a prior pledge to my daughter, and when I threaten to bring proceedings of a breech of promise, Darcy will rethink his promise to you."

Elizabeth did not know Mr. Darcy as well as she would like, but she did not think the gentleman would take well to his aunt's coercion.

"Although I witnessed your professions of Mr. Darcy's tacit engagement to Miss De Bourgh, the gentleman says otherwise. If Mr. Darcy is neither by honor nor inclination confined to his cousin, why is not for him to make another choice? And if I am that choice, why may I not marry him?"

"Because honor, decorum, prudence, nay interest, forbid it. Yes, Miss Bennet, interest, for do not expect to be noticed by his family or friends, if you willfully act against the inclinations of all. You will be censured, slighted, and despised by everyone connected with him. Your alliance will be a disgrace; your name will never even be mentioned by any of us."

Her Ladyship's warning stung more than Elizabeth would admit to anyone. She worked hard to keep guilt from her features. Elizabeth prayed her alliance would not bring such censure upon the gentleman's head.

"These are heavy misfortunes!" replied Elizabeth. "But the wife of Mr. Darcy would possess such extraordinary sources of happiness necessarily attached to her situation that she could upon the whole, have no cause to repine."

"Obstinate, headstrong girl!" Lady Catherine hissed. "Is this your gratitude for my earlier attentions? Is nothing due to me on that score? You are to understand, Miss Bennet, that I came here with the determined resolution of carrying my purpose; nor will I be dissuaded from it. I am not accustomed to submitting to any person's whims, nor am I in the habit of brooking disappointment."

"That will make your ladyship's situation more pitiable, but it will have no effect upon me."

Elizabeth's chin notched higher as she gathered her skirt to make her exit.

"You can have nothing further to say," Elizabeth spoke in resentment. "You insulted me in every possible method. I mean to, therefore, return to the house."

"You have no regard, then, for the honor and credit of my nephew? Unfeeling, selfish girl! Do you not consider that a connection with you must disgrace him in the eyes of everybody?"

"Lady Catherine, I have nothing further to say. You know my sentiments."

"You are, then, resolved to have him?"

Elizabeth wished Mr. Darcy would appear to bring an end to this madness. *Did she want to marry the gentleman? A resounding "yes" echoed in her head.*

"I am only resolved to act in that manner which will constitute my happiness, without reference to you or to any person so wholly unconnected with me."

"You refuse, then, to oblige me; you refuse to obey the claims of duty, honor, and gratitude. You are determined to ruin Darcy in the opinion of his friends and make my nephew the contempt of the world."

"Neither duty, nor honor, nor gratitude, has any possible claim on me in the present instance," Elizabeth quipped in frustration. "No principle of either would be violated by my marriage to Mr. Darcy. And with regard to the resentment of his family, or the indignation of the world, if Mr. Darcy expressed excitement at the prospect of marrying me, your condemnation would not provide me one moment's concern; and the world, in general, would possess too much sense to join in the scorn."

Lady Catherine's features hardened.

"And this is your real opinion! This is your final resolve! Very well! I shall know how to act. Do not imagine, Miss Bennet, that your ambition will ever know gratification. I came to this place to try you," Her Ladyship snarled. "I hoped to discover you a reasonable creature, but depend upon it, I will carry my point to London."

As Lady Catherine strode away, Elizabeth groaned in despair. Would Her Ladyship prevail? Could his aunt convince Mr. Darcy to call off? Although some censure would arrive at the gentleman's door if he chose such a course, it was possible Mr. Darcy would simply withdraw until the gossip died. A man of Mr. Darcy's wealth and ancestral lines would not long be censured for disposing of a minor indiscretion, as was Elizabeth.

Chapter 4

"MISS DARCY." ELIZABETH GREETED THE GIRL. "How kind of Mr. Bingley to escort you to Longbourn."

Miss Darcy offered Elizabeth a respectful curtsy.

"I begged my brother to permit me to come ahead. I hope you do not think me too presumptuous. I hoped to have the acquaintance of your sisters before the ceremony. William's negotiations delay his departure from London."

The girl's news grieved Elizabeth; she had yet to recover from Lady Catherine's vituperations.

"I am sorry to hear of Mr. Darcy's continued absence," she said distractedly.

Miss Darcy slipped a folded paper into Elizabeth's palm.

"Darcy sends you his regard."

The girl blushed as if Miss Darcy read her brother's words, but the wax seal remained in place.

"Come in and permit me to make you acquainted with my family."

As they entered the parlor, Miss Darcy shared, "My cousin, Colonel Fitzwilliam, will accompany Darcy to Hertfordshire."

Elizabeth responded without much enthusiasm.

"Yes, your brother spoke of a promise between the cousins

regarding weddings."

"It is my understanding the colonel will soon be required upon the American front to train new British recruits. It saddens me that my cousin will be from his family over the festive days and beyond."

Miss Darcy's countenance displayed the girl's affection for the colonel.

Elizabeth observed, "If the colonel must serve England, I would think him safer upon the Canadian border than with Wellesley upon the Peninsular."

"Yes…yes, I suppose," Miss Darcy said on a rush. "Even so, I wish the colonel was a simple country gentleman rather than a trained soldier."

After learning from Kitty of Lady Catherine's calling upon the Bennet household, Miss Darcy expressed concern in private to Elizabeth as the girl departed with Mr. Bingley.

"I pray Aunt Catherine spoke to you civilly," she whispered as Elizabeth waited with the girl for the coachman to bring Bingley's carriage around.

"Although my experience with Her Ladyship is limited, I believe Lady Catherine speaks her opinions without prompting," Elizabeth quipped.

She could not shake the feeling that Lady Catherine's prediction would know fruition.

"Oh, dear," Miss Darcy whispered anxiously. "Darcy will not be pleased with our aunt's interference."

The girl caught Elizabeth's hand to press the back of it.

"Please do not hold Darcy responsible for Lady Catherine's delusions. My brother does all he can to dissuade her."

"I assume your brother will possess another opportunity to do exactly that," Elizabeth said matter-of-factly. "Her Ladyship meant to press her point with Mr. Darcy."

Miss Darcy squeezed Elizabeth's hand a second time.

"Do not fear, Darcy will correct Aunt Catherine's miscalculations. My brother cares very deeply for you, Miss Elizabeth. Do not discount Darcy's resolve to make you his wife."

Elizabeth wanted desperately to believe the girl; yet, each time she counted the reasons Mr. Darcy would choose to marry her and the reasons he would not, the second list remained three times longer than the first. If they were in love–if they openly expressed their affections, mayhap then, Elizabeth could believe Mr. Darcy might withstand the pressure of his family and Society to deny their connection. It gritted against everything holy that Elizabeth recognized the truth of many of Lady Catherine's arguments, as well as the knowledge her rebukes to the gentleman in Kent could not be wiped from the slate recording their journey.

"Only novels bring the hero and heroine together after a bit of trouble," she told her foolish heart as she crawled into bed that evening.

The last three days had Darcy at his wit's end. In addition to the painstakingly slow negotiations with the stock company and two other investors, Darcy's confrontation with Lady Catherine occurred over part of Monday evening and twice more on Tuesday. Because of the interruptions into his private affairs, Darcy had yet to retrieve the wedding ring for Elizabeth.

On Tuesday, he sent the colonel to Netherfield to assist in chaperoning Georgiana for Mrs. Hurst had yet to join her brother to serve as his hostess, as well as to smooth the feathers of Darcy's future family for Georgiana sent an express chronicling the terrible rumors Elizabeth endured in his absence.

As Wednesday came to light, Darcy meant to be on the road to Hertfordshire.

Even that was not quick enough in Darcy's estimation. He missed Elizabeth with an ache he could not describe to those who never knew love. Darcy planned to claim her mouth several times this evening in anticipation of their exchange of vows on the morrow.

"Will there be anything else, Mr. Darcy?" the jeweler asked with a ready smile.

After examining the many sketches the jeweler showed him, Darcy studied the pieces upon a black velvet cloth. The craftsman knew his art: all were exquisite. At length, his eyes fell upon a simple, but elegant design incorporating an alternate row of topaz and creamy brown stones he did not recognize.

"Diamonds?" he asked as his finger traced the cut of the unusual stones.

"Yes, Sir. I purchased a handful of what the darkie called "cacao.' 'Like me,' he bragged."

Darcy flinched with the caustic remark, and his opinion of the jeweler's assistant lessened; even so, he kept his objections to himself. Rundell and Bridge held a reputation for excellence, and although Darcy recognized the prejudice following many from other lands, he knew his voice was in the minority. However, he would place a private word with the man's employer regarding the impropriety of the assistant's speech.

"I was uncertain whether anyone would think the stones worthy," the craftsman said as he nudged his assistant to the side, "but I find the cream of the stones play well with the golden tones of the metal and the topaz. Do you not agree?"

"The piece is perfection," Darcy murmured. "It reminds me of the cinnamon umber of my betrothed's eyes."

Thankfully, the jeweler did not pounce upon Darcy's comment. The man waited for Darcy's decision.

"Wrap it separately," Darcy instructed.

"Certainly, Sir," the man said with a deep sigh of satisfaction.

Darcy glanced up to note his carriage moving slowly past the shop. Customarily, his coachman would walk the team up and down the street in preparation for a journey. Keeping the horses warm meant fewer injuries than permitting them to stand for long periods.

With a look to his watch, Darcy hoped to be in the confines

of his coach and on his way to Elizabeth within minutes.

Unfortunately, that wish was not meant to be. The jeweler insisted on tightening two prongs upon the necklace's setting before wrapping the gift. If Darcy's heart was not set upon seeing the delight upon Elizabeth's face when he presented her the necklace, he would abandon the item to another day; but Darcy hoped to observe Elizabeth wearing it upon their wedding night: the necklace and little else.

In time, he secured both the ring and the necklace in an inside pocket of his jacket and stepped into the early afternoon shadows on what should be a busy street, but what was quite deserted except for the occasional street urchin and a house mistress. Darcy looked up and down Ludgate for his coach. A quick glance to his timepiece explained the abandonment of the street. It was well past time for the midday meal. He would be fortunate to reach Netherfield before the supper hour.

Another glance brought no sight of his carriage, and a frown claimed Darcy's forehead. If thoughts of the urgency of reaching Elizabeth's door did not distract him so, he might have taken note of the four men slowly surrounding him.

It was only when he heard the clicks of the two guns pressing into his back did Darcy recognize the danger the day held.

"You'll come with us," a menacing voice announced.

Darcy stiffened, but he kept his wits about him.

"If it is my purse you desire," he said evenly. "I will hand it over without a fuss."

"It be not yer purse Mr. Sloane requires," the group's spokesman announced.

"I assure you," Darcy said, keeping his eyes upon the street in hopes of assistance, "I hold no one named Sloane in acquaintance."

"That be not my concern."

The man nudged Darcy in the side with the gun.

"Step betwixt the shops and we'sll settle this."

Darcy wished for a different option, but he did as the man

instructed. It was essential to stall until Mr. Garner and Murray reappeared with the coach.

Yet, he possessed no opportunity to delay what was to come. Once in the safety of the narrow passage between the buildings, two of the men caught his arms, while the one before him struck Darcy square upon the chin, and the fourth punched him several times in the small of his back.

Darcy's legs did not know whether to stumble forward or to crumple. His mind chose the second, but before he could sink to his knees, the two holding Darcy's arms jerked him upward again, and a second and a third round of blows followed. He tasted his own blood, but there was no time to consider his split lip for one of the ringleaders' punches doubled Darcy over at the waist. This time the two who held him permitted Darcy to pitch forward into the slime dumped upon the hard ground. He did not wish to think upon what covered his freshly shaved cheek.

He knew when his attackers stepped back, and instinctively, Darcy brought his legs up to curl into a protective ball before a new onslaught ensued. He expected the men to rob him–to steal his purse. Without considering his actions, Darcy rolled more to his left side to protect the ring and necklace he meant to gift to Elizabeth.

"Elizabeth," he murmured. *At all costs, he must reach Elizabeth. Tomorrow was their wedding day.*

With a groan, he rolled to his knees, but before Darcy could stand to make an escape, the toes of a highly polished pair of boots came into view. A gloved hand caught Darcy's hair and lifted his head. Through what must be a cut eye, Darcy stared up into the scowling countenance of a gentleman. Darcy could not make out the man's features, for the shadows were too deep in this part of the passage, but he could smell the boot black and the man's sandalwood soap.

"What have you done?" the man growled as he released Darcy's hair.

Darcy collapsed to his forearms, his breath difficult to come by.

"As ye instructed," the ringleader responded in what sounded of fear.

Although he could not view the altercation, Darcy knew the instant the gentleman caught Darcy's assailant violently and shook the man.

"I told you to bring me that scoundrel Wickham," the man, who was likely the one called 'Sloane,' barked.

Wickham? Darcy thought. *How ironic! I took a beating mean for my long-ago chum.*

Darcy attempted to respond to the man's assertions, but he could not muster a breath to pronounce the words. A sharp pain in his chest accompanied each of his efforts.

"We follow this gent several times from the house ye claimed to be this Wickham fellow's," the assailant grunted.

"Then we erred," the gentleman insisted. "We must be rid of this one. If he identifies us to the authorities, we will all face hard labor or transportation."

Darcy wondered if they meant to kill him. One of his attackers answered his question. The man wrapped a large kerchief about Darcy's eyes and tied it off.

"We's take him to the country and dumps him. If'n he lives be it God's choice."

After the slightest hesitation, Sloane agreed, and Darcy was unceremoniously hoisted to his feet. His captors half carried and half dragged him to a waiting wagon. Darcy supposed the culprits meant to use the farmer's cart to transport George Wickham to what was to be his former friend's fate.

He could not see the flat cart, but Darcy could feel it when the men quite literally threw him into the back. Two of his attackers crawled in beside him and covered Darcy with a heavy cloth. Again, Darcy curled up in a ball of protection. He survived by not fighting back, and Darcy meant to continue the assumption of helplessness. Some would think him a coward, but Darcy knew otherwise. It took more courage to know when to walk away from a fight: He meant to survive and make his way to Elizabeth.

Later, Darcy would locate the unknown "Mr. Sloane," and the man would know Darcy's displeasure. Likely, Wickham dishonored the fellow's sister or wife or Darcy's oldest friend owed Sloane a gaming debt. Either way, Darcy would claim his justice upon another day; for now, Elizabeth's disappointment was of a greater concern.

Surely his betrothed would understand this situation was beyond his control. The license was valid for three months, and as quickly as Darcy could recover he would have her before Mr. Williamson and her family.

Elizabeth is a reasonable woman, he told his Reason. *She would recognize the irony of this attack coming at Mr. Wickham's hands.*

Thinking so, Darcy closed his eyes to bring forth his favorite image of his intended. *Survive for Elizabeth*, he repeated with each click of the wagon's wheels.

After what felt of hours, the wagon rolled to a halt. Once again his attackers carried Darcy to the destination they chose for him. More than once a branch slapped him in the face, but Darcy did not cry out. He counted the steps as best he could. He could feel the cool shadows as opposed to the warm sunlight upon his skin, and Darcy realized his attackers maneuvered him into some sort of woods. He concentrated upon only one thing: Being released so he could discover assistance to return to London and then onto Hertfordshire. Nothing else mattered.

"Where is the dastard?" Elizabeth heard her father demand of Colonel Fitzwilliam.

The colonel and Miss Darcy arrived at the church with the news that Mr. Darcy did not arrive at Netherfield last evening as they all expected.

Ironic, but Elizabeth knew he did not come. Even without being told, her heart said she would know disappointment. Nevertheless, Elizabeth permitted her mother and the others to offer a hundred reasons for Mr. Darcy's absence. How could she tell them she destroyed her happiness with a quarrelsome tongue?

"Perhaps Mr. Darcy took ill."

"Mayhap there was a carriage accident."

"More likely, the gentleman changed his mind, just as I predicted," Mrs. Connor declared in triumph.

Miss Darcy caught Elizabeth's hand, offering her support.

"You must know how dearly William cares for you," the girl pleaded.

Elizabeth did not wish to be cruel to Mr. Darcy's sister, but her pride smacked of the betrayal.

"Mr. Darcy cared more for his railroad than his intended," she snapped.

Fighting back tears, Elizabeth spoke privately to her father.

"Please, Sir, may we not return to Longbourn? I believe two hours is long enough to wait for Mr. Darcy."

Thankfully, her father recognized Elizabeth's fragile composure. As they made their exit to his waiting coach, Mr. Bennet discreetly requested that Mr. Bingley see the remainder of the Bennet family home. Inside the carriage, her father gathered Elizabeth in his arms to rock her to and fro.

"My dearest girl," Mr. Bennet whispered as Elizabeth permitted her tears free rein. "I will not tolerate this insult, not to my darling Lizzy."

"No!" Elizabeth sobbed. "Mr. Darcy is not worth our notice. Please say you will do nothing foolish. I could not bear it."

"I am but a country squire," her father declared, "but I am not without connections."

"Please, Papa. I simply wish to forget this slight. Do not exacerbate it."

Elizabeth buried her face in her father's cravat.

"It was my fault for aspiring to a match above my sphere. Lady Catherine said as much. Mr. Darcy likely realized the censure he would claim with our joining."

Mr. Bennet took umbrage with Elizabeth's remarks.

"I will not have you speak so, Lizzy. Any man would earn a brilliant match by claiming you."

Elizabeth attempted to control her tears. She wiped hard at her cheeks.

"Permit me my misery this day," she said through a choking sob. "I promise to know a wiser choice on the morrow."

"As you wish, Lizzy."

Her father gathered her closer to caress Elizabeth's back. It was comforting to know his love.

"I will forbid *all* from entering your room until you are prepared to face them. Take as long as you like. One day or a whole month of days. When you decide how you wish to proceed, send for me, and we will deal with this together. Even if you do not wish to force the marriage, I believe Mr. Darcy's name will know the shame of a breech of promise action."

Elizabeth did not argue with her father regarding the futility of such legal actions against a man of Mr. Darcy's stature. Instead, when they reached Longbourn, she hurried to her room to bury her tears in her bed pillow. She noted the worried look from Mr. and Mrs. Hill as she scurried past them. The servants and all her neighbors would know Mr. Darcy abandoned her at the altar.

Inside the room, Elizabeth kicked off her slippers, sending them flying across the room to slam against the wall. The action brought her a momentary surcease. She wished there was something else she could throw, or better yet, punch in a most unladylike manner. The thought of slapping Mr. Darcy's too masculine cheek was quite satisfying.

In frustration, Elizabeth ripped at the lace of her ivory wedding dress. She should summon a maid to assist her, but it did her well to hear seams rip and to have lace sleeves come loose in her hands.

With more anger than she knew possible, Elizabeth tore the gown from her body, strip by silken strip. She would never wear the dratted dress again, and seeing it turned to rags brought her the only delight this day could hold for her. Standing at last in nothing more than her shift, Elizabeth gathered the ribbon and pieces of cloth in an untidy heap and unceremoniously dumped them out her bedroom window. She watched as the material fluttered to the ground below, as flighty as her hopes of becoming Mrs. Darcy.

The realization brought another round of tears to her eyes, and Elizabeth jammed her fist into her mouth to stifle the cry of injustice rushing to her lips.

It was bad enough to know that Mr. Darcy only agreed to their marriage to save her from the damage of Maria Lucas's gossip, but to be so publicly shamed was beyond Elizabeth's comprehension.

"Maria's tale would be preferable to what occurred today," she sobbed aloud. "I might have convinced the girl to ignore the obvious, but now everyone knows the man's disdain for the Bennets."

"Lizzy?"

A soft knock at the door caught Elizabeth's attention: It was Jane.

"Are you...? Is there anything...?"

"No, Jane," Elizabeth called before biting down hard on her lip to keep from lashing out at her sister.

Jane would soon know the happiness of joining with Mr. Bingley. *How often had they hid in the copse to speak of the men they would love?*

"I am well," Elizabeth managed.

"Are you certain?" came her sister's voice of concern.

Anger returned.

"Why should I not be well?" she said with ill temper. "It was the pinnacle of my day to stand before friends and foes and permit them to witness my public humiliation." She paused, seeking control. "Just leave me be, Jane. I know you mean well, but..."

"As you wish," Jane said in what sounded of tears.

Silence followed her sister's departure.

Elizabeth could hear the buzz of voices below. She hoped

her father could keep everyone away. She imagined the chaos as Mrs. Bennet hustled servants to remove the wedding breakfast.

"The breakfast," she murmured through a new round of tears.

Curling in a ball upon the bed, Elizabeth covered her face with the pillow to muffle her misery.

"The breakfast where Mr. Darcy and I were to accept the congratulations of all our dear family and friends."

Darcy possessed no idea of how long he remained upon the ground in the glade. His attackers left him upon the grassy floor. Although he could not see the area where they left him, Darcy could smell the mossy surface, hear the crunch of leaves and twigs beneath the feet of his kidnappers, as well as the suddenly silent birdsong, and feel the sharp slap of the branches as they brushed across his body.

"Far enough," the one who served as the group's leader grumbled.

Without notice, they released him, and Darcy's knees buckled, sending him face first into the damp earth. Before he knew what to expect, one of the men on his left kicked him hard in the side. The air rushed from Darcy's lungs as the pain in his ribs screamed for succor.

"Leave him be," the leader snapped. "Tie his hands and let's be from this place 'for someone sees us."

One of the man's cohorts bent over Darcy to wrench Darcy's arms behind him. The movement increased the pain shooting through Darcy's chest. Too weak to resist the man, Darcy concentrated on how the man laced what felt of a leather strap about Darcy's wrists before tugging the constraint tighter.

And then they were gone.

Before Darcy could lodge a complaint, he heard their rapid retreat.

"Wait!" he called, but even to his ears his voice sounded

weak.

"Wait!" he attempted to call them back. "How am I to find my way from here?"

"Yer not," a voice announced from a distance.

A round of laugher and then sickening silence followed the man's pronouncement.

He was alone. Injured. Blindfolded. And restrained. Even if he could manage to stand, Darcy had no idea how he could discover assistance. The nearest farm or village was likely miles removed, and without his sight, Darcy would possess no means to find his way.

With an effort, he rolled upon his side and then paused to rest.

"Slow and deliberate," he announced to his waning spirits. "Find assistance and return to Elizabeth."

Three days passed, and Elizabeth thought it impossible that there were still tears to be shed. Mrs. Hill reported that Mrs. Bennet claimed her bed with a case of the 'nerves.' Elizabeth would like to offer her mother sympathy, but she could not. It was Elizabeth's life that Mr. Darcy ruined, not Mrs. Bennet's.

Jane slipped a note under Elizabeth's door to share the information that Miss Darcy and Colonel Fitzwilliam departed for London from the church with a promise to send word of Mr. Darcy's excuses, for Jane and the gentleman's family felt certain something far-reaching occurred to prevent Mr. Darcy's appearance. Jane wrote…

Mr. Darcy would never act in such a craven manner. I observed him in London, Lizzy, and the man holds you in deep regard. I do not err in this matter. Moreover, Mr. Darcy would never leave himself open to Society's condemnation, nor would he expose his family name to a public breech of promise suit. Mr. Bingley agrees. For all his faults and awkward mannerisms, Mr. Darcy is a gentleman.

"But no letter begging for my forgiveness arrived,"

Elizabeth told her badly bruised heart.

She knew for certain no message came by express or otherwise for Elizabeth's bedroom overlooked the drive before Longbourn's main door.

"No letter of forgiveness. No excuses. No pardons. Only open disdain. I thought better of you Fitzwilliam Darcy. Although I feared this very outcome, somehow I clung to the hope that you would act with honor and that your word was law. I am as foolish as Miss Bingley and Miss De Bourgh for you will neither marry for fortune nor family bloodlines nor love."

In the long hours without sleep, Elizabeth considered her future and came to necessary conclusions.

"A gentleman does not deliberately avoid the church where his fiancée awaits him," she reasoned. "At least, not if the man respects the woman he intends to marry. If Mr. Darcy wished to withdraw, he held multiple opportunities prior to the wedding to send me his regrets. His absence was meant as the ultimate revenge for my private snub of his attentions. It is painfully obvious the gentleman wished all to know a woman of my ilk could not occupy a place by his side."

With a heavy sigh of resignation, Elizabeth spoke to her reflection in the window.

"I was nothing more than a nuisance. My pleas for assistance fell upon deaf ears and upon a heart set against me.

"Even if Mr. Darcy crawled upon hands and knees and begged my forgiveness, I would never bend to his will.

"Tomorrow, I shall send for Papa and request his assistance. Mr. Darcy's actions placed me in a world of isolation. No man will think me worthy of his hand. The assumption will be that I am a woman of loose values for why else would a man call off a marriage he sought? I will grow old as the favorite aunt of my dear sisters' children. Yet, before that time I mean to see something of the world. To experience a bit of life before my future is so timely ripped from my grasp. I will know something of what makes others smile.

"I shall claim an adventure to last me a lifetime. With no concern for propriety's dictates, I want to enjoy the society of others. To know something in life of *my* choosing. Something beyond the walls of Longbourn. I shall tell Papa I wish to visit with Aunt Gardiner until this shame knows an end. I shall explain to Mr. Bennet that I require time to salve my disappointment."

Elizabeth turned from the window and paced the short distance to the door.

"Instead, I shall go to Brighton or Tunbridge Wells or Bath or any place, which will permit my heart a bit of freedom from the strictures I shall suffer until my dying days. A bit of fun and excitement and something from the ordinary before I return to Longbourn to tend my parents in their old age and before I beg for Mr. Bingley's benevolence when the Collinses claim Longbourn out from under me."

Chapter 5

DARCY SPENT NEARLY THREE DAYS in the woods before he found assistance in the form of a hound that first set up a howl upon discovering Darcy and then licked Darcy's cheeks with an exceedingly wet tongue.

All he accomplished the first day was to stumble into several trees and to trip over more roots than he thought possible. It was in the first night's middle when he finally loosened the kerchief enough for it to slip down his cheeks to encircle his neck. By rubbing his cheek against a smooth rock Darcy earned his sight. In that particular instance, he did not curse his tumble to the leaf-covered earth, but in all the others, Darcy wished Sloane and his men to the Devil.

Freeing his hands proved more problematic. Darcy realized he could not walk without supporting himself with his hands. Moreover, his injuries kept him from walking upright. So, despite wishing to speed his search for assistance, Darcy meticulously contorted his body to work his legs through his arms.

He sat upon the ground, his wrists tied behind his back. Then with determination, he edged backward to sit upon his fingers. The movement cost him dearly for in theory, his body should move easily through the flattened circle his arms formed, but the oval was not wide enough to accommodate the width of his hips. His long coat brought him to more than one moment of frustration for it caught on the binding holding his hands. Until he worked his way clear, Darcy imagined hunters finding his skeleton and wondering how any man could lie down and die in such a position.

Perhaps the task would not be so difficult if the slightest twist of his torso did not send shooting pains that robbed Darcy of his breath and his strength.

"Just think of Elizabeth," he repeated aloud. "She must be beyond worried, and your lady requires your protection."

With a string of curses and more than one cry for Divine intervention, Darcy prevailed. As dawn arrived on the day following his kidnapping, Darcy stood with his tied hands before him, rather than behind his back. He considered the change a victory declaring his survival. He used his fingers to free his private parts to relieve the need to urinate, a fact that baffled him.

"I had nothing to eat or drink since breakfast yesterday," he grumbled half aloud.

Even with his new mobility, finding his bearings was not an easy task. The woods were thicker than he expected. In his mind's eye, his kidnappers did not walk far in the countryside, and Darcy expected to reach the road without much difficulty. He counted some five hundred steps, roughly half a mile. He expected to reach the road, but several attempts proved fruitless. After wandering about for some two hours, Darcy realized he turned away from the road instead of toward it.

Looking to the way he came, with a sigh of resignation, Darcy came to the conclusion that he would never be able to recall accurately all the turns he made. Looking to the sun to determine its direction, he managed east and west. That led to a turn of his steps to the south. Darcy assumed his kidnappers drove away from London. He meant to encounter those traveling to the City and beg for their kindness.

Reaching a clear creek running through the landscape,

Darcy knelt painfully and drank his fill. The creek also provided a means to free his hands. Placing them in the chilly water, Darcy soaked the leather strap until it stretched enough to free one hand. He quickly untied the leather from the other before it dried again and shrunk tighter against his skin.

Rubbing feeling into his arms, Darcy surveyed the surrounding tree line.

"Another victory. Another challenge," he declared to bolster his resolve.

With that, he set out again. Darcy's trek was slower than he anticipated. Even after he discovered a sturdy branch to use as a staff, his gate remained painfully slow. He ate berries he recognized as safe, using his small penknife to cut away twigs. He rested more often than he wished, but there was no other way to go. Darcy remained weaker than he would like.

He spent the second night of his trek curled in the crack of a downed tree. Darcy wished for a flint where he might light a fire for although it was early May, the night held its chill. He tied the stiff kerchief about his head like a peasant woman to keep his head warmer and wrapped his jacket tighter about him. Closing his eyes for welcomed sleep, Darcy conjured up his favorite dream of Elizabeth–the one that started with a simple kiss and led to a heated night in his bed.

"Wait for me, Elizabeth," he murmured as sleep claimed his bruised body. "I will come for you soon."

And so he would for on the third day as Darcy set a more determined pace, he staggered into an open glade to discover a hound clawing at a rabbit hole under the raised roots of a mighty oak.

"Where is your master, Boy?" he demanded in a gravelly voice.

The hound turned to snarl at Darcy, but when Darcy sat heavily upon the damp earth, the dog approached warily. Only after sniffing Darcy's hands and shoulders did the animal nuzzle Darcy's leg.

"I shan't harm you," Darcy whispered.

He extended his hand slowly to scratch behind the dog's ears.

"Can you call for your master? I am in need of a strong shoulder upon which to lean."

As if the animal understood Darcy's request, the hound set up a mournful howl. When Darcy praised the animal's efforts, the hound rewarded Darcy with a wagging tail and a slobbering kiss. Within minutes, a rather rotund man called out to the dog before stepping into the opening.

"What have ye there, Chester?" the man asked in caution.

Darcy continued to stroke the animal's head. The motion calmed his nerves.

"A man seeking your assistance, Sir," Darcy pronounced on a breathy exhale. "Several men attacked me and left me to die. I wandered these woods for two days until your hound discovered me."

The man's eyebrow rose in skepticism.

"Why didnae ye walk to the road?"

Darcy thought to chuckle, but his cut lip would not curl.

"I asked myself that very question more than once. I do not seem to possess a sense of direction."

"Kin ye walk?"

The man edged closer, but he did not lower the long gun he carried.

Darcy gave the dog a final pat on the head.

"It depends on how far, as well as the pace you set."

Darcy planted the tree branch in the soft earth to use it as a staff to lift his weight, and the man caught Darcy's arm to lend his support.

"My ribs," Darcy hissed as the pain claimed his breath again.

"Me wife'll tend them. Me name be Tearlach Rogue. I own a piece about a half mile removed."

Darcy nodded his understanding.

"I can walk a half mile."

He prayed that was true for Elizabeth deserved better than to be left at the altar. He owed her a very public apology.

Surprisingly, her father was sympathetic to Elizabeth's plea.

"Time away from Longbourn might be best in this situation, but I will not have you travel by public coach unescorted. You will have my carriage."

Elizabeth did not like the idea of providing her father a deception, but if she did not seize this opportunity, she would spend a life in quiet solitude with no opportunity for travel or for marriage.

"I would not wish to deny you the use of your carriage. I do not mind the inconvenience of a public coach."

Her father countered, "How often do I have need of the carriage? With your mother taken to her bed, the coach is free. Moreover, how long will it take to travel to London? A few hours each way. I could be better spare the coach than a servant to accompany you."

"If I recall," Elizabeth said coyly, "Aunt and Uncle Gardiner mean to journey to the northern shires soon. Mayhap, I could go to London and travel with them. I am certain uncle would see his way clear to assist. Uncle Gardiner appeared quite incensed by the outcome of Mr. Darcy's courtship."

Mr. Bennet's scowl deepened.

"Your uncle felt responsible for permitting Darcy his manipulations."

Elizabeth did not wish to ask, but she needed to know the truth of Mr. Darcy's complete abandonment in order to close that particular door.

"Then there is no word from the gentleman?" she asked through a small voice.

"*Gentleman* is not the proper word for the wastrel," Mr.

Bennet hissed. "And I pray you change your mind regarding my claiming a portion of Mr. Darcy's fortune for your future. With Longbourn entailed upon Mr. Collins, you must have an allowance upon which to live."

Elizabeth never thought of Mr. Darcy's fortune, not in the way many women did. She knew him wealthy, but Elizabeth knew after giving the man her heart that she would accept Mr. Darcy even if he were one of the tenants upon Pemberley estate, rather than the property's master.

"I shall consider your suggestion, but for now, I wish to hear no more of Mr. Darcy."

"Then this is farewell."

Mr. Bennet rose to gather Elizabeth in his embrace.

"You are my most precious Lizzy. If I could bear your pain, know that I would claim it gladly."

Even after Darcy reached the Rogue's cottage, it was another day before Rogue departed for Town with a message for Darcy House. With Rogue possessing no more than a donkey cart to his name, Darcy contented himself with the idea that someone from his home would come for him post haste when they received news of his recovery.

Rogue's wife tended Darcy's many wounds and fed him simple meals, but Darcy would not know contentment until he could offer his excuses to Elizabeth. His intended never left his mind. He thought once their engagement became known that his obsession to claim the woman would ease, but Darcy erred. Elizabeth's essence clung to him like a second skin.

"Yer betroth be pretty?" Mrs. Rogue asked as Darcy crawled across the straw mattress to claim a bit of rest.

"Many believe Miss Elizabeth is not as fair of face as her elder sister, but I find the lady the most handsome woman of my acquaintance."

Mrs. Rogue chuckled.

"Ye be the only one who matters to the lady, and she to you."

Restless to reunite with his family and Elizabeth, Darcy was awake when Rogue returned to the cottage well after dark.

"Ye've a fine home, Mr. Darcy," Rogue announced when Darcy joined the couple in the large room, which served as parlor and kitchen. "They come fer ye in the morning."

"You spoke to my sister? To Miss Darcy?"

Darcy prayed Elizabeth joined Georgiana in Town, but he doubted the Bennets would think anything but the worst of him. They would not permit Elizabeth to come to London.

"Yer sister 'ent ye a message."

Rogue handed Darcy the note, and Darcy accepted it gladly.

"I thank you for your kindness, Mr. Rogue. You own my undying loyalty."

"Ye've paid me well fer me inconvenience," Rogue protested. "Me and Mrs. Rogue hold plans fer a barn with yer gratitude."

"I will leave you to yer sleep," Darcy allowed as he returned to the small storage room serving as his bedroom.

Inside the space, he relit the rush candle he snuffed out earlier so he might read Georgiana's letter.

Settling heavily upon the thin mattress, Darcy unfolded the page to read the familiar script.

William,

Praise God you survived. I shall send for the colonel as soon as this note is on its way to you. You must know my anguish at your sudden disappearance. I could not bear your loss. Colonel Fitzwilliam knows no rest, searching for every possible lead to your whereabouts. Our dear family will know elation at your survival.

I know you wish news of Miss Elizabeth, but I fear

I cannot tell you more than to speak of your betrothed's complete desolation at your absence. Neither the colonel nor I spoke to any of the Bennets after our return to London. In truth, my thoughts remained solely upon your fate, and I doubted any at Longbourn would pray for your safety. Even Mr. Bingley appeared incensed by the slight of his sister to be.

Thankfully, you may now reclaim Miss Elizabeth's affections and set the world aright, but first you must permit me to tend to your recovery. Until tomorrow, with all my love…

Georgiana

From the moment she departed Longbourn, Elizabeth planned how she would make her escape. Thankfully, her father did not realize the Gardiners meant to travel to Oxfordshire to visit with one of Aunt Gardiner's nieces, who recently welcomed a son. The Gardiners would attend the child's christening. In a letter to Elizabeth shortly after she and Jane arrived at Longbourn, their aunt confirmed the date for Elizabeth's nuptials to avoid a conflict with her grandnephew's naming day. Therefore, Elizabeth thought she could maneuver the appearance of visiting with her aunt and uncle. The difficulty would be to purchase a coach ticket to Brighton.

She thought to explore Tunbridge Wells, but Elizabeth had no desire to return to Kent. In addition to the possibility that Lady Catherine would learn of Elizabeth's presence in the neighborhood and arrive on Elizabeth's doorstep to gloat on Mr. Darcy's snub, there was the likelihood the gentleman himself returned to Rosings Park to claim his cousin. Elizabeth thought long on it: If Mr. Darcy married Miss De Bourgh, his abandonment of her would be readily forgiven. An endogamous marriage was much preferred by the aristocracy over connections to one such as she.

The chance encounter of Mr. Darcy in London was the chief reason Elizabeth refused to take solace with the Gardiners. Elizabeth's heart was too badly bruised to face Mr. Darcy so soon. She required time to harden her heart to the man.

And so when her father's coachman stopped at a coaching inn on the outskirts of London, Elizabeth claimed her opportunity to purchase a ticket to the seaside resort of which she heard so many tales.

"Yes, Miss?"

The inn's proprietor approached.

Elizabeth glanced about to make certain Mr. Lester still tended her father's horses before responding.

"Is there a coach to Brighton later today?"

"One leaves here at five," the man pronounced with authority.

It was near one. Elizabeth could disembark in Cheapside and be back at the inn by three at the latest.

"I hold business in my...in my late husband's name in the neighborhood," she said with more calm than she felt.

Elizabeth thought to say "my father," but the idea of passing herself off as a war widow would provide her the freedom that being a gentleman's daughter would not.

"When I complete the task of meeting with my husband's solicitors, I must travel to Brighton to rejoin my family. Would a seat be available?"

"I cannot hold a seat in reserve, Miss. The line to Brighton be quite popular."

"Certainly not," Elizabeth declared. "I would not expect you to do so. I shall purchase my fare now and return later for the journey."

And with a few coins, she took the first step into her future.

"A small victory," Elizabeth murmured as she returned to her father's coach. "A new challenge."

Darcy made himself as presentable as he could in clothes he wore for nearly a week. He looked forward to a proper bath and a shave. By half past ten in the morning, the crunch of carriage wheels upon the rocky path serving as the road to the Rogues' small farm had him lifting his weight from the chair to greet his dear family. He did not wish Georgiana to think him an invalid.

A sharp rap on the door announced that his cousin accompanied Georgiana. Within seconds, Mrs. Rogue admitted them into the large room.

"My God, Darcy," Fitzwilliam gasped. "What did you endure?"

"Hush, Colonel," Georgiana chastised. "My brother's bruises will heal fast enough. I shall tolerate nothing less."

His sister's gaze slid over Darcy.

"I thought to claim the comfort of your embrace, Brother, but you appear too weak for such affections."

Georgiana's voice indicated his sister's qualms.

Darcy raised his hand to stifle her movements.

"Mrs. Rogue kindly bound my wounds, but my movement is quite limited.

Georgiana shot a quick glance to the Rogues.

"Please forgive my lack of manners. Your Christian generosity speaks well of you. Our family is in your debt, and I speak earnestly of the gratitude I experience with the return of my brother."

Mrs. Rogue presented Georgiana an awkward curtsy.

"We didnae often have such fine company. May I's offer ye a cup of tea?"

Darcy did not permit Georgiana time to respond. He knew his sister would accept the woman's offer, but after being with the Rogues for some forty hours, Darcy was well aware the Rogues owned little. Accepting tea from the woman would mean the lady would do without later.

"If you do not consider it too rude to do so, I will beg your pardon for our speedy departure. I must be to London and make arrangements to speak to my fiancée," Darcy declared.

He leaned upon the twisted branch to support his weight.

"Colonel, if I might claim your arm," Darcy continued, "we will leave the Rogues to their day. I brought enough chaos to their lives."

Georgiana reached for a small bag she carried.

"The Darcy House staff asked me to present you with this. It is not much, but your effort to protect Darcy did not go unnoticed by his servants. They each added a few pence to the bag. Please accept it with their gratitude."

Darcy knew as much surprise, as did the Rogues.

"Yer brother must be a fair master," Rogue observed. "Makes me proud to take Mr. Darcy's acquaintance."

The man accepted the small sack of coins.

"Convey me thanks to yer people."

With that, Darcy made a slow and painful journey to his waiting coach. It took both the colonel and Murray to hoist him into the carriage. What was a common movement, one performed almost daily, became a test of Darcy's well-honed fortitude.

The colonel followed Darcy into the carriage to assist Darcy to the bench seat.

"We must summon your physician when we reach London," Fitzwilliam hissed in disapproval. "If I knew the extent of your injuries, the man would have accompanied us at this moment."

His cousin withdrew a small flask from an inside jacket pocket.

"A bit of brandy will ease your pain."

The colonel lifted Darcy's legs to the seat so Darcy could lean against the side of the coach.

Darcy uncorked the flask and took a sip of the warm blend. The heat of the drink raced through his veins, and for the first time in days, Darcy felt human. He closed his eyes to think upon Elizabeth while his cousin settled Georgiana in the carriage. The brandy and an image of Elizabeth settled Darcy's nerves. He knew what he must confide regarding Wickham would bring Georgiana more distress, but Darcy would require the colonel's assistance in learning more of the man called "Sloane" and what deception Wickham practiced.

Elizabeth avoided the Gardiners' servants by insisting that Mr. Lester set her down near the mews. They argued when the coachman meant to carry her bags into the house. Elizabeth literally placed her foot down, tapping her toe to indicate her displeasure.

"I shall not permit one of Mr. Bennet's most trusted servants to carry my unmentionables. You are like a trusted uncle, Mr. Lester. Your kindness to my sisters and to me is more than generous. I look upon you as an intimate, as extended family. Mr. Gardiner's staff will execute the task."

The words "unmentionables" and "intimate" had the coachman hemming and hawing.

"If'n you insist, Miss Elizabeth," he pronounced with a blush.

"I do, Sir."

Elizabeth knew a bit of anguish at her manipulations.

"Now set a course for home. If you leave now you should know Longbourn before dark." She paused before adding, "Tell my father I am grateful for his benevolence."

When Mr. Lester pulled away from the community mews, Elizabeth looked about her. She did not wish any of her uncle's servants to recognize her. Although her family was away, the servants would report her presence to Uncle Gardiner if she were seen. Pulling the brim of her bonnet lower to conceal her countenance, she summoned a young groom to her aid.

"A coin for you if you locate a hackney willing to drive me to the coaching inn near the village of Meniste."

"The driver'll charge more fer the distance, Miss," the lad clarified.

"I would expect nothing less," Elizabeth retorted. "Now be

about the task or I shall find another who wishes my patronage."

When the youth rushed away to do her bidding, Elizabeth breathed easier. She edged into the shadows of the covered stall constituting the mews and waited for what felt to be an eternity, but was likely no more than ten minutes.

She looked up at the sound of a carriage to view a hack squeezing through the tight passage. The young groom clung to the side of the coach. Once things were settled between her and the driver, the boy hefted Elizabeth's trunk into the hack before she crawled inside. She presented the boy an extra penny for his efforts, and then the carriage pulled away, returning her to the road and the coaching inn and freedom. As the coach turned toward the open road, Elizabeth sighed heavily. This was not what she wished for her life, but, at least, this adventure would be of her own making, not the design of her father or of a domineering husband.

"And so you think Wickham claimed Darcy House as his residence?" Fitzwilliam asked in what appeared to be fury.

"The man who attacked me told the one called 'Sloane' that he followed me about Town," Darcy explained. "That as I acted as the master of Darcy House then he assumed me to be Mr. Wickham."

The expression on the colonel's features spoke of his cousin's ire.

Darcy noted how Fitzwilliam tenderly claimed Georgiana's gloved hand to offer his comfort. Darcy doubted his cousin realized his action. The colonel always was most protective of Georgiana, and all the talk of Wickham had Darcy's sister appearing as pale as Darcy.

"I wish to know if Mr. Wickham remains with the militia from Meryton. When I called upon Mr. Bennet, Elizabeth father informed me that the militia planned to depart for Brighton. Such is the reason I permitted Georgiana to travel to Meryton without my escort. I would not permit my sister to encounter Mr. Wickham on her own.

"I also wish to learn if Mr. Wickham's joining the militia had anything to do with the threat of meeting Mr. Sloane on Hampstead Heath."

Darcy paused to convey his need for the colonel's understanding.

"Do you possess knowledge of a man who might learn something of this unknown 'Mr. Sloane'?"

The colonel nodded his affirmation.

"A former sergeant recently ended his service with Saunders Welch. Thomas Cowan possesses a brilliant analytical mind."

Darcy insisted, "And the character of discretion?"

"Most assuredly," Fitzwilliam announced. "You may count upon Cowan."

Darcy relaxed into his coach's squabs. Before he could take action against Sloane, Darcy required more information on the man.

"Then would you speak to me of Miss Elizabeth's disappointment? I must discover a means to reclaim my intended."

Chapter 6

ELIZABETH ARRIVED AT THE COACHING INN before three of the clock and joined several other riders in the common room to wait for the various coaches coming and going from the busy inn, which offered access to the London Road and those leading west, as well as to the southern shires. Elizabeth often stopped at the inn when she traveled to and fro from the Gardiners' London home for the inn was a reputable establishment. Even so, she never entered the inn alone before this day.

Elizabeth paused before crossing to a table tucked close to the window to remind her faltering resolve that a widow would not think twice of taking tea alone in the company of strangers.

Once seated, Elizabeth studied the inn's customers and wondered which ones would be her traveling companions and which chose other destinations.

At length, her eyes fell upon a woman cuddling an infant upon her shoulder, while a young boy no more than three played with a wooden horse at the woman's feet. The woman's drab brown hair framed what was a surprisingly expressive face. When she noted Elizabeth's interest she smiled weakly.

"To where do your journeys take you?" Elizabeth asked without a proper introduction.

The woman possessed a friendly countenance, and Elizabeth thought if the mother was set upon Brighton, they might accompany each other for security.

"I hardly know," the woman responded in so soft a voice that Elizabeth knew surprise at hearing her over the rumble of voices in the inn.

The woman's response brought a flush of embarrassment to Elizabeth's cheeks.

"I meant no offense. I…"

She glanced to the boy and fought back another round of tears. For a brief moment Elizabeth wondered upon the look of the children she wished to bear Mr. Darcy, before she could shake off the maudlin.

"I…I simply thought we might keep each other company if we were traveling the same way. Not many women are counted among those waiting."

The woman's bottom lip trembled, and Elizabeth suddenly noticed the track of dried tears upon the woman's cheeks.

"Oh, my," Elizabeth said in sympathy.

She carried her teacup to the woman's table and assumed the empty seat before catching the woman's free hand.

"You are distressed," Elizabeth declared, "and we are strangers, but I am of the persuasion that it is best to speak the words aloud if your anguish is to know an end."

Elizabeth realized she ignored her advice when it came to her feelings for Mr. Darcy, but she thought the woman knew nothing of abandonment. Two children spoke of the affection some man held for the woman.

"My name is Miss Elizabeth Bennet. Would you care to share your name?" she coaxed.

The woman studied Elizabeth's gloved hand.

"Yer a fine lady."

Elizabeth smiled encouragingly.

"My father is a country squire, but I do not claim the peerage."

Again, the thought of Mr. Darcy's connections brought a pang of regret, but Elizabeth placed those musings aside.

"I be Alice Bylane," the woman explained.

Elizabeth smiled in encouragement.

"Why do we not order a pot of tea and bread and butter?"

A look of panic crossed the woman's features.

"I possess no coin for such luxury, Miss Bennet."

Before departing Longbourn, Elizabeth planned how much she could spend each day of her journey. She saved her coins for over two years to purchase a special book for her father's fiftieth birthday, and she held the few funds Mr. Bennet slipped into her hand when Elizabeth left her home. The money was meant to allay the cost of her traveling with her aunt and uncle to the northern shires, and Elizabeth's father would be sorely disappointed if her knew of her excess; yet, she would face Mr. Bennet's disapproval upon another day.

Calculating the expense in her head, Elizabeth announced, "Then it shall be my treat. I am certain your son would enjoy a bit of bread and butter, would you not, Darling?"

Elizabeth leaned over for a closer look at the child.

Mrs. Bylane spoke with both gratitude and embarrassment.

"It is too much, Miss Bennet. Although young William would know delight, I cannot permit it."

"William?" Elizabeth whispered. "My favorite name."

She swallowed hard to force her tears away.

"My gesture is not one of charity, Mrs. Bylane," Elizabeth confessed. "I am uncomfortable traveling alone. Please permit me to do this.'

Mrs. Bylane looked lovingly upon her son's upturned countenance.

"Very well, Miss Bennet."

Within minutes, the inn's mistress delivered the tea and bread. Elizabeth held the sleeping baby girl while Mrs. Bylane prepared a weak cup of tea for the boy and placed a slice of buttered bread before the child. The woman made a like cup of tea for herself before she retrieved her daughter from Elizabeth's arms.

Elizabeth discovered how she felt bereft of the child's closeness. Of late, she permitted herself the dream of children, but Mr. Darcy's betrayal ruined her hopes.

"I am to Brighton on holiday," she told Mrs. Bylane. "If I may be so bold to ask, where do you travel?"

Mrs. Bylane caressed the back of her son's head.

"I remain uncertain. Me and the children were to travel to Portsmouth for me husband's ship was to dock there today. It's been more than a year since we seen our Jamie."

Elizabeth frowned with confusion.

"Did you hope someone would take pity upon you at the inn?"

Mrs. Bylane shook off the suggestion.

"I save me pennies. I be the cook for Mr. Joneston, but the rector find a new woman in service when I told him of Jamie's return. I cannot return to me work, and I cannot make my way to Brighton before Jamie discovers me missing."

Elizabeth shook her head as if to clear it.

"I remain confused, Mrs. Bylane. I thought you said Mr. Bylane was to dock at Portsmouth, not Brighton."

"I did, Miss Bennet. I be so distraught I not think with a sound head. Mr. Bylane sent word that the *Screaming Scotsman* would dock at Brighton instead of Portsmouth, exceptin' I's already paid me fare to Portsmouth. That be the reason I have no pennies remainin' for tea."

Tears filled the woman's eyes, and she looked away so as not to frighten her child.

Elizabeth patted the back of the woman's hand.

"Will not the innkeeper return your money or permit you to convert your fare to Brighton? I am certain the fare to Portsmouth is more expensive due to the distance, but it seems to me it would be worth accepting the difference as a loss if you could reunite with Mr. Bylane."

Mrs. Bylane glanced to where the innkeeper kept company with what appeared to be two tradesmen.

"I asked if'n I might trade me place for another, but the innkeep say the Brighton coach be full. I am to wait for another traveler who wishes to journey to Portsmouth. Then the innkeep will sent the gent my way. I's likely not recover me full fare, but I kin claim enough to travel to Brighton. There be another coach going south tomorrow.

"It is good of the innkeeper to make the offer," Elizabeth observed.

"The man has a business," Mrs. Bylane said without emotion. "But I could be long waitin' fer another to ask of Portsmouth. A coach only goes to the western shires every other day, and the innkeep say it not be full until it reach London."

Mrs. Bylane touched her finger to the butter upon the bread and slipped the tip of her smallest finger into the babe's mouth. The infant sucked greedily upon it.

"If there be no takers soon, I must set out fer Brighton on foot."

"Will not Mr. Bylane come searching for you?" Elizabeth asked in concern. "Could you not wait for your husband's calling? Surely there must be another means than walking to Brighton."

The woman looked off wistfully.

"If'n Mr. Bylane thinks I not come he might rejoin the crew. Even if'n he do look fer me, Mr. Bylane will turn his steps toward Staffordshire, to where me family lives. Me husband knows not I's took employment in Hertfordshire. That be the reason his message arrived too late."

"I could..." Elizabeth began, but Mrs. Bylane shook off the suggestion before Elizabeth offered.

"I accepted the tea and bread for William's sake, but I kin take no charity, Miss Bennet. I's have me pride."

"Pride is a sour meal," Elizabeth countered.

She and the woman sat in silence for several minutes, each lost in her musings. At length, Elizabeth removed the scrap of paper the innkeeper presented her earlier from her reticule and slid it across the table to Mrs. Bylane.

"I find I always wished to visit Portsmouth," she said in a voice calmer than she felt. "Would you do me the great honor, Mrs. Bylane, of trading places with me?"

Elizabeth knew very little of Portsmouth other than its seafaring renown, but surely it offered a variety of entertainments for gentlemen in the navy and their families. The town would not possess the pomp of Brighton's connection to Prince George, but if she wished an "adventure," Portsmouth would be one no one would expect.

"Miss Bennet, I did not speak me tale to bring ferth yer sympathies," Mrs. Bylane protested.

Elizabeth spoke in earnest.

"I experienced a loss of late, and I require some private time before I return to my family. It does not matter whether that private time comes in Brighton or in Portsmouth. Yet, marital felicity does depend upon your being in Brighton. Now, no more arguments. Take William and your daughter to reunite with Mr. Bylane. Claim a bit of happiness."

"Darcy, you cannot," the colonel declared when Darcy attempted to dress.

"I must go to her, Fitzwilliam," Darcy protested. "Miss Elizabeth must be made to understand I did not desert her."

The colonel scowled his disapproval.

"You can barely walk without assistance," his cousin reasoned. "If you persist in this madness, you could suffer dire consequences."

After the physician tending Darcy's many wounds departed, Darcy had a long talk with Georgiana. His sister's assessment of Elizabeth's disappointment frightened Darcy more than had his assailants. Elizabeth was not the type to succumb to tears. Darcy expected her anger to send Elizabeth into as shrewish rant, but the idea of her displaying an emotional attachment to him had his hopes praying for succor.

Was it possible Elizabeth held feelings for him? It was a question Darcy could not shake.

"Elizabeth must despise me," he whispered in anguish tones.

The colonel caught Darcy's arm to turn Darcy's steps toward the bed.

"I cannot be both guard and spy at the same time," the colonel insisted. "You must choose as to whether my occupation will be caretaker or will I search out news on Wickham?"

"You know my response," Darcy grumbled as he eased his weight onto the bed.

The colonel spread the linens across Darcy's lap.

"I will bring you ink, pen, and pager," his cousin instructed. "You will write Miss Elizabeth your regrets, and I will ferry it to Longbourn. Promise the lady you will be on her doorstep as quickly as you recover."

Darcy sighed heavily. The colonel's suggestion was all that was reason, but Darcy's heart ached to know Elizabeth would still be his.

"You will send an express detailing Miss Elizabeth's willingness to hear my apology," Darcy confirmed.

"If it is your wish," Fitzwilliam placated. "Now, permit me to retrieve your ink well and paper. You write while I speak to Cowan regarding Mr. Sloane. Then with your letter in hand, I will set a course for Hertfordshire."

It took Elizabeth another quarter hour to convince Mrs. Bylane to accept Elizabeth's offer. Only when the innkeeper announced the arrival for the coach set for Portsmouth did the woman relent. Elizabeth wished the woman well, and with a feeling of excitement and a bit of trepidation, she boarded the coach to a town of which Elizabeth held little knowledge. She felt the exhilaration of claiming a bit of freedom. Surprisingly, no one took note to her traveling unescorted, providing her the privacy to enjoy the journey: Elizabeth's eyes were open to the absolute beauty of the English countryside.

From Hertfordshire to London, then the coach crossed Bucks and the southern most points of Oxfordshire before entering Berkshire for the passengers to spend the night at a small coaching inn. Having heard horror stories of women attacked upon the road, Elizabeth stayed to her room for the evening.

In the morning, she was the only occupant of the coach until a naval officer joined her at the second stop. If Elizabeth had her choice, the coach would pass close to Windsor and the royal castle so she might enjoy the splendor of the signts, but coming from the north, it only made sense to a make a large arc toward Reading and Basingstoke and Winchester.

The gentleman appeared to take up more than his share of the coach, although, in truth, he kept himself very compact. Elizabeth studied his weather-beaten face with interest. His eyes missed few of the objects outside the coach's window, but Elizabeth thought he truly did not see the rolling countryside or the dense forest. She wondered if, like her, the officer thought of another.

The gentleman's frame was square, much in the look of Colonel Fitzwilliam, rather than that of Mr. Darcy's lanky form. The man's eyes were a cross between a dark brown and a metal gray. His mouth, set in a tight line, displayed the firmness of his rank: A captain, if Elizabeth correctly recognized the insignias.

When the coach stopped for a change of horses and a stretch of the passengers' legs, they spoke for the first time.

"May I assist you, Ma'am?"

The officer reached to steady Elizabeth's balance upon the coach's narrow steps.

"Thank you, Sir."

She placed her gloved hand in his and knew a twinge of disappointment that the gentleman's touch did not affect her composure, as did Mr. Darcy's. Even when they both wore gloves, Mr. Darcy's caress of the back of her hand with his thumb always set Elizabeth's heart fluttering.

"Captain is it not?" she said with practiced politeness.

The officer released her when Elizabeth claimed solid footing. He offered a bow of respect.

"Yes, Ma'am."

He glanced about as if seeking someone.

"As there appears to be no one about to provide a proper introduction, I pray you will forgive my gauche behavior. I am Captain Wentworth."

A second bow followed the gentleman's declaration.

Elizabeth smiled warmly at him.

"Although we should claim propriety, as we are the only two passengers, such appears foolish. We are likely denying ourselves stimulating conversation because of Society's strictures. I am Mrs. Elizabeth..."

She hesitated, not wishing to use her family name. Instead, she chose a form of the surname of the woman Elizabeth left outside of Watford.

"Mrs. Elizabeth Bryland."

The captain's eyebrow rose in curiosity.

"Does your husband not travel with you?"

Elizabeth rushed to say, "Mr. Bryland lost his life upon the Continent. I am newly from my widow's weeds."

The idea of being a widow appealed to Elizabeth for travel purposes, but the idea of creating a story of a lost husband and family was not to her liking. She always considered herself an honest person. In fact, speaking her mind often vexed her dear mother and sisters. *Yet, Mr. Darcy found your quick tongue refreshing.* The thought of her former betrothed brought a frown to her mouth.

"I can see you still grieve for the late Mr. Bryland," the captain said in concern.

Elizabeth shook off her thoughts of Mr. Darcy.

"I do," she murmured, and then with a squaring of her

shoulders, she added, "I believe I shall walk along the road for a bit. I fear I am unaccustomed to a sedentary life."

"Do you desire my company?" the captain offered.

"I assure you, Sir, I am stout enough for a steady walk. I thank you for your concern."

Captain Wentworth smiled easily at her.

"I hold no doubt, Ma'am."

He glanced to where the grooms brought fresh horse to harness to the coach.

"Do not go far. The coach will not wait for you, and I would dislike being denied your 'stimulating conversation.'"

It was a full day before Darcy stepped down before the Gardiners' Town house in Cheapside. His sister objected to Darcy's leaving his bed so soon, but after receiving the colonel's express, Darcy waited only long enough for proper calling hours before he rapped upon the Gardiners' door.

Darcy refused the laudanum the physician ordered for he did not like the way the opiate ripped control from his hands. As he waited for one of the Gardiners' servants to respond, Darcy shifted his weight to better tolerate the pain in his chest. It was difficult to breathe. Moreover, his cheeks and chin and much of his body held bruises in various shades of green and purple.

"Yes, Sir?"

A familiar maid bobbed a curtsy.

He kept his chin down so the girl could not observe his battered face.

"Mr. Darcy to speak to Mr. Gardiner," he announced.

Darcy would prefer to speak to Elizabeth first, but he knew he must assuage her family's ire before they would summon Elizabeth to speak to him.

"I be sorry, Sir," the maid said with a look of unease, and Darcy wondered if the Gardiners meant to send him away. "Mr. Gardiner be not at home."

Darcy sighed heavily.

"Then might I speak to Mrs. Gardiner?"

"The mistress be not at home either, Sir," the girl pronounced.

Darcy attempted a third approach.

"Perhaps Miss Elizabeth is available."

The maid's features crunched up in confusion.

"The master's niece not be within, Sir, since the lady's return to Mr. Bennet's home more than a month removed."

It was Darcy's turn to know puzzlement.

"I received word from Hertfordshire late yesterday stating that Miss Elizabeth rejoined the Gardiners' household a week prior," he insisted. "It is of the utmost importance I speak to the Gardiners or Miss Elizabeth. I mean to wait."

The girl blocked Darcy's forced entrance into the house.

"I beg your pardon, Sir, but I cannot permit your presence in the master's house without Mr. Gardiner present. If you care to call the beginning to the next week, I be certain the master will entertain your urgency."

Darcy's frown deepened.

"Why next week? Are the Gardiners from London? I understood your master departed Hertfordshire after…"

He would not say the words: The ones that announced the failure of his wedding day.

"The master and mistress," the maid declared in self importance, "attended the wedding of their niece and then they were to Oxfordshire for the christening of the mistress's grandnephew. They'll return within the week."

Darcy thought an error occurred, but it did not appear to be at the Gardiners' hands. Did the Bennets practice some sort of deception? He must uncover with whom the error rested before Darcy could discover the whereabouts of his wayward fiancée.

Returning to Darcy House, he wrote to Bingley to ascertain whether his friend held knowledge of Elizabeth's leaving Longbourn. The express from his cousin said the colonel spoke to Mr. Bennet and explained to Elizabeth's father that Darcy still meant to meet his obligation to the Bennet's second daughter.

Fitzwilliam's letter described the hostility the colonel experience at Mr. Bennet's hands, but the colonel indicated that he thought Bennet would hold no objection to Darcy's renewal of his intentions as long as Elizabeth knew satisfaction.

"Mayhap Bingley knows something of Elizabeth's absence from Hertfordshire. If Elizabeth chose to confide in anyone, it would be Miss Bennet, and the lady would confide in Bingley," Darcy reasoned aloud as he constructed the hasty note to Bingley. "That is assuming Mr. Bennet did not offer the colonel a deceit."

Darcy remained unconvinced that Elizabeth was not under her father's roof.

"You may experience difficulty discovering an appropriate hotel for a woman of your station," Captain Wentworth explained as they shared a late afternoon meal at their last stop before reaching Portsmouth.

The gentleman assumed the role of Elizabeth's protector after two more passengers joined them in Reading. She knew gratitude at the captain's thoughtfulness.

"You know Portsmouth, Captain?" Elizabeth asked as she poured the gentleman more tea.

"I sailed in and out of the port more times than I care to remember. It is a difficult maneuver if a man is not familiar with the sound. I am to meet up with two of my junior officers. We take possession of a new ship. I mean to enjoy what society Portsmouth has to offer before I return to the war."

The man hesitated, and Elizabeth wondered of the brief glimpse of desolation she discovered in the captain's eyes.

"I would be honored, Ma'am, if you would permit me to escort you upon the town and to give you the acquaintance of Commander and Mrs. Harville and Commander Benwick."

Elizabeth paused to consider the prudence of accepting the captain's offer. She knew little of the man other than what

Wentworth shared, and Elizabeth learned a hard lesson from Mr. Darcy regarding first, second, and third impressions. Even so, she trusted the captain's sincerity: A man of Wentworth's consequence was not the type to play a woman unfairly.

"Yours is the best offer I had today," she teased.

"If another offers you his escort," the captain responded with a twinkle in his eye, "I must prime my dueling pistols. I claimed your company first, Mrs. Bryland, and I am not of the persuasion to share you with rascals."

Chapter 7

THE RETURN LETTER FROM BINGLEY did little to allay Darcy's qualms regarding Elizabeth's disappearance. In confidence, Bingley questioned Mr. Bennet's coachman, who swore he delivered Elizabeth to the Gardiners' home. Mr. Lester explained how he thought it odd that Elizabeth asked to disembark in the mews behind the Gardiners' Town house and how she did not permit Lester to carry her bags into her uncle's home.

"What deceptions do you practice, Elizabeth Bennet?" Darcy murmured as her reread Bingley's message.

With a sigh of resignation, Darcy sent Bingley a reply. He offered his friend his gratitude and praised Bingley's initiative in the matter. Darcy again assured Bingley, and likewise Elizabeth's family via Miss Bennet that Darcy's affections for Elizabeth remained unchanged, and then he asked Bingley another favor.

If possible, keep your inquiries from the Bennets. I do not wish to alarm Miss Elizabeth's father if what I suspect proves true. Moreover, please ascertain if Mr. Lester stopped at any of the available inns to change horses or to permit Miss Elizabeth a stretch of her legs. I require a starting place in my search for my betrothed.

"I could not," Elizabeth protested when Mrs. Harville offered Elizabeth a room in the house the woman and Harville let.

"What of Commander Benwick?"

"Benwick may stay with me," Captain Wentworth declared. "I will take rooms at the inn upon Cornwall Street. Benwick cannot remain with the Harvilles once Fanny returns from Devon."

In the introductions, Elizabeth learned that Commander Benwick meant to make Fanny Harville his wife once the gentleman earned his fortune. Elizabeth thought the situation quite romantic, which did not please her stubborn disposition of late. Until she received Mr. Darcy's letter, Elizabeth never considered herself the romantic type. She was not of Charlotte Collins's pragmatic nature, but Elizabeth did not consider love possible. Although she often professed the notion that only the deepest love would persuade her into matrimony, Elizabeth knew marriages were rarely based upon deep affection, and the thought of all her losses brought the return of maudlin to her chest.

"You must permit us to serve you, Mrs. Bryland," Mrs. Harville pressed. "You are alone in Portsmouth, and even a widow is susceptible to those who speak half truths or practice pretexts."

Elizabeth thought again of Mr. Darcy and how easily the gentleman manipulated her.

"If you insist, Mrs. Harville," Elizabeth acquiesced. "I shall be grateful for your kindness."

"Are you certain the lady in question asked you to locate a hackney?" Darcy asked the young groom.

Darcy made a call upon the mews behind Gardiners' home.

"Aye, Sir. The lady gives me a coin fer findin' the hack and another to 'ssist with her bags."

Darcy knew admiration at Elizabeth's stealth. His future wife was quite resourceful.

Darcy presented the youth one of his cards. He did not think the boy could read, but there were others about who could.

"If you find the same hackney driver and bring him to the directions on that card, there will be more than a shilling for each of you. Do you understand?"

"Aye, Sir. I knows the driver well."

Darcy said in warning, "I am not a patient man. If I do not hear from you by today's end, I will no longer be generous."

His threat worked. Within three hours, the coachman and the groom called in at the servant entrance to Darcy House. Darcy stepped outside to speak to the pair, and within a half hour of their departure, he was on his way to the coaching inn some ten miles outside of London proper.

"Then you recall the lady?" Darcy asked the innkeeper.

"Many travelers pass through these doors, Mr. Darcy," the man said in self-importance. "I cannot recall them all."

Irritated by the man's ploy for payment, Darcy 'suggested' in his best Master of Pemberley voice, "Perhaps you should look at your coaching log four days prior. I do not imagine many unchaperoned females claim passage upon the line coming in and out of Hertfordshire."

Grumbling, the innkeeper found the page upon which he recorded the fares.

"Ah, here be two among the passengers."

Darcy swallowed his impatience.

"And which is the lady I seek?"

"Can't be certain, Sir. I recall these two. One purchased her fare early on and returned later."

Darcy thought that made sense if Mr. Lester stopped at the inn. Elizabeth could travel the distance to the Gardiners' house and be back at the inn in a little over two hours, three at the most.

"The lady said something of business in her late husband's name," the innkeeper continued. "Purchased the fare to Brighton."

Brighton. Darcy's heart slammed into his ribs. *Reportedly, Mr. Wickham was in Brighton with the militia. Did Elizabeth seek a reunion with Darcy's long-time enemy?* He had yet to relay what he knew of Wickham to Elizabeth. *Was she in the dastard's embrace at this moment?*

"And the other woman?" Darcy asked.

He prayed there was a logical explanation for Elizabeth's disappearance other than a renewal of her connection to George Wickham.

"The cook for the local vicar. Mrs. Bylane and her wee ones were off to reunite with her sailor husband. Purchased fare for Portsmouth."

Darcy calculated the chances of Elizabeth traveling to Portsmouth and rejected the idea.

"It appears I am to Brighton," he murmured before slipping a coin into the innkeeper's hand. "At any rate, Fitzwilliam is in Brighton. My cousin can assist in my search," he confirmed as he returned to his coach. "Perhaps, the colonel will agree to serve as my second when I put a bullet through Mr. Wickham's deceitful heart."

※

Elizabeth adored Millie Harville's generosity; the woman reminded Elizabeth of Jane, except this "Jane" possessed the backbone of Lady Catherine De Bourgh. Some of what the woman shared shocked Elizabeth's virginal awareness, and she had to remind herself that "Widow Bryland" would know something of a man's lust.

"Ye blush as prettily as an innocent," Mrs. Harville declared when Commander Harville entered the small parlor wearing nothing but his trousers and a shirt.

"My...my late husband," Elizabeth stammered, "guarded my experiences."

"I meant no offense, Ma'am," Harville offered. "Ye be so quiet like your presence slipped my mind."

"It is your home, Commander," Elizabeth said judiciously. "I present you no censure."

"Commander Harville and Commander Benwick are most anxious to return to the sea," Mrs. Harville explained in a change of subject. "They expect the war to know an end soon."

Harville agreed, "The prize purses be harder to come by with Napoleon finding himself a grave. Benwick wishes to marry my sister, and we both hope for a promotion before we retire on half pay."

"I do not wish Thomas to return," Mrs. Harville admitted. "But a man must feed his pride."

Elizabeth considered how she attacked Mr. Darcy's pride with her refusal and how the gentleman shredded her pride with his absence.

"I am of the persuasion that a woman's pride can be as easily wounded," Elizabeth declared.

"Aye," Millie Harville was quick to add.

"Yet, a man's pride is the skeleton of his very being," Harville insisted. "Some men possess the favorable side of pride. They know the discipline to recognize what is just and act upon the way God would wish them to perform. A man with 'good' pride is vulnerable to shame and to failure because dignity and self respect define him."

Elizabeth felt the rush of tears and worked hard to blink them away.

"And what of the sin of pride?" she asked softly.

Commander Harville tapped his chin with steepled fingers.

"Such pride displays a lack of character. Although pride is his motivation, a man of this demeanor knows no personal satisfaction. Because such a man stands in isolation, he can know no humility. He deceives himself in his worth. He invokes no loyalty in his dealings with others. A man who takes his delight in worldly self-fulfillment and in self-pity and in self-conceit cannot present God with the credit for the good in his life. A proud man is never a grateful man for when he does not receive what he believes he deserves, he blames others."

Despite her best efforts Elizabeth recognized Mr. Darcy possessed the first rank of pride, while Mr. Wickham held the marks of the evil of pride.

"My dearest sister Mary is fond of saying that vanity and pride are different things, though the words are often used synonymously. A person may be proud without being vain. Pride relates more to our opinion of ourselves; vanity, to what we would have others think of us."

Why did Elizabeth not listen to Mary's advice? Perhaps if she had she would not have disparaged Mr. Darcy to her dear family. Miss Bingley told Jane that the gentleman was remarkably agreeable with his intimate acquaintances, but because Mr. Darcy mortified her pride–her self-pitying pride–with his snub at the Meryton assembly, she claimed an offense. If she only recognized her attraction to the man…

"If you will pardon me." Elizabeth stood to make her leave. "I find the journey was more tiring than I expected."

"Certainly," Mrs. Harville agreed. "Do not forget Captain Wentworth and Commander Benwick plan to join us early. We will be a happy party taking in the sights of old Portsmouth."

"I shall be quite prepared," Elizabeth said with a show of enthusiasm, but as she left the Harvilles to their devices, she questioned the sensibility of her impetuous adventure. Elizabeth hoped for a bit of retribution for Mr. Darcy's rejection, but she discovered her manipulations in alignment with Mr. Wickham's attempts to discredit Mr. Darcy. Moreover, she did not understand why even after all that passed between them that she did not despise Mr. Darcy.

"I tell you, Darcy," the colonel declared in adamant tones, "I followed Wickham about the town for three days, and the steward's son has not met with Miss Elizabeth."

Darcy discovered his cousin at a familiar inn in Brighton.

The Earl and Countess of Matlock often took rooms at the inn when they attended events hosted by the Prince Regent.

"But the innkeeper was certain Miss Elizabeth purchased a ticket to Brighton," Darcy protested.

"Did the man observe Miss Elizabeth board the coach?" Fitzwilliam countered.

Darcy jammed his fingers into his hair in frustration.

"I did not ask, and the innkeeper did not volunteer the information," he admitted.

A long silence followed before Darcy asked, "Is there a chance Miss Elizabeth is in the town without Mr. Wickham's knowledge?"

The colonel appeared as confused as Darcy.

"Most assuredly, it is possible. Mayhap your betrothed no longer seeks the connection to those from Meryton. Surely some of the militia are aware of your absence from the ceremony. I would not imagine Miss Elizabeth would wish to encounter possible censure," the colonel reasoned.

Darcy accepted the obvious.

"I must know without a doubt whether she is here."

The colonel nodded his understand.

"We will begin a search after breaking our fasts on the morrow. We will call upon each inn, boarding establishment, and hotel. If Miss Elizabeth is in Brighton, we will discover her."

"What would you care to see, Mrs. Bryland?" Captain Wentworth asked with a proffered arm.

Elizabeth slid her hand about his elbow.

"I am delighted simply to visit a new place. I am at your disposal, Sir. What do you suggest?"

"Do not ask Wentworth his preference," Commander Harville teased, "or we will spend the day watching the ships building the new breakwaters."

"Such sounds fascinating," Elizabeth admitted.

"Perhaps the first time one views it," Harville continued his taunt. "Or even the first hour upon occasion."

"I am not obsessed," Wentworth protested good-naturedly.

"Mayhap on another day, Captain," Elizabeth suggested, "you might show me the works."

"You will regret your choice, Mrs. Bryland," Harville protested with a hand to his heart in a mocked wounding. "Wentworth is a thinking man and a man who enjoys history. Trust me, the captain will shower you with the dimension and armaments of every ship in port."

Elizabeth smiled at the easy camaraderie between the men.

"I can think of more miserable ways to spend an afternoon. I once listened to a particular young lady extol the qualities of a truly accomplished woman. Surely Captain Wentworth's vast knowledge of ship will be more interesting than the insipidity of the perfect lady."

"And what are the characteristics of a truly accomplished woman?" Mrs. Harville asked with a mischievous smile.

Elizabeth laughed lightly.

"Permit me to quote the lady."

She assumed the same stance as had Caroline Bingley when Miss Bingley attempted to entice Mr. Darcy.

"No one can be really esteemed accomplished who does not greatly surpass what is usually met with."

Elizabeth mimicked Miss Bingley's toplofty intonation.

"A woman must have a thorough knowledge of music, singing, drawing, dancing, and the modern languages, to deserve the word: and besides all this, she must possess a certain something in her air and manner of walking, the tone of her voice, her address and expressions, or they will be but half-deserved."

Elizabeth and the others burst into laughter when she finished.

"You are correct, Mrs. Bryland," Harville declared with another chuckle. "Wentworth's descriptions of the ships are preferable."

Mrs. Harville wiped at the happy tears blearing her eyes.

"And this advice came from a princess or a duchess or a countess?"

Elizabeth returned her hand to Wentworth's arm.

"Someone even better."

She beamed with satisfaction.

"The daughter of a wealthy tradesman who had her sights set upon a landed gentleman with a vast fortune."

"I am much impressed with your connections, Mrs. Bryland," Mrs. Harville said in her best aristocratic tones before bursting into laughter again.

"And why were you not among the landed gentleman's choices?" Commander Harville asked in earnest. "It would seem to me you would be the superior choice for a man of the gentry. Or were you attached to Mr. Bryland at the time?"

"I held no connections to Mr. Bryland when this encounter occurred," Elizabeth said softly in remembrance of her foolish deception. If she only recognized Mr. Darcy's intent at Netherfield perhaps she would not be seeking her last opportunity for enjoyment.

"The gentleman contradicted the woman's definition of accomplishments by adding his desire for a woman who improved her mind by extensive reading."

A secret smile claimed Elizabeth's lips: Mr. Darcy described her.

With a sigh of resignation, she added, "The gentleman in question also objected to my connections. My father is a country squire, but my mother's family is also in trade. So you see, the gentleman could not seriously consider claiming my hand."

They called in at every possible abode in which Miss Elizabeth could claim rooms, as well as at many establishments well below a woman of Elizabeth's ilk, but there were no sightings of the woman. Darcy's frustrations rose incrementally higher with each denial.

"Where in bloody hell could she be?" he grumbled as he and Fitzwilliam took a late afternoon meal. "I was so certain Elizabeth was in Brighton. I possess no idea where to look next."

Fitzwilliam studied Darcy's expression before offering a carefully worded suggestion.

"If the lady does not wish to be found, perhaps you should return to London and your life. Miss Elizabeth is only one of many comely females."

Darcy squeezed his eyes shut to ward off his cousin's best intentions.

"How do I explain?" he asked without opening his eyes. "Loving Elizabeth Bennet is the most gut-wrenching act I ever practiced. It is the most exquisite form of self-destruction."

Darcy looked again upon his cousin.

"But even if the lady never holds affection for me, I cannot abandon my need for Miss Elizabeth in my life; for although my love for Elizabeth sometimes brings me pain, it is also the most beautiful emotion I ever knew. It fills me. It completes me."

Fitzwilliam did not respond for several elongated moments.

"I did not realize."

Darcy chuckled in irony.

"Neither did I until it was too late to mend my bridges, but there is the hope… If I can only claim the lady…"

He could not express what was essentially a foreign emotion for Darcy.

"If Elizabeth becomes my life partner, then perhaps my love will be enough for both of us."

"What will you do?"

Darcy sighed heavily: Inevitability claimed his demeanor.

"Return to Longbourn and beg Mr. Bennet to disclose Elizabeth's whereabouts."

Visibly uncomfortable with Darcy's confession, Fitzwilliam busied himself with refilling his plate a third time from the offerings on the table.

At length, his cousin spoke again.

"It seems to me that before you go racing off after your lady love, we should address Mr. Wickham's latest offense to the man himself."

Wickham was the least of Darcy's worries at the moment, but he knew the colonel correct. If Darcy did not act against his long-time enemy, Wickham's next offense would be worse.

"Can you bring Wickham here tomorrow? I do not wish to confront him before the officers from Meryton with whom I dined often while residing with Bingley at Netherfield. Moreover, rumors of my missing the wedding are likely well known among Colonel Forster's men."

"I will call upon Forster in the morning," Fitzwilliam assured. "Wickham will not be happy to see me, but I will take delight in renewing our acquaintance."

"I should have known," Wickham said as he shrugged off Fitzwilliam's hand from his shoulder. "Only the Master of Pemberley could entice an earl's son to play the role of henchman."

"Trust me, Wickham, any retribution I exact upon your being has nothing to do with your offenses against Darcy," Fitzwilliam growled. "Instead of offering my cousin one of your caustic barbs, you should show your gratitude to Darcy. If not for the *Master of Pemberley*, I would have run you through long ago. For my opinion, the world would be a better place without you in it."

With the heel of his boot, the colonel dragged a straight-legged chair close.

"Now sit, and if I were you, I would consider speaking the truth for a change. Darcy and I are well aware of your latest maneuvers to dodge your creditors."

Darcy wished he possessed Fitzwilliam's indifference when it came to Wickham, but every time Darcy looked upon the companion of his youth, he experienced a pang of regret at

Wickham's continued betrayal and Darcy's failure in intervening in Wickham's life before Mr. Wickham's fall into depravity. It would grieve Darcy's father to observe his godson's path.

"What do you wish, Darcy?" Wickham asked in what sounded of insolence.

Darcy shrugged his shoulders in resignation. How often had he and Wickham sat as such? How many confrontations would it take to remove Wickham from his life?

"Mr. Sloane and his associates paid a call upon my person," Darcy said with false calmness.

It amazed Darcy how Wickham did not portray any *sign of guilt*. What became of that youth who wished to conquer the world? Whose eyes shined with excitement when he discovered a line of slate in the rock formations surrounding the estate? Who defended Darcy when the locals meant to tease Darcy for being the "young master"?

There was no raised eyebrow. No twitch of a muscle in Wickham's cheek. No flinch or a flexing of a fist. No hint of culpability or of satisfaction in Wickham's tone when he responded in denial. No humanity.

"I fear I know no man by the name of 'Sloane.'"

Darcy nodded his new understanding.

"Then it is Miss Sloane with whom you hold an acquaintance?" he charged.

Wickham's smile widened with taunting admiration.

"I must remember to guard my words with you, Darcy. It slipped my mind how you are not only the 'master' of Pemberley, but also of the double entendre."

Darcy schooled his expression.

"You avoid my question, Mr. Wickham."

"Why is it, Darcy, that you never call me 'Wickham'? Surely our lengthy acquaintance indicates a more familiar form of address."

Darcy long ago dropped the informal manner of speaking to George Wickham. In Darcy's estimation, "Mister" kept Wickham at arm's length; their dealings remained purely business. None of what they shared previously involved their transactions.

"It is what I prefer," Darcy responded evenly. "Now, speak to me of Miss Sloane."

"I assure you, Darcy, I hold no acquaintance by that name."

Wickham smiled wryly, indicating Darcy's former friend would disclose nothing of interest in that particular vein.

Darcy's brows drew together.

"If there is no Miss Sloane, then you provided the directions to Darcy House to strangers to disguise your lack of funds," Darcy accused.

Wickham heaved a disappointed sigh.

"You place unjust blame upon my shoulders," Wickham asserted. "You offer me another offense. If not for my affection for the former Mr. Darcy, I…"

Darcy's patience snapped.

"If not for *my* affect for *my* most excellent father, you would be in debtor's prison. Because of you, I was left to die in the woods outside of the Capital. I will tolerate no more of your perfidy, *Mr. Wickham!*"

"So what Captain Denny and the others shared is true," Wickham gloated. "You did not appear at the wedding ceremony to exchange vows with Miss Elizabeth."

The muscles of Darcy's jaw knotted as fury claimed him, but Wickham took no notice.

"I am glad to learn that you did not dampen Miss Elizabeth's exuberance. The lady deserves better than the likes of you. Even being the Mistress of Pemberley could never earn the lady's heart."

Wickham spoke to Darcy's greatest fear: Elizabeth would reject him. His absence from the wedding doomed Elizabeth to more censure than the rumor of her accepting an intimate letter from him would have done. Elizabeth Bennet could now deny an alliance she never sought.

"Miss Elizabeth may deserve better, but she will be Mrs. Darcy soon," Darcy hissed.

Fitzwilliam stepped between Darcy and Wickham.

"We waste our time with these games," the colonel insisted. "Know this, Wickham. Your days are numbered. We have yet to inform Sloane of your whereabouts, but your lack of cooperation and your conceit names your days. Sloane's men will not be fooled a second time. When you encounter Sloane again, the man will turn your clock to midnight."

Darcy stood and turned his back on the pair.

"I will not pay your debts again, Wickham. Your latest offense against my family is your last. Whatever path you carve is yours alone. I wash my hands of you."

Chapter 8

WICKHAM DEPARTED IN A HUFF, and Darcy knew the weariness of a never-ending loss.

"What if it is as Mr. Wickham says?" Darcy asked on a sigh of defeat.

He knew his cousin studied him, but Darcy did not turn about. He had yet to regain his resolve.

"Surely Miss Elizabeth recognizes the advantage of an alliance to the Darcy name. Your marriage would elevate her sisters' standings in Society, as well as secure the future of her widowed mother."

Darcy said dryly, "Mr. Bingley will provide for Mrs. Bennet."

He did not address the prospects of the other Bennet sisters, for in truth, Darcy paid them little attention except to find fault. As sad as it was to acknowledge, he thought only of his and Elizabeth's future. If Elizabeth Bennet accepted his hand, Darcy would take a greater role in her sisters' lives. He would actively search out appropriate matches for the girls.

"I suppose," Fitzwilliam said in what sounded of frustration. A long pause followed.

"I am confused, Darcy. Last evening you spoke eloquently

of your affections for Miss Elizabeth. Today, you permit Wickham to be the voice in your head. Are you now of the mind to abandon the lady?"

Darcy did not respond–could not admit he was at a loss as to how to approach Elizabeth.

"Wickham spoke the truth," he said, at length. "I assumed my position in Society would blind Miss Elizabeth to my faults. I took her agreement for granted. I never thought to woo the woman. Thinking my opinions superior, I permitted Elizabeth to overhear my disparagements of her and of her family. Then I expected the lady to overlook my shortcomings just because it is what others would do.

"Miss Elizabeth is likely one of the few women in England who does not accept the fact that I am considered a viable choice as a husband. I am not the *prize* the lady desires."

Darcy turned to encounter his cousin's stunned look.

"You did not respond to my earlier question. Will you leave Miss Elizabeth to her own devices?"

Darcy shook off his cousin's suggestion.

"I cannot."

Darcy made a silent vow that when he discovered Elizabeth's location he would spend time courting her. Somehow, he would convince Elizabeth that he was the only man who could make her happy.

"Even if pursuing another would prove just as well," Darcy declared, "I mean to make Miss Elizabeth Bennet my wife. I will have no other."

Surprisingly, Fitzwilliam put up no objections.

"Then let us be about discovering your lady love. I possess a suggestion if you care to hear it."

"I am all ears," Darcy said with a twitch of bemusement.

"When I called upon Colonel Forster to seek out Wickham an idea occurred to me. The steward's son often uses names not his own when he avoids his latest round of creditors. What if Miss Elizabeth used an assumed name in securing quarters? I do not imagine the lady would wish to bring more shame to the family name, and by her father's admission, Mr. Bennet believes his second daughter resides with the Gardiners in London."

"If Miss Elizabeth uses a name not hers, how will we discover her?" Darcy questioned, but his mind was already searching for possible names.

Fitzwilliam's anticipation rose quickly.

"Even a woman of Miss Elizabeth's intelligence would use a name with which she was familiar."

"Collins or Lucas or Bingley," Darcy suggested.

His cousin added, "Gardiner, Fitzwilliam, De Bourgh, Forster, Denny, or Darcy."

Darcy would relish the idea that Elizabeth would choose to use his name in her deception, but then another name crept in to spoil the moment.

"Or Wickham," Darcy said in disgust.

Thankfully, Fitzwilliam ignored Darcy's bit of pity.

"What of the other woman at the coaching inn?" the colonel suggested. "If the woman and your betrothed exchanged pleasantries at the inn, Miss Elizabeth might consider a name of which none of us are aware. Do you recall the woman's name? Did the innkeeper mention the woman's identity?"

Darcy's brow tightened in deep lines of concentration.

"Butler? No."

He searched for the name.

"Landon?" No."

Again, Darcy paused to look off, searching for something not quite apparent.

"Definitely began with a 'B.'"

He replayed the conversation in his head.

"Boland. Borland. Something similar. I cannot be certain."

Fitzwilliam nodded his understanding.

"It is enough, Darcy. We will revisit each establishment and ask after anyone with the names we listed. We might also offer a description of Miss Elizabeth. No possibility will be ignored."

"We called upon two days prior in search of a young lady," Darcy encouraged as he spoke to the innkeeper.

They had yet to discover a connection to Elizabeth, but his heart encouraged him to persevere.

"I's recall," the man said suspiciously, "but there be no females stayin' alone in me establishment. I's dinnae let to women less they be with family."

Darcy assured, "I did not think otherwise. Yet, as the lady's family worries for her safety, I must ask if you have anyone by the mane of Collins or Darcy or Bingley?"

The man shook his head in the negative to each of Darcy's suggestions.

"What of Boland?" Fitzwilliam interjected.

The innkeeper's lips turned down in a scowl.

"There be a Mr. and Mrs. Bylane, but the woman be no young miss. She be a mother with two wee ones. The gent jist arrived on a ship."

Darcy's heart leapt with anticipation. The innkeeper's story paralleled the one he learned in Watford.

"Would it be possible to speak to Mr. and Mrs. Bylane?"

Darcy slid a coin across the grimy bar.

"Tell Mr. Bylane there is a like coin awaiting him if he will give me five minutes of his time."

"I doubt the gent be cordial." The innkeeper pocketed the coin. "But I's ask."

Within a quarter hour, a burly man of short stature appeared at the table Darcy and the colonel shared.

"Ye wished to speak to me," the man mumbled.

Darcy gestured to an empty chair.

"Please join us," he commanded.

Darcy placed the promised coin upon the table.

"I possess a few questions, which I believe you hold answers. I offer you no trouble beyond those strictures."

The man whose face spoke of the years at sea, scowled deeply.

"I'll listen to yer tale, but I make no promises."

Darcy nodded his acceptance and waited upon the man to assume the seat.

"I am searching for a woman with whom I believe your wife took an acquaintance in Hertfordshire. The lady I seek purchased fare from Watford to Brighton, but did not board the Brighton coach. I hope Mrs. Bylane knows something of the lady's change of plans."

Bylane eyed Darcy in wariness.

"Mayhap Mrs. Bylane do and mayhap she don't. Why is it ye seek this lady? I be certain me wife would not wish any woman to know the spite of an angry husband or a strict master."

Without admitting knowledge of Elizabeth, Mr. Bylane confirmed Darcy's suspicions.

"I mean the woman no harm," Darcy assured.

He decided upon sharing a version of the truth.

"The lady and I were to be married, but footpads attacked me in London and left me for dead. Because I did not show for the ceremony, the lady believes me indifferent. She risks her good name with her impetuous leave-taking. I mean to discover her and return her to her family so we might exchange our vows."

Again, Bylane studied Darcy's countenance.

"Ye bear the mark of yer attack upon yer cheek."

"As well as upon other parts less visible," Darcy guaranteed.

Bylane indicated his decision with a curt nod.

"Me missus encounters this lass in the coaching inn. The woman purchases bread and tea so me son and wife not go without."

"I would expect nothing less from the lady," Darcy declared. "My intended possesses a tender heart."

Mr. Bylane replied with much gravity.

"When ye discover yer lady, extend me deepest gratitude. She showed charity when others would not."

Darcy accepted the comment graciously.

"Does Mrs. Bylane hold knowledge of my betrothed beyond sharing tea and bread?"

"Me ship was to dock in Portsmouth," Bylane explained. "So the missus spent the last of her wages on the fare to the port, but news come late to Mrs. Bylane of us arriving at Brighton. I sent word as best I could, but the seat be bought before me wife learns of the change.

"The innkeeper in Watford said if another meant to travel to Portsmouth he would give me wife the man's fare, and she cud purchase 'nother to Brighton. She be without the price of food fer our wee ones and no means to send werd to me. Yer lady took pity on my Alice and gave me wife her Brighton fare while yer Miss Bennet departed on the Portsmouth coach."

Darcy had no doubt that Bylane spoke the truth, and he wondered why he did not consider the possibility earlier. He held knowledge of Elizabeth's benevolent nature.

"I will assure my betrothed knows of Mrs. Bylane's safe journey to Brighton," Darcy said with a bit of satisfaction.

He added a second coin to the one he offered and slid them across the table.

"I assume you possess skills beyond those you acquired at sea."

"Aye, Sir. I be a carpenter."

Darcy stood and added his card to the coins.

"If you call at either direction on the card and tell my steward I sent you to him, he will assist you in finding proper employment."

Bylane scrambled to his feet.

"I doesn't know me letters, but I's find someone who does. Thank ye, Sir. It'll make Mrs. Bylane happy not to worry over young William and me daughter."

Darcy paused as he reached for his hat and gloves.

"Your son is named 'William'?"

"Aye, Sir. Yer lady say it be her favorite names. Please Mrs.

Bylane greatly."

Darcy could not hide the smile claiming his lips.

"It is a family favorite for me as well."

He wondered if Elizabeth thought of him when she spoke of her pleasure in the name. With a spark to his step, Darcy exited the inn: He meant to discover the answer to his question in person.

Elizabeth and Captain Wentworth sat together upon a rock formation studying the comings and goings of flat ships loaded with rocks and cable. She had spent five days in Portsmouth, and although Elizabeth enjoyed each of her encounters with the Harvilles, Commander Benwick, and Captain Wentworth, her heart remained in Hertfordshire and with a certain gentleman.

Elizabeth worried that when her father learned of her deviousness that Mr. Bennet would know disappointment in her choices.

"You are excessively pensive, Mrs. Bryland," Captain Wentworth said with what sounded of a mix of concern and amusement.

"I was simply considering how very small England feels when looking out upon the vastness of the ocean."

The captain's eyes remained upon the spot where the ships dropped stones to form the Breakwater, but he spoke with a growing intimacy. They were in each other's company for several hours each day for the last week.

"You spoke previously of a wish to know more of the world, Mrs. Bryland. Have you ever considered the possibility of living abroad ship and claiming the likes of the Americas or the Continent?"

Elizabeth did not move a muscle. Although she recognized the captain's growing interest in her, Elizabeth hoped to return to Hertfordshire before the good captain thought to approach her.

"Mine is but a wish, Captain," she replied in false innocence of what Wentworth insinuated. "I doubt I would be so brave as to take to the sea, Sir."

Wentworth looked to her in curiosity.

"You are braver than you claim, Ma'am. I find it remarkable you chose to travel unescorted and your acceptance of the kindness of strangers. Most women would be too timid."

"Some women possess no choice in such matters, Captain," Elizabeth protested.

"True," Wentworth gave her, "but in my experience there are women who blame al that befalls them upon others, and there are women who accept what they cannot change and find a means around the obstacle. You are of the second nature, Mrs. Bryland."

Elizabeth chuckled at the captain's brashness. Despite the fact that she did not hold blossoming affections for the man, Elizabeth enjoyed the captain's company immensely. He was a refreshing change from the drawing room chatter.

"I believe the same could be said of the male species."

Wentworth barked a laugh.

"Most assuredly, Mrs. Bryland."

Elizabeth turned the conversation.

"How often have you sailed into Portsmouth Sound?"

"More times than I care to count," Wentworth said in good-natured ease.

"From this point, such maneuvers appear quite dangerous," Elizabeth observed.

"It is that, Ma'am," Wentworth said as he pointed out spots along the shoreline. "Coming into Portsmouth Sound is not for the faint of heart."

The captain accepted Elizabeth's ruse and made his explanations, which she suspected were meant to impress her.

"The present day Breakwater is at the mouth of Plymouth Sound between Boyisand Bay on the east and Cawsand Bay on the west. The efforts we observe today will create a Breakwater some three thousand feet in length and ten feet above the low water.

"The Breakwater will offer the coast protection from weather and the effects of the backwash. Without it, the ocean will reclaim the shore."

"I would never consider the possibility," Elizabeth admitted.

"The sea is a strict mistress," Wentworth observed, "and if we do not protect the land the oceans will steal back, inch by inch, the very soil upon which we tread."

Elizabeth watched as the captain shook off what appeared to be maudlin, after which he shared a tale only a man who loves the sea could tell. Wentworth's story of the first time he sailed into Portsmouth Sound had her gasping and laughing aloud.

"I gnawed a hole in my cheek as the crew of the *Golden Horn* navigated past a wreck of a hull on the Boyisand coast. My knuckles were white from my grip on the rail. I expected us to run aground at any moment," he said with a mischievous grin.

"Do not bam me, Captain, you enjoyed every hair-raising second of the adventure," Elizabeth declared.

"I did at that, Ma'am."

Wentworth glanced to the sky and then at his watch.

"Pardon me, Mrs. Bryland. I did not realize how the time might slip away when in the company of a charming woman. If you hold no objections, Ma'am, I will see you to the Harville's residence. I am to meet with a man from the Admiralty regarding a new assignment."

The captain haphazardly dumped the remains of their impromptu picnic into the basket Mrs. Harville provided.

Elizabeth slapped his hands away.

"You go along, Captain. I am quite capable of finding my way to Commander Harville's home."

"I will not hear of such a thing, Ma'am. This is a bustling port city, not a country lane. It is too dangerous."

"Perhaps I might be of service to the lady," a familiar voice announced.

Elizabeth did not know how she did not sense Mr. Darcy's presence until he was behind her. On legs, which meant to buckle, she stood to face him.

"Mr. Darcy," she said in a voice, which irritated Elizabeth for its lack of composure.

"Mrs. Bryland," he said with a brief bow. "Perhaps you would care to introduce me to your escort."

Mr. Darcy knew of her deception.

Elizabeth wished at that moment to be one of the sailors upon Captain Wentworth's ship so she might utter the curse word rushing to her lips. If only the ground would open up to swallow her, Elizabeth would know satisfaction. She had but five days to mark a lifetime of spinsterhood.

"Certainly, Sir."

She managed a brief glance to Mr. Darcy's calm countenance. His dark silver eyes spoke of his displeasure at discovering her with another.

"Mr. Darcy, permit me to give you the acquaintance of Captain Wentworth."

Wentworth ignored Elizabeth's introduction.

"Are you familiar with the gentleman, Mrs. Bryland?" the captain asked in concern

Elizabeth glanced first to Darcy and then to the captain. Both men eyed the other with a look of feral cunning upon their countenances. Suddenly, Elizabeth realized she was the prey.

With a clearing of her throat, she managed, "Most assuredly, Captain. Mr. Darcy and I are long time acquaintances. I spent much of the early spring with my cousin in Kent. Mr. Collins holds a living presented to him by Mr. Darcy's aunt, and Mr. Darcy joined Her Ladyship to tend to her business affairs. Moreover, we anticipate a betrothal between Mr. Darcy's intimate friend and my eldest sister. The gentleman and I are often in company."

She swallowed hard to drive away the feeling of unreality.

"If Mr. Darcy is willing to serve as my escort, you should know no qualms in turning me over to him, Captain. Mr. Darcy would protect me with his life."

Elizabeth spoke the truth: Mr. Darcy would protect her so he might have the pleasure of destroying her again and again.

"I will call for you at seven," Captain Wentworth said in a tone of possession. "I told the Harvilles we will take in the play at the Theatre Royal."

Mr. Darcy did not even flinch, which told Elizabeth he was most vexed with the captain. The gentleman remained as stiffly cold as he was at the Meryton assembly.

"How delightful," Mr. Darcy said in practiced politeness. "I took rooms at the Royal Hotel. Perhaps we will encounter each other again." Mr. Darcy's eyes shifted to her. "Might I assist you with the basket, Mrs. Bryland? Then we may renew our acquaintance."

"Until this evening, Captain," Elizabeth said to speed Wentworth on his way.

She thought it possible that Mr. Darcy would take delight in disclosing her ruse.

"I enjoyed our afternoon."

"As did I, Ma'am."

Wentworth caught Elizabeth's gloved hand to bow over it before he offered Mr. Darcy a silent warning and a curt nod of his head.

With Wentworth's exit, Elizabeth dropped to her knees to gather the last of the cutlery to add to the basket. She could feel Mr. Darcy's eyes upon her back, but she refused to look over her shoulder at him. At length, she lifted the basket and turned to meet Mr. Darcy's steely gaze.

"If you mean to replace me with Captain Wentworth, Elizabeth, you erred," he said in cold warning.

"You forfeited the right to know with whom I may or may not associate when you forgot the small matter of our wedding," she snapped.

The gentleman's eyes flashed with anger.

"You remain my betrothed."

Elizabeth knew her chin notched higher. Sometimes she thought Mr. Darcy brought out the worst in her.

"Another item you denied with your absence, Sir."

"I did not..." Mr. Darcy began but quickly halted his refutation. "Your sensitive situation with the letter remains. You and I will marry despite your protests."

Elizabeth's heartbeat hitched higher. To know Mr. Darcy still meant to marry her filled Elizabeth with joy, as well as with a good dose of dread. Meanwhile, the realization he could reject her a second time outweighed any goodwill she could muster for the man. How could she face those in Meryton again? Everyone would think her father forced Mr. Darcy to keep his promise. Elizabeth did not want a marriage forged in ice.

"Did Mr. Bennet send you to recover me?" she demanded. "Are you here to prevent a very public breech of promise charge? If so, you may return to Hertfordshire and tell my father I will have none of you."

"I have not spoken to Mr. Bennet or to a barrister representing him. I cam to Portsmouth to reclaim the woman I mean to marry," he insisted.

A shake of her head did little to clear Elizabeth's thinking.

"I possess other plans, Mr. Darcy," Elizabeth said as she pushed past him. "I shall enjoy my limited days in Portsmouth with my new companions. Then I will return to my father's household and assume the role of devoted daughter."

"This is ridiculous, Elizabeth," he insisted. "You would prefer to live out your days as a spinster rather than to be the Mistress of Pemberley."

"I would," Elizabeth declared. "Now, I beg your indulgence. I must return to the Harvilles so I might change for the theatre this evening."

She started away, but Mr. Darcy stepped before her.

"I said I would escort you to your destination," he hissed. "Now, present me the basket and join Murray at my carriage. I will follow."

Elizabeth had not noticed the servant in the Darcy livery until Mr. Darcy pointed out his man.

"You wish me to ride in your carriage without an escort?"

she charged.

"I expect *Mrs. Bryland* to ride in a carriage with her fiancé," he said in a low warning.

Elizabeth smiled in mockery.

"*Mrs. Bryland* prefers to walk, Mr. Darcy. Good day, Sir."

As she rushed away, Elizabeth prayed her rejection would stick. She did not think she could tolerate many more encounters with Mr. Darcy without bowing to his wishes.

Darcy regretted his confrontation with Elizabeth, but it was deuced annoying to discover her with another man. And not just any man, but an officer in the Royal Navy!

Upon arriving in Portsmouth and learning she was not in residence at the Royal Hotel, Darcy set out to call upon the other inns in the old city to search for her. It was only by chance that he looked out his coach's window toward the Sound to spot the figure of the woman who haunted his dreams.

It took him longer than he liked to reach Portsmouth for Darcy stopped often along the coaching route to make certain Elizabeth traveled to the end of the line rather than to take another route. It was from those inquiries that Darcy learned "Mrs. Bylane" transformed into "Mrs. Bryland."

When he approached Elizabeth earlier, Darcy hoped she would welcome his return, but Elizabeth's shrewish tongue returned. In truth, Darcy could not blame her. He would know a like anger if Elizabeth did not show for their nuptials, but could she not observe the marks upon his face from his encounter with Sloane's henchmen?

"Instead of lashing out, Elizabeth should have demanded an explanation," Darcy reasoned aloud; yet, he knew her nature as well as he knew his own.

Darcy lips twisted with wry amusement.

"So my betrothed thinks she will claim spinsterhood or perhaps the affection of her captain."

Darcy's smile spread when he thought of the spark of defiance in her eyes.

"First, I will learn something of Captain Wentworth," Darcy summarized, "and then I will develop a means to win *Mrs. Bryland's* heart. If Elizabeth wishes a man to court her, then she will find me prepared to quote poetry and to bring her flowers. The woman will wear my ring and bear my children. I will tolerate no other alternative."

Chapter 9

CAPTAIN WENTWORTH AND HIS PARTY occupied a box, but not one of the upper ones. The officer and two other naval sorts escorted Elizabeth and another woman. Darcy watched Elizabeth exclusively throughout the performance. He knew when she discovered him sitting alone in an upper box for Elizabeth quickly withdrew her eyes and turned her attention to Wentworth.

When she walked away from him earlier in the day, Darcy sent Murray to escort her to her residence and to carry the picnic basket for Elizabeth struggled from the weight of it as she crossed the wooden walkway toward the main streets of old Portsmouth.

Darcy's faithful footman reported that Elizabeth refused Murray's assistance until the footman hinted that he did not wish to know Darcy's ire for failing to do as his master instructed.

Murray kept his wits about him when Miss Elizabeth demanded the return of the basket and sent the footman on his way when they approached the row house, where she later entered. From a concealed location, Darcy's servant observed Elizabeth's destination; afterwards, Murray asked others of the occupants of the house before returning to the hotel to report to Darcy.

"There be a naval officer, his wife, and two children," Murray shared.

As Darcy watched the occupants of the captain's box, it did not take long for him to determine the married couple. The second officer, who Darcy had yet to learn his identity, sat to Elizabeth's right and Wentworth on her left.

Wentworth nodded in Darcy's direction, a silent challenge, when their eyes met across the theatre. Darcy returned the nod, as they took each other's measure. For a moment, Darcy wished Elizabeth chose Mr. Wickham, as her gallant, for Darcy knew he could prove a better man, but Wentworth was another matter. Darcy's discreet inquiries of the man proved the officer both heroic and quite intelligent. Wentworth also reportedly amassed a substantial fortune for his action in battle.

Darcy recognized the captain's resolve, but his own held steady. He came to Portsmouth to reclaim his bride to be. If anything, Wentworth's attentions confirmed the necessity to whisk Elizabeth from the man's grasp and return her to Hertfordshire. Darcy held no doubt Mr. Bennet would soon learn something of his wayward daughter's choices. If Darcy possessed any hope of witnessing Elizabeth once again at Longbourn before scandal claimed her reputation, it must be soon.

At the intermission, Darcy waited until Wentworth escorted Elizabeth toward the refreshment table before he departed his box to join the small crowd in the theatre front. Casually, he circled the gathered audience, his eyes never leaving Elizabeth's profile.

She braced for his approach, and Darcy purposely kept his distance until Wentworth and the unknown officer stepped away.

"Good evening, Mrs. Bryland."

Although she did not offer it, Darcy caught Elizabeth's hand to bring the back of it to his lips. He permitted his warm breath to invade the silk gloves she wore.

"You are stunning this evening, Ma'am. I have not viewed you so delightfully attired since we stood up together at the ball at Netherfield," he said meaningfully.

It did him well to view a flush of color claiming Elizabeth's cheeks. Even so, she had the presence of mind to give her hand a little tug so Darcy would release her fingers.

He smiled at her maneuver.

"Perhaps I might impose on you to introduce me to your new friends."

Darcy noted Elizabeth's resistance, but good manners demanded she acquiesce.

"Mr. Darcy, permit me to give you the acquaintance of Commander Harville and Mrs. Harville."

"I am pleased Mrs. Bryland discovered those with whom she shares a variety of interests. Life in Portsmouth is more diverting than to what the lady is accustomed in Hertfordshire."

"I forgot that you mentioned something of Hertfordshire, Ma'am," Commander Harville remarked. "You appear to enjoy the southern shires."

Darcy read Elizabeth's irritation: She did not want her new acquaintances to know of her life before becoming "Mrs. Bryland."

"I do, Commander, and as for my life in Hertfordshire, it was long ago," she said in what sounded of regret.

With a fake smile upon her lips, Elizabeth challenged, "And you, Sir, are well aware Mr. Bingley praised me as a studier of character. I find many things diverting."

Darcy smiled easily at her quick recovery of her composure. The woman would make him an excellent wife for Elizabeth innately knew when to prompt and when to withdraw: Only once had he viewed her without control of her emotions, and the fault of much of that scene rested on his shoulders.

"Most assuredly, Ma'am. I recall your finding intricate characters most amusing."

Darcy noted how Mrs. Harville studied their exchange. Perhaps her husband was less astute, but the lady recognized the history between Darcy and Elizabeth.

"Would you not agree, Mrs. Bryland, that there is not the variety of subjects in the country as one might find in the city and townships?" the woman offered with a teasing tone.

"I believe Mr. Darcy once held a similar opinion, and both

you and the gentleman express a common thought, but I am of the persuasion that people alter so much over time that there is something new to be observed in them forever."

"I must take your word for it, Ma'am," Mrs. Harville said with a bemused smile before turning to Darcy.

"How do find the performance, Mr. Darcy?"

The play was *Petruchio and Katherine*, a Shakespearean comedic romp.

"I find it most enjoyable, Mrs. Harville," he said evenly. "What could be more entertaining than a woman with a shrewish tongue? Such is a well worn plot twist, but one which never disappoints."

From his eye's corner Darcy noted a lift of Elizabeth's eyebrow.

"As well read as you are, Mr. Darcy," his intended said in challenge, "I imagine your repeating the lines with the actors."

"As you are aware, Mrs. Bryland, I place a value on reading," he responded.

"Mrs. Bryland shared a tale of an acquaintance enumerating the qualities of an accomplished lady," Mrs. Harville suggested with a wry twist of her lips.

The woman's remark proved that Mrs. Harville knew that he and Elizabeth held more than a casual acquaintance.

"Did she?" Darcy said with an equally teasing life in inflection. "I always find Mrs. Bryland's observations delightfully accurate."

Mrs. Harville probed deeper.

"Yes, our dearest Elizabeth claims such qualities as a graceful walk, a knowledge of several languages, and a certain air to the lady's carriage essential."

"Mrs. Bryland is well aware I hold the belief a lady must add something more substantial in the improvement of her mind by extensive reading. Such is one of the reasons I hold Mrs. Bryland in great consideration."

Elizabeth could not respond for Wentworth and the other

officer returned with lemonade for the ladies.

Wentworth scowled his greeting.

"I did not realize you joined us, Mr. Darcy."

"I could not pass on the opportunity to speak to dear acquaintances, Captain," Darcy said with a look of impervious calm.

"Are you in Portsmouth long, Mr. Darcy?" Harville asked.

Darcy was certain the commander recognized the hint of animosity in Darcy's and Wentworth's tones. Odd that the officer did not take note of Darcy and Elizabeth's familiarity: Perhaps it said something about the differences in men and women.

"I come to Portsmouth often for I hold investments in both the shipyards and the import and export business."

Darcy would not admit he came to the port city to reclaim his bride to be.

Elizabeth said in surprise, "I was unaware of your interests in shipping, Sir."

Darcy smiled easily at her. Elizabeth Bennet made his heart swell with happiness; even when she was cross with him, Darcy still adored her.

"I have no doubt, Mrs. Bryland. Such is not meant for drawing room conversations. It is not as if I keep my business interests a secret or do not share investment negotiations with my intimates. I would, for example, speak to Bingley or Colonel Fitzwilliam of my interests, and I expect to share the extent of my holdings with my wife if I should marry."

Again, a blush rushed to Elizabeth's cheeks. His betrothed knew something of his negotiations for the railroad expansion for his home shire. Elizabeth understood Darcy's meaning perfectly.

"We should return to our seats," Wentworth suggested.

Darcy bowed to Elizabeth's party.

"I apologize for monopolizing your time. I extend my gratitude for your fine company. Being alone in Portsmouth is quite discomforting. Perhaps I could convince you to join me one evening for supper at the Royal Hotel. It would do me well to engage in intelligent conversation. And I would be most interested in the gentlemen's views on the progress of the war, that is, if the ladies hold no objection to the subject."

Mrs. Harville glanced to her husband, who nodded his agreement.

"We would consider it an honor, Mr. Darcy," the commander accepted the invitation.

"Shall we say tomorrow evening at seven?" Darcy pressed

He had no intention of waiting four and twenty hours to see Elizabeth again, but the supper invitation would divert her anxiousness.

"Agreed, Sir," Harville continued as the group's spokesman.

Wentworth bowed his exit and placed Elizabeth's hand upon his arm. Even so, Elizabeth glanced back to Darcy as the captain led her away. A combination of longing and confusion crossed her features before Elizabeth disappeared into the shadowy passage to the captain's box.

Darcy thought to return to his quarters at the hotel and analyze the successes and failures of his encounter with Elizabeth, but Darcy knew his removal from his let box would lead Wentworth to think the captain won their latest skirmish. Darcy would not permit the man the upper hand.

Instead, he returned to his seat to spend his time fantasizing over the pleasure of claiming Elizabeth Bennet as his wife.

Despite her best efforts, Elizabeth's gaze drifted often to the box where Mr. Darcy sat, looking upon the performance, but appearing distracted, nonetheless.

When she spotted him among the theatergoers, Elizabeth expected another confrontation, but Mr. Darcy proved himself the consummate gentleman. As she anticipated, Mr. Darcy included more than one reference to their relationship, but he surprised her, nonetheless.

Purposely Elizabeth glanced to Captain Wentworth. The

gentleman's obvious interest in her was flattering. Wentworth was a thoughtful companion, treating her with tenderness and never as an afterthought, but her senses did not tingle with anticipation from the captain's touch.

Multiple times over the last week, the captain claimed her hand to rest it upon his arm, but it was the brush of Mr. Darcy's lips upon her gloved hand, which caused Elizabeth's knees to buckle.

It was deuced frustrating to be susceptible to Mr. Darcy's masculinity. For some time now, Elizabeth realized she felt an attraction for the man from the start of their acquaintance. She permitted her righteous pride to deny her feelings for the man, but she now understood her indignation at the gentleman's snub at the Meryton assembly. It was because Elizabeth found the man exceedingly handsome. In that matter, Elizabeth was as misguided as Mr. Darcy in her opinions.

Up until his absence from the church, Elizabeth spent more than one night considering the possibility of resting in Mr. Darcy's embrace. They shared but one kiss prior to her leaving London for Longbourn.

Of late, she banished thoughts of sharing intimacies with Mr. Darcy from her repertoire; however, Elizabeth expected a return of her musings were at hand. She feared if Mr. Darcy chose to court her, she would succumb to the dream again and would know more heartache for her weakness.

Darcy waited until Captain Wentworth and Commander Harville departed the residence before he made his appearance upon the Harville threshold.

"Mr. Darcy, how good of you to call upon us this day," Mrs. Harville said as she accepted his hat and cane and ushered Darcy into a small parlor at the front of the house. It did not surprise Darcy to discover Elizabeth with a cup of tea in hand. It was the way he always imagined her in his home: He and Elizabeth enjoying a cup of tea in the morning after a night of intimacies–her face aglow with affection for him.

Unfortunately, Elizabeth quickly withdrew the pleasure in his appearance and replaced it with a look of disapproval.

"May we offer you tea, Mr. Darcy?" Mrs. Harville asked to fill the awkward pause.

Darcy belatedly recalled his purpose in calling upon Elizabeth today. Too often his innate fear of Elizabeth's rejection had him hesitating just long enough for Elizabeth to interpret the momentary pause as his censure. Darcy meant to change the lady's opinion.

"There is no need to bother with a fresh post, Mrs. Harville. I broke my fast at the hotel."

Darcy accepted the chair to which Mrs. Harville gestured.

"You must pardon my impetuous call, Ma'am. I was on my way to the shipyards to view the repairs on a yacht I recently purchased, and I thought perhaps you, Mrs. Bryland, and the officers might care to view the work. Mrs. Bryland appeared quite surprised to learn of my interests in the neighborhood. I thought to rectify that fact."

"My opinions were never to your liking, Sir," Elizabeth declared in suspicious tones. "Why would my disbelief in your motives be of concern? I cannot imagine your giving them a second thought."

Ah, she was back to despising him again. Darcy schooled his features to display no knowledge of Elizabeth's intent. On the day she crossed the marker to claim her place at his side, Elizabeth Bennet would learn there was a thin line between love and hate.

"You erred, my dear. I always value your opinions. I tended most earnestly to your insistence that your elder sister held Mr. Bingley in true regard, and I recently spoke to Mr. Wickham."

Elizabeth flushed with color. She knew exactly which opinions he referenced.

"Mr. Wick...Mr. Wickham?" she stammered.

"Yes, the son of my estate's former steward recently traveled to Brighton with the Hertfordshire militia. Surely you were aware of Colonel Forster's withdrawal."

Darcy prayed he did not overplay his hand by reminding Elizabeth of Mr. Wickham.

"No...I was...not aware of the militia's removal. Certainly my younger sisters mentioned the possibility, but I held no knowledge of the actuality. I was in Hertfordshire for only a few weeks after being so long removed, and I was...I was..."

"Occupied with a task of some importance," Darcy supplied.

"Yes," she said simply before diverting her eyes. All the same, Darcy noted how Elizabeth blinked away her tears.

Darcy thought to make further observations, but the presence of tears in her eyes played hard with his heart. Therefore, he offered Elizabeth no explanation to his business with Mr. Wickham. There was time enough for that once they were safely at her home.

"Then may I prevail upon your good nature, Mrs. Bryland? It would please me to show you the ship. I believe you would find pleasure in the experience."

Elizabeth looked to Mrs.. Harville.

"Captain Wentworth and Commander Harville have business with the Admiralty this morning. Mrs. Harville and I planned to take the children to the park today."

Darcy shook off Elizabeth's objections.

"The invitation, Mrs. Bryland, was for Mrs. Harville to accompany us. I am certain you would offer me a most stern reprimand if I thought to escort you about town without a chaperone, and as to the children, if Mrs. Harville believes they would enjoy viewing the ship, I hold no objections to their presence. I am quite fond of children."

Elizabeth appeared shocked by his willingness to acquiesce, but there was a hint of yearning when she looked upon him. The thought was most satisfying.

"What say you, Mrs. Harville?" Elizabeth asked tentatively.

"Commander Benwick remains at the inn to write another

letter to Fanny so we hold no concerns in that corner, and as to young Thomas and Harry, the boys love the sea as much as their father. To greet a gentleman who owns a vessel would make their outing quite special."

"Then it is decided," Darcy said with a smile. "My carriage is outside when you ladies are prepared to depart. I promise you both a 'charming' day."

As Elizabeth and Mrs. Harville rushed away to freshen their clothing, Darcy prayed they would not be long. He wished to be away from the house before Captain Wentworth returned to spoil Darcy's plans.

As Elizabeth changed her day dress, she wished for the hundredth time since Mr. Darcy's arrival in Portsmouth that she brought at least one fashionable gown with her. She chastised the anticipation, which filled her heart. The intensity of Mr. Darcy's stare during last evening's performance had warmth creeping through Elizabeth's veins.

The dratted man occupied her thoughts too often of late. Elizabeth reminded her foolish heart to claim annoyance as its partner. If she could keep Mr. Darcy at a distance long enough, the man would tire of his pursuit and accept her refusal for an answer.

Unfortunately, the genuine smile, which claimed the gentleman's lips when Elizabeth entered the parlor, had her bracing for the flash of satisfaction warming her heart. The man's smile, so rarely present upon Mr. Darcy's lips, had her thinking of the sun lighting the room with its brilliance.

"You look quite fetching, my dear," Mr. Darcy said softly.

Elizabeth protested the compliment.

"There is no need for flattery, Mr. Darcy; pretty words shall not alter my decision."

Although in truth, Elizabeth would welcome the "pretty words" of Mr. Darcy's letter.

"You must know, Elizabeth, that it was not my choice to

leave you at the altar," he said in regret.

"I am certain," Elizabeth said with more hurt than she wished to convey, "that Lady Catherine was quite persuasive. Or perhaps it was the Earl of Matlock's objections that you found viable."

"I am not so easily persuaded, Elizabeth. No unsolicited opinions could keep me from you."

Mr. Darcy's words were more than a bit unnerving.

"Whatever the cause," Elizabeth said with a shake of her head to drive away the maudlin, "the significance wanes. You did me a service, Sir."

Mr. Darcy's scowl lines deepened.

"How so?"

"I would never have the resolve to experience the world on my terms. I would always be Mr. Bennet's daughter or Mr. Darcy's wife. As Mrs. Bryland, I possess the freedom the world would deny Elizabeth Bennet."

Before they could speak further, the loud clop of two boisterous boys upon the stairs brought their conversation to a close. Elizabeth knew both remorse and relief with the entrance of the Harvilles.

"If you ladies are amenable, we should depart," Mr. Darcy said through tight lips. "I told Mr. Brownley I would call by eleven."

As Darcy assisted Mrs. Harville, the children, and Elizabeth to his carriage, he was thankful for all the difficult business negotiations he experienced over the years. They taught him on how best to disguise the turmoil claiming him.

Elizabeth Bennet was not meant to be an eccentric spinster aunt; yet, the woman refused to forgive him. Needless to say, if Darcy explained the attack upon his being, Elizabeth would accept her error, but Darcy foolishly desired Elizabeth's choice to be he. Darcy reasoned if she came to him of her own volition, their joining would possess the chance of affection.

"How long have you owned a yacht, Mr. Darcy?" Thomas Harville asked with eagerness.

Darcy placed his qualms aside. His "battle" with Elizabeth was far from over: they were simply at a stalemate.

"I own a large one I keep docked closer to my country estate, but when I saw this one, I knew I must claim it. She requires a bit of a kind hand, but I believe her an excellent choice."

"May we go aboard, Sir?" Harry Harville begged.

"As she is out of the water for repairs, I see no reason you could not have a look around. Needless to say, you must hold Mrs. Harville's permission."

"May we, Mama?" Harry pleaded.

"If Mr. Darcy thinks it is safe," Mrs. Harville said as she straightened her son's jacket.

Within minutes, Darcy assisted the children from the coach.

"You must stay close," he warned the boys. "And listen to the instructions Mr. Brownley provides. There are many men employed in the area, and they are not accustomed to children and ladies about."

"Yes, Sir," the boys chorused.

Within minutes, Brownley appeared, and Darcy sent Mrs. Gardiner and her sons on a tour of the ship.

"Nicely done, Mr. Darcy," Elizabeth said with sarcasm.

Darcy maneuvered her from the way of two men carrying strips of lumber for repairs to another vessel.

"I admit I wished time alone with you," he whispered. "You are my affianced, Elizabeth. You cannot think I could enjoy searching the English countryside for you."

"You thought I ran off with Mr. Wickham," she accused. "You traveled to Brighton to catch me with another!"

Darcy flinched internally. Although he did not wish to consider the possibility, the thought of Elizabeth with Mr. Wickham crossed his mind.

"I did not offer you an untruth. Colonel Fitzwilliam was in

Brighton before I learned of your disappearance from Longbourn. As to Mr. Wickham, I delivered a message from Mr. Sloane to my former friend."

"Why would this Mr. Sloane contact you regarding Mr. Wickham? It has been years since you two claimed an allegiance," Elizabeth charged.

"Your precious Mr. Wickham," Darcy hissed, "owes Sloane an exorbitant debt, and this is not the first time Mr. Wickham cultivated a dangerous enemy. Such is the man you chose to defend to me."

Darcy clamped his jaw together before he could say more.

Again, Elizabeth had him acting as an oaf.

With a deep sigh of resignation, Darcy whispered, "I injured you again. It is never my purpose, but I am often from step when it comes to you. I wish to remain dispassionate; unfortunately, I am weak when under you spell, Elizabeth."

"Mr. Darcy?" she murmured in what sounded of regret. "I do not know what to believe," she admitted.

"Your eyes or your heart?" Darcy breathed the words.

She did not look at him, but a slight nod of affirmation told Darcy she understood.

"Permit me to show you something of this vessel," he said softly.

He turned Elizabeth so she faced away from him. Darcy rested his hands lightly upon her shoulders as he murmured his explanation into her ear.

"I had business in Hull in February when I came across this ship. She limped into port, and many among the men who viewed her thought she would never prove herself, but I was of a different mind for you see I fell in love with her the moment I took in her beauty and her grace.

"So while my companions criticized the lack of perfect symmetry in her form, I noted a vessel pleasing to the eye, and while others spoke of her awkward lines, I knew real admiration for the potential she promised."

Darcy pointed to the name upon the ship's side.

"After months of anguish of my own making, I took a leap of faith and accepted this ship as a sign from God. When I learned you resided with your cousin at Hunsford Cottage, I asked Mr. Brownley to move the yacht to Dover. I wished to show you my devotion after you accepted my hand. I had it all planned, but my cursed tongue ruined what could have been."

"It is *Lizzy's Delight*," she said softly.

Darcy smiled in wry amusement.

"Yes, *Lizzy's Delight*. Such was what I expected. I thought any woman would be delighted to be 'Mrs. Darcy,' but you humbled me for the better. My conceit proved false, but I promise, Elizabeth, if you will provide us another opportunity, I will make this right."

Chapter 10

"YOU LOOK VERY WELL," Mrs. Harville observed when she joined Elizabeth in preparation for their evening at the Royal Hotel.

Elizabeth glanced to her reflection in the oval glass.

"I wish we did not agree to join the gentleman this evening," she admitted.

Since her encounter with Mr. Darcy earlier in the day, Elizabeth's emotions remained off kilter. Mr. Darcy's disclosure regarding his purchase of the yacht had Elizabeth in turmoil. Even if the dratted gentleman was the handsomest man of her acquaintance, it did not justify why her insides turned somersaults like a carnival performer.

"Do you dislike Mr. Darcy so very much?" Mrs. Harville inquired. "I find the gentleman quite affable, especially for a man who claims an earl as his uncle."

"Yes, I suppose so," Elizabeth said distractedly.

"But you did not always think so?" Mrs. Harville asked as she added a beaded band to Elizabeth's hair.

Elizabeth sighed heavily with resignation.

"No. I cannot say I always thought well of Mr. Darcy, although upon hindsight, I would admit to enjoying the quickness of the man's mind."

Elizabeth shrugged her shoulders in disbelief.

"Mr. Darcy once remarked that I was tolerable, but not handsome enough to tempt him."

Mrs. Harville halted her administrations to look seriously upon Elizabeth.

"I imagine such a comment did little to advance your relationship with the gentleman. Yet, it is quite obvious Mr. Darcy affects you, I doubt his appearance in Portsmouth has more to do with your presence in the port city than to do with his business interest."

Elizabeth protested, "I would be perfectly happy if Mr. Darcy withdrew."

Mrs. Harville retrieved her shawl from the back of a chair.

"I believe, Mrs. Bryland, that you offer yourself a falsehood. I do not know your true connection to Mr. Darcy, but like it or not, the man engages your affections."

The woman's tone switched to warning.

"I shall ask one thing of you: Do not lead Captain Wentworth to believe you would accept his attentions if you cannot give of yourself completely. Our dearest Frederick gave away part of his heart to a woman some years past. Captain Wentworth never speaks of the lady or what occurred, but a woman easily recognizes the great pain of disappointed hopes in another.

"Frederick has not shown serious interest in any woman until the captain took your acquaintance. Do not encourage him, Mrs. Bryland, unless you mean to accept Wentworth's hand. He is a good man, and he deserves a woman to complete him."

Over supper, Elizabeth guarded every word she uttered. She avoided the challenging smile of Mr. Darcy and the man's all too confident air. Likewise, Elizabeth ignored the raw sensuality of Captain Wentworth. She thought her journey would provide her a bit of freedom, but Elizabeth felt as a trapped animal.

Upon their entrance, Mr. Darcy claimed Elizabeth's hand, and with masculine determination brought it to his lips. She attempted to pull her hand free, but the gentleman tightened his grip upon her fingers.

"I am pleased you could join me," Mr. Darcy said to the group as he placed Elizabeth's hand upon his arm to escort her to the private dining room. Elizabeth was sorry to admit the sound of Mr. Darcy's breathing was in tune with the beat of her heart.

The conversation swirled around her, but Elizabeth had difficulty in attending to any of the details. She sat between Darcy and Commander Benwick, while Mrs. Harville claimed her husband and Captain Wentworth as tablemates.

"It appears Benwick will not be part of my next crew," Wentworth shared. "He has been with me since serving as a lieutenant upon the *Laconia*."

On a jaundiced note, Benwick added, "It will seem odd not to have Wentworth as my commanding officer, but I have the promise of a promotion with a successful mission. If so, Miss Harville and I can claim our joining sooner. I cannot think the war will last much longer."

"Although I will grieve for the loss of your good sense, Benwick, anything which brings you closer to claiming Harville's sister cannot be ill," Wentworth assured.

Elizabeth's attention returned to the conversation.

"Does this mean you and Commander Harville will continue your service soon?"

Despite knowing these men engaged in the King's business, Elizabeth did not think upon the possibility until this very moment that they were destined to return to the war. The thought that they might die as a result sent a shiver of dread down her spine.

"With gratitude to Wentworth, I will also claim a rise in rank when we return to sea," Harville declared.

"I am much pleased for your good fortune, Commander," Elizabeth said with genuine affection.

With the exception of Mr. Darcy, the people about the table took her in when she could claim nothing but immediate family.

Wentworth explained, "Without the assistance of Harville,

I would never have brought the *Asp* safely into port. Many men would have died that day."

"The gale set upon us before the small boats took all the crew ashore," Harville explained in the way of all men relating a tale of adventure. "The rain and the wind lasted four days. If we were still at sea, we would be on the ocean's bottom."

In spite of her best efforts to remain unaffected, tears of empathy misted her eyes.

"We never had two days of foul weather in all the time we were at sea, and the *Asp* stood strong against the French frigate we captured," Wentworth assured.

Harville chuckled.

"Face it, Wentworth, the *Asp* knew better days before you took command of it."

"Aye, the Admiralty entertains itself, now and then, with sending a few hundred men to sea in a ship not fit to be employed," Benwick shared. "But they have a great many for which to provide, and among the thousands who may just as well go to the bottom as not, it is impossible for the Admiralty to distinguish the very set who may be least missed."

"You best not permit my Brother Croft hear you make such statements," Wentworth teased. "The Admiral believes there was not a better sloop than the *Asp* in her day."

Harville grumbled, "The Admiral did not serve upon the *Asp*."

"When do you return to the sea, Sir," Mr. Darcy inquired.

"I will depart for Liverpool by week's end," Benwick answered.

"And Wentworth and I take up the stern of the *Resolve* within a fortnight," Harville added.

"So soon?" Elizabeth remarked before she could stifle the words. "And what of you, Mrs. Harville? Will you remain in Portsmouth?"

"At least for the foreseeable future. Miss Harville is traveling to Portsmouth, and I cannot depart until my sister in marriage arrives."

Elizabeth turned to Benwick.

"Please say Miss Harville will arrive before you depart. It would be a shame not to be permitted a farewell."

Benwick's eyes took on one of longing.

"I can only add my prayers to those who wish to claim the loves of their lives."

Elizabeth squeezed the back of the man's hand in consideration.

"I shall add my prayers to yours, Sir. I wish you and Miss Harville many years of happiness."

Although Elizabeth enjoyed the afternoon with Captain Wentworth and the Harvilles, she found herself looking over her shoulder for Mr. Darcy, but the gentleman did not appear on the day after her party joined him at the Royal Hotel, nor did he send a note of explanation for his absence.

A small part of Elizabeth was glad for his withdrawal, but a more important part, that of her heart, knew great disappointment.

Mr. Darcy walked back to the Harvilles' residence with her party last evening, and in spite of her decision to deny the man her acceptance, Elizabeth walked beside him.

"What is our future, Elizabeth?" Mr. Darcy asked softly as they trailed the others.

"There is no 'our' in my future, Sir," she said with less enthusiasm that previously.

They walked in silence for several minutes before Mr. Darcy said, "You wish my withdrawal?"

Elizabeth could not bring herself to say the words, which would lead to their permanent separation.

"I wish you the same freedom as I hope to claim."

"Does that freedom include Captain Wentworth?"

"The captain deserves a woman who affects him."

Mr. Darcy slowed their steps to maintain the gap between

them and the Harvilles.

"If I leave you in Portsmouth, your reputation will know ruin. We can be in the same city as you stay with the Harvilles, but your situation becomes more problematic if you permit a gentleman of whom Mr. Bennet holds no knowledge to escort you about town."

"My reputation is an illusion at best," Elizabeth protested. "Your leaving me at the altar sealed my fate, Mr. Darcy. I mean only to claim a bit of society and a few precious memories before I return to Longbourn to become 'Aunt Lizzy' to my sisters' offspring."

"A woman of your magnificence as a spinster is a waste," Mr. Darcy argued. "Surely you wish more than such a fate."

"You mean surely I wish to be Mrs. Darcy," Elizabeth charged.

She could feel Mr. Darcy's gaze skimming her form.

"Would being Mistress of Pemberley and the mother of my children be such a cross to bear?"

An image of several children dancing about, all with the look of Mr. Darcy filled Elizabeth's mind. It was a dream she experienced often of late.

"No, Sir," she whispered. "Both were once a lovely prospect, but I am of a practical nature. Dreams are for fools."

They approached where the others awaited them.

"Elizabeth," Mr. Darcy said without looking at her, "please do not discredit a chance for happiness just because you are frightened to trust."

"Frightened?" Elizabeth hissed. "Surely you grasp at straws, Sir."

"Perhaps," he pronounced in what sounded of exasperation. "Yet, despite your objections, I believe in our complementary natures. You cannot view the affection I hold for you, but it exists just the same."

With that, Mr. Darcy made his farewells to the group and turned away. Elizabeth accepted Commander Benwick's arm as they crossed to the Harvilles' door. To take Captain Wentworth's arm smacked of betrayal.

When Darcy returned to the Royal Hotel, a message awaited him, and so at dawn he set out for Hertfordshire. In his grasp, Darcy clutched his cousin's note while he cursed his lack of foresight in dealing with George Wickham.

"Any fool could predict that Mr. Wickham would act without honor when Fitzwilliam threatened to inform Sloane of Mr. Wickham's whereabouts. I was too consumed with my need to discover Elizabeth," he grumbled under breath, "to think with reason."

Darcy looked up from his dark thoughts when his coach turned into the land leading to Longbourn. Darcy regretted not informing Elizabeth of his task, but he knew his fiancée well enough to know Elizabeth would insist upon returning to Hertfordshire with him. As foolish as it would sound to others, Darcy could not trust himself alone in his coach with her for so many hours. He would permit Mr. Bennet to return her to the manor for their traveling together would bury Elizabeth further in shame. As it was, only he and she knew of her impetuous decision. Darcy would insist Mr. Bennet practice discretion.

"Mr. Darcy," Mr. Bennet met Darcy before the main house, "what brings you to Hertfordshire?" Mr. Bennet's tone was everything but welcoming.

"I learned something of your worries for Miss Lydia, and I thought to offer my assistance. I dealt with Mr. Wickham on multiple occasions."

Mr. Bennet's disdain continued.

"Why does that particular fact not surprise me? You ruin my second daughter and your former friend ruins my youngest. What is it about the men from Derbyshire, which grants them privilege over others?"

Darcy's temper flared, but he spoke with practiced calmness.

"Miss Elizabeth's reputation is safe. It is my intention to make her my wife; however, Miss Lydia's foolish decision is more problematic." He gestured toward the house. "Perhaps we might step into your study to speak in private."

Mr. Bennet shrugged with resignation before turning to lead the way into the house.

Miss Bennet, who accepted Darcy's hat and gloves, met them.

"I am pleased you came," the lady offered. "Mr. Bingley believes you hold intimate knowledge of Mr. Wickham, which will assist Mr. Bennet's efforts."

"I pray so," Darcy spoke in kindness.

Elizabeth's eldest sister always looked to the best in every man. He glanced to where Mr. Bennet made his way toward his study.

"If you would send word to Netherfield and ask Mr. Bingley and Colonel Fitzwilliam to join your father and me, I would appreciate the kindness. I did not call at Netherfield before I came to Longbourn."

Miss Bennet followed Darcy's gaze.

"Mr. Bennet suffers greatly," she confided. "First Lizzy's shame and now Lydia's. While Mrs. Bennet declaims her nerves for all to hear, our father takes each incidence as a sign of his failure as a parent."

Darcy kept his opinions of the Bennets private. When he married Elizabeth, the couple would become part of Darcy's family, and he would exercise his influence over the Bennets at that time.

"I am certain Mr. Bingley shared my desire to keep my engagement with Miss Elizabeth," Darcy confessed. "Please know I spoke to your sister recently and expressed my expectations."

Tears misted Miss Bennet's eyes.

"Mr. Bingley promised you would not forsake Elizabeth without good reason."

"The reason is tied to this business with Mr. Wickham,"

Darcy confided. "Therefore, I should join Mr. Bennet so we might devise a plan to recover Miss Lydia."

With that, Darcy trailed Mr. Bennet along the passage to the man's private room. He pointedly closed the door and without permission, assumed a seat before Mr. Bennet's desk.

"I asked Miss Bennet to send word to Bingley and Colonel Fitzwilliam to join us," Darcy announced.

Mr. Bennet's eyebrow arched in disapproval.

"You are very free with your instructions in another man's house."

Darcy smiled in wry amusement.

"Why do we not discuss Miss Elizabeth's future before the others arrive? It would not do for us to be sniping at each other."

"What is there to discuss?" Mr. Bennet quipped. "Other than my dearest child's life is relegated to that of a spinster, what concerns might I possess?"

Darcy permitted his ire free rein.

"Did I not say five minutes prior that I mean to make Elizabeth my wife. Perhaps you should spend less time bemoaning what occurred a sennight prior and set your mind to making alternate plans for Miss Lydia's future?"

"Why do you not explain 'what occurred a sennight prior'?" Bennet charged.

"I thought my cousin offered you an explanation," Darcy insisted.

"When Colonel Fitzwilliam called upon Longbourn after that disastrous day, I was not of the mind to listen to his pledges upon your behalf. I heard bits of the story via Miss Bennet, but I would prefer to hear 'the truth' from you, Sir. You have no idea how my Lizzy suffered from your rebuke. Elizabeth rarely cries; yet, my dearest girl spent some four days doing little beyond grieving your absence at the church."

Bennet's words went a long way in explaining Elizabeth's stubborn resistance to renewing their understanding. His fiancée protected her heart: The realization provided Darcy hope.

"Very well," Darcy said evenly. "The day before the wedding I made a call on Rundell, Bridge, and Rundell for I commissioned a ring specifically designed for Elizabeth. When I exited the shop, several men *insisted* I join them in a nearby alley. I offered them my purse, but they did not mean to rob me. A man hired my assailants to deliver a message to the gentleman residing at Darcy House."

"What offense did you practice?" Bennet accused.

Darcy frowned his response.

"You possess little respect for me."

He paused in purposeful warning.

"Perhaps that is best. It will make the fall more dramatic."

With a shrug of indifference, Darcy continued, "The man erred, a fact he readily noted when he joined his hirelings in the alley. It appears Mr. Wickham was the real culprit. Wickham claimed Darcy House as his, and the gentleman's henchmen followed me by misstep. Wickham and I are of a similar stature.

"The gentleman ordered his men to bind me and drop me off in the woods outside of London. They left me with bruised ribs and multiple cuts and bruises. Once I managed to work my restraints free, I walked until a farmer and his hound discovered me. Once I returned to London, the surgeon forbid me to travel."

"Why did you not send word to Elizabeth?" Mr. Bennet demanded.

"It was several days after the wedding before I achieved a rescue. I sent Colonel Fitzwilliam as my courier, but by then Elizabeth left Longbourn. It took me several days to locate her."

"Then you spoke to Lizzy in London. Did Elizabeth forgive your slight?" Mr. Bennet asked through tight lips.

Darcy tired of Bennet's posturing. He responded with a hint of steel.

"You are behind the times, Bennet: Your daughter Elizabeth is not with your Brother Gardiner."

"What mean you by this nonsense?" Bennet hissed. "Mr. Lester left her in Cheapside."

"No nonsense," Darcy said with perverted pleasure. "Miss Elizabeth perfected a ruse at your coachman's expense. Your daughter hired a hack to return her to the coaching inn at Watford. There she purchased the fare to Brighton."

"Elizabeth cannot be in Brighton," Bennet insisted. "If she were, someone from Meryton would have noticed her and informed Colonel Forster."

"Very true," Darcy said smugly. "I doubt if Miss Elizabeth thought upon the Meryton militia being housed at Brighton when she considered the Prince's favorite watering hole. From what I understand, Miss Elizabeth wished a bit of freedom before claiming a life as a spinster."

"Do not speak so gaily of Lizzy's prospects," Bennet ordered.

"I find nothing in Miss Elizabeth's choices to my liking," Darcy retorted.

"Then if Elizabeth is not in London or in Brighton, where pray tell is my daughter?"

Darcy stretched out his legs in comfort. The conversation shifted to his control.

"Miss Elizabeth's kind heart sent her upon another adventure."

Darcy chuckled when he considered his betrothed's impetuous nature. He would spend a lifetime in amazement at his wife's daring.

"At Watford, Elizabeth took the acquaintance of Mrs. Bylane, a woman set for Portsmouth to reunite with her sailor husband. After the woman purchased her fare, Mrs. Bylane learned said husband would come ashore in Brighton instead."

Mr. Bennet closed his eyes and shook his head in disbelief.

"Elizabeth traded the coaching fares with the woman," Bennet said in affection.

"Oh, yes, Miss Elizabeth set out alone for a port city of which she held no knowledge," Darcy disclosed in equal regard.

"Does Elizabeth remain in Portsmouth?" Bennet asked in

concern.

"I saw her last evening. She resides with Commander and Mrs. Harville, a good-hearted couple who let her a room so Miss Elizabeth would not be alone in a strange city."

Darcy sat forward to press his point.

"As Commander Harville is to return to the sea soon, it would be best to retrieve Miss Elizabeth before someone discovers she is not 'Mrs. Bryland.'"

"Mrs. Bryland?" Bennet asked with amused interest.

"Yes, your daughter pretends to be a widow, but Miss Elizabeth did not realize a widow is as fair a target as any woman," Darcy explained. "The Harvilles cannot continue to offer their protection."

"Does it bother you, Darcy, that others find Elizabeth desirable?" Bennet taunted.

"Do not think for a moment that I do not desire your daughter," Darcy declared baldly.

Bennet's frown lines deepened.

"I would prefer not to dwell upon that image," Elizabeth's father admitted.

Darcy ignored Bennet's continued objections.

"You will retrieve Elizabeth from Portsmouth while I track Miss Lydia's whereabouts," Darcy instructed. "I want my affianced under your roof so we may set another date for the wedding."

"And if I ignore your orders?" Bennet challenged.

"I will leave you to your dilemma with Miss Lydia and wish you well with Mr. Wickham's manipulations. Meanwhile I will return to Portsmouth, gather Miss Elizabeth to me and set sail for Scotland."

Darcy smiled in sardonic amusement.

"You see I moved my newest yacht to Portsmouth when I learned of Miss Elizabeth's presence in the city. Did I mention the ship's name? It is *Lizzy's Delight*: The perfect name for what I plan for Miss Elizabeth's future."

Chapter 11

"MAY I INQUIRE AS TO WHEN Miss Lydia traveled to Brighton?" Colonel Fitzwilliam directed his question to Mr. Bennet. "I was in Brighton for several days and was unaware of your youngest daughter's presence in Colonel Forster's household."

Darcy and Mr. Bennet came to a truce of sorts while they waited for Bingley and Fitzwilliam to arrive. After he tolerated Bennet's animosity directed squarely at Darcy, Darcy now took pleasure in watching Elizabeth's father squirm under Fitzwilliam's close scrutiny. The colonel knew how to bring the proudest man low.

"The household was at sixes and sevens after…"

Bennet shot a tentative glance to Darcy.

"After my lack of an appearance," Darcy finished Mr. Bennet's statement.

The man nodded his affirmation.

"Lydia is most difficult to manage when confinement is necessary; with Mrs. Bennet taking to her bed and Elizabeth to her quarters, Mrs. Forster's offer appeared prudent to eliminate Lydia's protestations. I knew Forster to be a sensible man. The invitation showed itself as ideal."

Bingley's frown lines deepened.

"Even so, I would not say Mrs. Forster, who is but nineteen, possesses the maturity to serve as a proper chaperone for Miss Lydia. Mrs. Forster is younger than Miss Bennet and Miss Elizabeth and the same age as Miss Mary. One should not extend Forster's reputation for responsible actions to his wife; Mrs. Foster is known to be quite flighty."

Darcy kept the smirk from his lips. One reason he and Bingley became ready intimates was they held similar values. Despite the differences in their upbringings, they were both firstborn sons, meant to assume their family's assets. Such responsibility hones a man's preferences. Bingley admired Miss Bennet's handsome face, but more importantly Darcy's friend spoke often of the lady's good sense. Likewise, Darcy admired Elizabeth's quick wit and astute opinions as much as he did her alluring attractions. A man who chose a partner purely for her comely appearance lived to rue the day.

"Mrs. Bennet thought the idea a fine one," Bennet offered in excuse.

Their group offered Bennet no more censure. It would prove fruitless to beat a dead horse: The Bennets were not likely to change their parenting skills or the lack thereof.

"Where do we go from here?" Darcy asked, at length.

Fitzwilliam shared, "Mr. Wickham and Miss Lydia left Brighton together on Sunday night and were together almost to London, but not beyond; they certainly are not gone to Scotland."

"Then I think you and I should be to London," Darcy confirmed. "I know something of Mr. Wickham's haunts, and you can move among his associates in the militia."

"What of me?" Bennet inquired.

"You and Colonel Forster should return to Brighton. Question Captain Denny and Wickham's other intimates. Plead with Mrs. Forster to share what Miss Lydia said of the event. Someone among Wickham's companions possesses knowledge of his whereabouts."

Darcy paused before adding a truth Mr. Bennet had yet to

consider. Bennet was thinking only in terms of an elopement.

"Most recently, Mr. Wickham raised the ire of several powerful men," Darcy explained. "The man who set his hirelings on me is among them. I fear Wickham runs scared, and Miss Lydia is a useful tool to evade the creditors."

Mr. Bennet paled.

"Surely you must see it is unlikely that any young man should form such a design against a girl who is by no means unprotected or friendless and who was actually staying in his colonel's household. Could Wickham expect Lydia's friends would not step forward? Could the cad expect to be noticed again by the regiment after such an affront to Colonel Forster? His temptation is not adequate to risk."

Bingley added, "It is really too great a violation of decency, honor, and interest for Wickham to be guilty of what you insinuate, Darcy. I realize you have long been at odds with the man, but I cannot think so very ill of Wickham."

"Not, perhaps, of neglecting his own interest; but of every other neglect, I believe Wickham capable," Darcy countered. "If, indeed, it should be so! But I dare not hope it. Why should Mr. Wickham and Miss Lydia not go on to Scotland, if that is the case?"

Bingley challenged, "There is no absolute proof that they are not gone to Scotland."

"Oh, but their removing from the chaise into a hackney coach," Fitzwilliam interjected, "is such a presumption! Moreover, no traces of them were to be found on the Barnet road."

"Supposing them to be in London," Mr. Bennet thought aloud. "They may be there, though, for the purpose of concealment, for no more exceptional purpose. It is not likely that money should be very abundant on either side; and it might strike them that they could be more economically, though less expeditiously, married in London than in Scotland."

"But why all the secrecy?" Darcy argued. "Why any fear of detection? Why must their marriage be private? You would offer few objections, Sir. You knew nothing of my concerns, and Miss

Elizabeth is not at Longbourn to speak against the joining.

"Moreover, by Colonel Forster's account, Mr. Wickham told others he was not persuaded to marry Miss Lydia. In my opinion, Wickham will never marry a woman without money and connections; he cannot afford to do so. Surely Miss Elizabeth spoke of Mr. Wickham's desertion of her for Miss King's sudden inheritance."

Mr. Bennet's features hardened. Darcy would bet this situation would make Elizabeth's father more circumspect.

"You are saying Lydia possesses little beyond youth, health, and good humor to make Wickham forego every chance of benefiting from a well-placed marriage."

Elizabeth's father spoke barely above a whisper as reality claimed the man's composure.

Darcy nodded his agreement. He did not wish to deflate Bennet's hope, but Elizabeth's father never previously dealt with a man of Wickham's temperament. If they were to recover Lydia Bennet, they must not carry delusions into the fray.

Bingley asked in awe, "Can you think that Miss Lydia is so lost to everything but love of Mr. Wickham as to consent…?"

Darcy's friend did not finish his question, but each man in Bennet's study understood the implication.

Mr. Bennet sighed heavily in resignation.

"I permitted my youngest too much latitude. I fear Lydia is given up to nothing but amusement and vanity. I am sorry to say that since the militia first quartered at Meryton, only officers filled Lydia's head."

"And Mr. Wickham possesses every charm of person and address to captivate a woman," Fitzwilliam said in harsh tones.

Darcy knew his cousin thought if not for providence Georgiana could be in Miss Lydia's position.

Darcy spoke boldly and honestly.

"I know Wickham as he really is. He is my father's godson and my most constant youthful companion. As much as it pains me to say so, Mr. Wickham is profligate in every sense of the word;

he possesses neither integrity nor honor. Mr. Wickham is as false and deceitful as he is insinuating."

Bingley had yet to abandon hope.

"When they all removed to Brighton, did you have no reason to believe Miss Lydia and Wickham fond of each other?"

Acceptance of the truth scarred Mr. Bennet's features.

"Not the slightest. No symptom of affection on either side brought notice, and you must be aware that with a family of six females, had anything of the kind been obvious, it could not be thrown away. When Mr. Wickham first entered the corps, Lydia was ready enough to admire him, but so all were. Every girl in or near Meryton was out of her senses about Wickham for the first two months."

Bennet's description struck a sour note with Darcy for he knew Elizabeth among those who sought Mr. Wickham's attentions.

"Wickham never distinguished Lydia by any particular attention, and, consequently, after a moderate period of extravagance and wild admiration, Lydia's fancy for Mr. Wickham gave way, and others of the regiment, who treated Lydia with more distinction, again became my youngest daughter's favorites."

Mr. Darcy remained absent from Portsmouth, and Elizabeth's desolation returned. She cursed her stubbornness for sending the gentleman away. Her determined distance proved the straw to upset Mr. Darcy's cart.

"What can I say?' she murmured as she looked out upon the sound from a point on the hill looking down on the town. "I am not one to trust easily. Too often when I do permit my guard to slip, I am proved mistaken. Mr. Wickham is a prime example. Although I do not know the extent of Mr. Wickham's offenses, I do know Mr. Darcy is not capable of the ill will of which Wickham accuses him.

"Mayhap I would be less susceptible to the least of Mr.

Darcy's criticisms if I did not desire his good intentions."

"Talking to yourself?" a familiar voice came from behind her.

Elizabeth spun around to discover Captain Wentworth not six feet removed.

"I did not hear your approach, Sir," she said in embarrassment.

The captain came to stand beside her.

"I meant no offense, Mrs. Bryland. I searched you out. Mrs. Harville told me of your intentions to climb to the look out point today."

"I am fond of a hearty walk," Elizabeth offered in explanation.

Wentworth smiled easily.

"You are of a healthy disposition, I assume."

"Only once did my mother worry for my well being. A measles outbreak claimed me and two of my sisters, while Mama was in London on errands. Needless to say, my mother did not approve of my father's lack of care of his children."

"Men hold no sense in these matters," Wentworth claimed in sympathy.

Elizabeth's eyebrow arched in a challenge.

"Then humanity must succumb to the diseases of the world for physics and surgery are the domain of men."

"Touché, Mrs. Bryland," the officer said with a wry twist of his lips.

Elizabeth returned her attention to the Sound.

"It is so beautiful," she said wistfully. "I always wished to know more of the world. Before I traveled to Portsmouth, all I ever knew was Cheapside, Hertfordshire, and a bit of Kent. There is so much yet to learn and so much I will never see. It makes me quite sad to think upon it."

Elizabeth felt the warmth of Captain Wentworth's breath across her cheek as the man moved closer.

"It is still possible for you to possess your wish," he said softly.

Elizabeth recognized what would follow; she knew because Mrs. Harville alerted Elizabeth of the captain's intentions. Such was the reason she sought her own company for the last few days rather than sharing the outings planned by the Harvilles.

"I fear not, Captain," she said without turning her head in his direction. "I must return shortly to my father's household. My world ends at these shores."

The captain edged nearer still.

"You possess other alternatives, Mrs. Bryland."

Swallowing her pride, Elizabeth turned to look up into the captain's weathered countenance.

"You are one of the kindest gentlemen of my acquaintance, Sir, and I can never repay you for the protection you extended upon my behalf, but I would be remiss if I permitted you to extend your protection beyond my stay in Portsmouth. In two days time, I shall reclaim my childhood home and accept my role in life."

Wentworth scowled with her declaration.

"You are a vibrant woman, Mrs. Bryland, and it would be against all things holy for you to know a life of doldrums. Do you hold no aspirations to marry again?"

Elizabeth could not stifle the sigh that rushed to her lips.

"I once considered myself the pragmatic one in my family, but I fear I am as consumed with stories of knightly heroes as my sisters."

The captain's ironic humor returned.

"I cannot imagine Mr. Darcy in chain mail."

Elizabeth accepted the image as her own.

"You err, Captain. Mr. Darcy possesses all the qualities of Sir Gawain of King Arthur's table. Do you not recall Sir Gawain's honor when tempted by the Green Knight's wife? Gawain even wore the girdle he accepted as protection against the Green Knight as a symbol of the temptation to which he succumbed. Mr. Darcy protects all who mean to bring deception to those he affects and even to those he does not."

"You hold Mr. Darcy in regard?" the captain questioned.

Elizabeth closed her eyes against the truth: Despite her best efforts, her bottom lip trembled, and she paused to gather her composure before continuing.

"I did not think it possible," she admitted. "Have you ever known deep affection, Captain?"

Surprisingly, Wentworth flinched. Elizabeth's question evidently lanced a wound the captain did not wish to reopen.

"I did not mean to press you," Elizabeth said in consideration.

Wentworth shook off her apology.

"It is only fair. I asked of your attachment to Mr. Darcy."

He gazed at Elizabeth with uncertainty.

"There was a woman," he said in reflection, "some six years prior. Our relationship was short lived–the matter of only a few months. I spoke of Miss Anne to no one beyond my brother Edward, not even to Harville or Benwick."

"Sometimes it is easier to share with strangers what we cannot say to those we trust most." Elizabeth managed a weak smile. "Did the lady refuse you?"

She knew something of the sting of refusal.

"Not initially," Wentworth admitted, at length. "She was the daughter of a baronet, and I had yet to know either my current rank or the fortune I earned as prize money for French captures. Miss Anne was persuaded to give me up."

Air seeped slowly from Wentworth's lungs.

Elizabeth spoke in irony.

"Did I ever tell you Mr. Darcy's maternal uncle is an earl and the gentleman can trace his ancestral roots back some six hundred years?"

Wentworth cocked a brow.

"That explains much of the gentleman's demeanor."

Elizabeth presented him a long, slow look.

"We are a miserable pair, are we not, Captain?"

Darkness appeared to burn Wentworth's soul, and Elizabeth wondered if she would one day know similar emotions.

"We are a *pair*, Mrs. Bryland, and I would consider it an honor if you would permit me to show you something of the world."

Mayhap if the captain addressed his offer to *Elizabeth Bennet* rather than to the fictitious *Mrs. Bryland*, Elizabeth might have thought twice before refusing. Captain Wentworth would make some woman an excellent husband, but it would not be she. Her heart was engaged elsewhere.

Although she never thought of herself as fanciful, Elizabeth could not *settle* for anyone other than the author of a love letter tucked away in her traveling case. She never dreamed of a man who could inspire her feminine hopes, but Elizabeth discovered him in the form of the Master of Pemberley.

Elizabeth could feel the captain's gaze heating her face. Her heart pinched at the ache gnawing away in her chest.

"I thank you for your thoughtfulness, Captain, but I would prefer to think of you knowing the contentment of a woman who returns your affection. I am very fond of you, but I am resolved to return to my father's household. I owe my parents my allegiance."

Dutifully, Wentworth escorted Elizabeth upon her return to the Harvilles' residence. No more was said of the gentleman's offer. Instead, the captain told her of his latest command, *The Resolve*.

"It is a fine sloop, so much better than any I captained previously."

They approached the Harvilles' door, and Elizabeth glanced up to note a familiar carriage upon the street. She stumbled to a halt and clutched at the captain's arm for support.

"What is amiss, Ma'am?" the captain asked in concern.

"A carriage from home," Elizabeth murmured.

Releasing her hold on Wentworth's arm, she rushed through the Harvilles' entrance. With each step, Elizabeth pronounced a silent prayer that something ill did not plague Mr. Darcy. *Odd*, she thought. *In less than a month the man became more important to her than her immediate family.*

"Mr. Bingley," she said as she entered the parlor. "I did not expect to find you here. I pray all is well in Hertfordshire."

Elizabeth bit her tongue to keep from saying, *And Derbyshire*.

"I am sent to fetch you home, Mis… Mrs. Bryland."

Elizabeth's breath caught in her chest. So, Mr. Darcy schooled his friend in Elizabeth's deception.

She swallowed her anxiety from a few moments prior.

"Permit me to give you the acquaintance of my escort, Captain Wentworth, and then you may explain your charge from my family."

Bingley glanced to the captain in disapproval before agreeing to Elizabeth's stipulations.

"Certainly."

He bowed to the room.

Elizabeth turned to Wentworth.

"Captain, may I present my eldest sister's particular friend, Mr. Bingley."

She would not customarily add the description to her introduction, but after spending nearly a fortnight in Wentworth's company, Elizabeth knew the captain would not easily leave her unless he thought Elizabeth safe in Bingley's care.

"Mr. Bingley, my recent acquaintance, Captain Wentworth of His Majesty's Royal Navy."

Bingley said all that was necessary, as did the captain before Wentworth excused himself.

With Wentworth's exit, Elizabeth directed Bingley to return to his seat.

"Speak to me what brings you after me. Is it Papa? Jane? I assume Mr. Darcy sent you to find me."

Bingley shot a quick glance to the still open door before lowering his voice.

"Miss Bennet and your father are in health," he assured, "but Jane requires your assistance with Mrs. Bennet and the neighborhood."

Elizabeth frowned deeply.

"I do not imagine I could be of service."

"You do not understand. Mr. Bennet and Colonel Forster are in Brighton, while Darcy and Colonel Fitzwilliam are to London. They search for Mr. Wickham."

Elizabeth sucked in a ragged breath.

"What offense has Mr. Wickham offered Mr. Darcy this time?"

"It is not Darcy who Wickham insults," Bingley protested. "It is your family. Wickham and Miss Lydia ran off. The initial thought was they would travel to Scotland, but that has not occurred."

"I do not understand," Elizabeth began.

Bingley hastened his response.

"We possess time enough to detail all that occurred on our return to Hertfordshire. How quickly may you be prepared to depart? I promised Miss Bennet we would return in a timely manner. Unfortunately, I was delayed overnight near Reading because of an issue with the coach's back wheel. If we depart soon, we could be at Longbourn before midnight."

Elizabeth stood to do as Mr. Bingley bid.

"I shan't be long. I planned to travel to Longbourn in two days' time, and so I previously organized my things. I shall hurry."

Bingley followed Elizabeth to her feet.

"Everything will be well. Darcy and Mr. Bennet will discover a means to bring Wickham up to snuff."

A few minutes later found her folding the last of her items to place them in her traveling trunk; Elizabeth's mind raced from one point to another.

How did Mr. Darcy become involved in her family's business? Did he depart Portsmouth specifically to aid her father? Could the gentleman's actions mean Mr. Darcy still cared for her?

Would her father know disappointment with her deception?

What if Mr. Wickham refused to oblige his duties to Lydia? And even if Mr. Wickham acted with honor, how could Mr. Darcy think to continue his understanding with her if Wickham was to be the gentleman's brother in marriage?

Elizabeth feared giving her hopes free rein again, and so she pulled harder against her defenses.

As Elizabeth made her farewells to the Harvilles and Captain Wentworth, she knew guilt for not worrying more upon what Lydia suffered. Yet, her relationship with Mr. Darcy held precedence. As she threw a retrospective glance over the whole of their acquaintance, so full of contradictions and varieties, she sighed at the perverseness of those feelings would now promote its continuance and would formerly rejoice in its termination.

Wishes for the gentleman's presence at her side proved vain, and the most Elizabeth could achieve was to amuse herself with them in the hurry and confusion of their departure from Portsmouth. Had Elizabeth been at leisure to be idle, she would remain certain that all employment was impossible to one so wretched as she. Less than an hour saw the whole completed, and there was nothing to be done but to go. Elizabeth, after the tension of the morning and a refusal of Captain Wentworth's honest proposal, found herself, in a shorter space of time than she could suppose, seated in Mr. Bingley's carriage and on the road to Longbourn.

Chapter 12

"FIRST, WE SHOULD SEEK OUT COWAN to learn what he discovered on Mr. Sloane," the colonel reasoned.

Darcy and Fitzwilliam arrived in London to organize their search for Mr. Wickham. Uncharacteristically, they argued upon their return to Darcy House.

"What will you do if Wickham abandons Miss Lydia?" the colonel asked after they greeted Georgiana.

Exhausted by the drama of the situation with the attack upon his person and the resulting disappearance of Elizabeth from Hertfordshire, Darcy spoke with more venom than he intended.

"I assume you wish to know if I intend to keep my commitment to Miss Elizabeth if her younger sister knows ruination."

The colonel's inflection rose in challenge.

"Will you?"

Darcy glanced away from his cousin's steady gaze. His mouth assumed a grim line.

"Tell me, Colonel, if it were Georgiana who knew ruination at Wickham's hands, would you and the rest of the Fitzwilliam family turn from my sister?"

"Wickham took advantage of Georgiana's immaturity," his

cousin argued.

"And I assure you, Miss Lydia holds not a fraction of Miss Darcy's good sense, and Elizabeth's sister is but months Georgiana's senior."

"You will welcome the chit into your family?" Fitzwilliam accused.

Darcy heaved a sigh of resignation.

"I will assist Mr. Bennet in securing Miss Lydia's future."

"What if Mr. Bennet insists that Mr. Wickham marry Miss Lydia? Will you call Wickham 'brother'? Will you force Georgiana to call Wickham 'brother'?"

Darcy conscience lashed him.

"I will speak to Georgiana of the possibility of a distant alliance to Mr. Wickham."

"The man's debtors will forever be at your door begging for succor!" Fitzwilliam protested.

"Do you think I am not often plagued with such pleas?" Darcy countered. "Nothing will change except I will have Elizabeth at my side."

Wariness draped his cousin's expression.

"You affect the woman that much?"

A tiny tendril of emotion wormed its way into Darcy's being, and a smile claimed his lips.

"Miss Elizabeth is my heart of hearts."

Once upon the road Mr. Bingley wasted no time in describing Lydia's foolish decision to elope with Mr. Wickham. Initially, Bingley "danced around" the more scandalous assumptions her father and Mr. Darcy made, but Elizabeth insisted upon knowing the absolute truth.

At length, she asked the question to which she most desired to know the answer.

"How did Mr. Darcy become involved in my father's business?"

"Darcy sent Colonel Fitzwilliam to deliver his apologies to you and your relatives after the colonel and Miss Darcy recovered Darcy from a farm some ten miles removed from London."

"I know nothing of a farm," Elizabeth admitted. "What was Mr. Darcy doing outside of London? Did he mean to hide until Mr. Bennet's ire subsided?"

Why she never asked of what detained Mr. Darcy, Elizabeth held no idea except to present credit to her stubborn denials.

"Does this have something to do with the bruises upon Mr. Darcy's cheeks?" she asked in regret.

Elizabeth assumed the marks were the result of some altercation at one of Mr. Darcy's clubs or perhaps time spent in fisticuffs under the watchful eye of Gentleman Jackson.

"Four men accosted Darcy outside a jeweler's shop. After a physical beating," Bingley explained, "the men bound and blindfolded Darcy and left him to die in the woods outside the Capital. According to the colonel, Darcy's ribs were badly bruised and cracked. Did you not notice the remnants of his cut lip and eye?"

She lifted her head to look upon Bingley's familiar countenance.

"I did not wish to see the obvious," Elizabeth murmured.

What she assumed as untruths proved to be reality.

"Again, how did Mr. Darcy become involved in Lydia's recovery?"

Elizabeth would spend time in deep consideration of the abuses she flung at Mr. Darcy's head, but for now she needed to concentrate on something other than how thoroughly she ruined her chances with the gentleman.

"When Fitzwilliam informed Darcy that you departed Longbourn, Darcy sought you out at the Gardiners' residence only to learn you took a carriage to a coaching inn upon the Hertfordshire route."

"Did Mr. Darcy and the colonel travel to Brighton to find me, thinking I sank into a tryst with Mr. Wickham?" Elizabeth demanded.

Although the evidence was most compelling in his favor, she did not wish to find Mr. Darcy completely blameless. Elizabeth's pride demanded she find another with whom to discover fault.

"The colonel traveled to Brighton to learn something of Wickham and the man that arranged an attack on Wickham," Bingley explained. "Unfortunately, the assailants mistook Darcy for Mr. Wickham. From what I know the colonel was several days in Brighton before Darcy arrived."

Elizabeth released her breath in a frustrated sigh. She possessed no idea who or what to believe.

"Then it was only Mr. Darcy who held no faith in me?"

Mr. Bingley's brow wrinkled in disapproval.

"Darcy affects you, Miss Elizabeth," he said in defense of his friend. "But even if Darcy did not know jealousy, how could you think he would act otherwise. In truth, Miss Bennet wondered aloud if you thought to reclaim Mr. Wickham's attentions while you were in London. If your most cherished sister holds such thoughts, how could you imagine that others would not do so likewise. You made it quite apparent that you considered Mr. Wickham the superior choice."

Regret crept deeper into Elizabeth's being: Her impetuous actions would be easily misconstrued. If she did not run away from her misery, this separation from Mr. Darcy would not be resolved.

"None of us realized," Bingley continued, "you thought to go to Brighton until Colonel Fitzwilliam returned to Netherfield, and the colonel only confided in me when we learned of Miss Lydia's elopement. Fitzwilliam assisted in locating the woman with whom you exchanged your fares. The colonel says Darcy was frantic in his search for fear you would encounter danger upon your journey."

Bingley's words brought another round of self-doubt to Elizabeth's already confused thoughts. She attempted one more sally against Mr. Darcy.

"I am Mr. Darcy's property," she said in disillusionment.

Bingley's mouth tightened into a firm line.

"I never heard such foolish talk coming from you, Miss Elizabeth. Darcy offers you an exulted position in Society. He rebukes the criticisms of those who would claim your connections below his. Do you not recognize how Darcy meant to protect you by traveling to Portsmouth? It was fortunate that Darcy held a prior acquaintance of the Harvilles. Placing you with the family of friends protected you until the exchange of vows."

Ah, Elizabeth thought, *so Mr. Darcy took credit for the Harvilles' benevolence.*

"Darcy's search was more than a resentful man reclaiming his recalcitrant intended. Darcy had no means of knowing if Sloane's attack upon him was an aberration or whether you, too, were in danger by association with him and Mr. Wickham. It was brilliant to have you assume the name of *Bryland*. If news of your retreat becomes common knowledge, a ready excuse will protect your reputation. Darcy considers only your well being."

Elizabeth grew quiet after that. She realized Bingley only repeated what Mr. Darcy told him, but Mr. Bingley's estimations ate away at Elizabeth's purpose. Was there any truth in Bingley's assumption that Mr. Darcy affected her?

They traveled as expeditiously as possible and reached Longbourn earlier than expected. It was a comfort to Elizabeth to consider that Jane was not wearied by long expectations.

Elizabeth jumped from Bingley's coach and hurried into the vestibule, where Jane, who came running down stairs from her mother's apartment, immediately met her.

Elizabeth, as she affectionately embraced her, lost not a moment in asking whether anything was heard of the fugitives.

"Not yet," replied Jane.

Elizabeth glanced behind her where Bingley stood by the still open door.

"I shall leave you to your "good evenings" with Mr. Bingley. I plan to look in on our mother. It is late, Jane, and we shall speak in the morning." To Bingley, she added, "More than words can express, I appreciate your kindness, Sir."

With that, Elizabeth climbed the steps to her quarters.

Tomorrow, she would face the ramifications of her recent choices, as well as her family's fragile position in Society. This evening Elizabeth meant to dream of the warmth of Mr. Darcy's breath upon her neck and the heat of his touch upon her skin.

Even as he approached the house upon Edward Street, Darcy's thoughts remained with Elizabeth. He wondered how she reacted to Mr. Bingley's arrival in Portsmouth to escort her to Longbourn.

"Likely more kindly to Bingley than the lady would be to me," he grumbled under his breath.

Darcy wondered how Elizabeth took to the story he spun of seeing her to his "friends," the Harvilles, until this mayhem with Wickham, Mr. Sloane, and now with Miss Lydia knew a conclusion. He did all he could to protect Elizabeth's reputation from his intended's foolish choices, but Darcy was not certain his efforts would be enough to earn a bit of Elizabeth's heart.

"What if she chose to accept Wentworth?" he murmured as he raised his hand to release the knocker.

Darcy held no reason to believe Wentworth would not speak his proposal. All Darcy could pray was Bingley whisked Elizabeth away before Darcy's lady could accept another man. Although he still considered Elizabeth his fiancée, in truth, with his absence from the church, Elizabeth was free to choose elsewhere.

"Yes, Sir?"

A young servant girl cracked the door to peer out at him, and Darcy forced his musing of Elizabeth to the back of his mind.

"Mr. Darcy to speak to Mrs. Younge," he said in a voice few would dare challenge.

"This way, Sir," the girl said with downcast eyes.

The girl led him to a small parlor near the rear of the house and gestured him inside before scurrying away. The room was dimly lit, but even so, Darcy's eyes fell upon the woman who once betrayed his trust.

He erred in choosing Mrs. Younge as Georgiana's companion. Darcy took his sister from school and formed an establishment for Georgiana in London, with Mrs. Younge overseeing Georgiana's care. When his sister requested permission to visit Ramsgate, Darcy granted it. Little did he know Mrs. Younge was an intimate of Mr. Wickham. Darcy's long time friend followed the ladies to the resort.

By her connivance, Mrs. Younge permitted Wickham to recommend himself to Georgiana, whose affectionate heart retained a strong impression of Wickham's kindness to her when Georgiana was but a child. Mr. Wickham convinced Georgiana of his affection for her, and his sister consented to an elopement.

Thankfully, I arrived in time to bring Wickham's plans to an abrupt halt, Darcy thought, as Mrs. Younge rose to her feet to greet him.

Something like surprise, or was it satisfaction, crossed Mrs. Younge's features before she captured the emotion to school her expression.

"Mr. Darcy?" she pronounced with the practiced tongue of an educated woman. "How kind of you to call upon me, although I am all amazement that you frequent this neighborhood."

"I doubt your *amazement*, Mrs. Younge," Darcy responded in false amicability. "As your servant did not ask your permission to show me into your home, I suspect you held expectation of my appearance."

Mrs. Younge forced a quick amused glance to Darcy before she indicated a chair near the one she recently vacated.

"A woman is entitled to her expectations, Mr. Darcy," she responded in what sounded of bitterness.

Darcy placed his hat and gloves upon a nearby table as he sat.

"All those who hold expectations of Mr. Wickham know

disappointment," he warned.

Mrs. Younge stiffened, regarding Darcy with customary wariness.

"I learned some time ago my acceptance of Mr. Wickham's manipulations provides me little happiness, the inverse of my expectations," the woman admitted.

"I wish I held empathy for your lack of wellness," Darcy spoke without emotion. "Hopefully, when you confide in me directions for Mr. Wickham's location, not only will your soul praise your benevolence, but your purse will be fuller."

Mrs. Younge closed her eyes, the truth of Darcy's words obviously weighing heavy upon her shoulders.

"The young lady with Mr. Wickham?" she asked softly.

"The daughter of a dear acquaintance," Darcy supplied.

The woman managed a sad smile

"I should have known the chit held a connection to you. Whenever the world presses Wickham for his debts or demands that he atone for his liberties, George concocts a plan to make the Darcy family pay for his failures.

"Wickham blames you for all the miserable choices he makes," she declared. "George's woes serve him well. Most women will champion a man of fine countenance when they believe him beset upon. Mr. Wickham learned that lesson early on."

Darcy easily recalled Elizabeth's defense of his former friend.

"As your allegiance to Mr. Wickham brought you upon hard times, I would think you would wish to sever the connection."

"Not so easily done, Mr. Darcy, but I shall not trouble your lack of empathy with a tale of misplaced connections."

Mrs. Younge barred her teeth in a parody of a smile.

"I shall accept your kind offer of a payment for my services, Sir. As always, Mr. Darcy, it is a pleasure to be the recipient of your patronage."

Elizabeth called upon her mother early before Mrs. Bennet broke her fast.

"You are home, at last," her mother said with ritualistic drama.

"It was late when I arrived last evening. I looked in upon you, but you slept so I claimed my bed also."

Elizabeth caught up the brush resting upon Mrs. Bennet's dressing table.

"Why do I not style your hair while you wait upon Mrs. Hill to bring you a tray?"

Her mother pushed up in the bed, and Elizabeth slid in behind her. She released the cloth holding Mrs. Bennet's long braid to run her fingers through her mother's hair.

"Your hair is so beautiful," Elizabeth murmured as she worked the tats from Mrs. Bennet's locks.

"Little good it does me," her mother declared with a tut of disapproval. "The only use of a full head of hair is to attract a gentleman. Unfortunately, once a woman reaches a particular age, society demands she cover her head with a mobcap or a turban or some such nonsense."

Elizabeth smiled at her mother's distraction. She heard Mrs. Bennet bemoan the eccentricity of society on more than one occasion.

"It would seem to me in your own home that you might choose to style your hair as you wish. I imagine Mr. Bennet would approve," Elizabeth mused.

Her mother huffed her disbelief.

"Mr. Bennet would order me to my quarters!"

Elizabeth taunted, "Mayhap he would follow you there."

"Elizabeth Bennet!" her mother exclaimed. "Who taught you of such intimacies?"

As predicted, Mrs. Bennet blushed, but Elizabeth noted the secret smile upon her mother's lips: An idea took root.

"I know nothing of intimacies," Elizabeth swore. "However, I like the idea that my parents hold an affection for each other."

"Mr. Bennet finds me a foolish woman," her mother said in regret. "Take my lesson to heart when you marry, Lizzy. I failed Mr. Bennet by not producing an heir for Longbourn. Any affection your father once held for me is long absent."

Elizabeth braided her mother's hair before she responded.

"Knowing Papa, I would imagine Mr. Bennet considers his failures, not yours. Mayhap as your daughters leave home to claim marriage, you might remind Mr. Bennet what brought you together. If Mr. Collins is to know Longbourn, it would do me well if you and Mr. Bennet saw a bit of the world at the good cleric's expense. I am not suggesting you bring ruin to Mr. Bennet's tenants; yet, no reason exists for you and Papa not to enjoy the fruits of your labors as good masters of your land."

"When did you become so wise, Lizzy?"

"I possess my father's analytical mind, as well as my mother's passion for life."

Elizabeth spent the next quarter hour assuring her mother than Mr. Bennet searched for Lydia and that her father recruited the assistance of Mr. Darcy and his cousin, Colonel Fitzwilliam.

"As we all well know, Mr. Darcy and the colonel hold an acquaintance with Mr. Wickham since childhood," Elizabeth reminded Mrs. Bennet.

"Do you think it possible the gentlemen erred in their estimation of Mr. Wickham's character? Surely Wickham intends to marry our dearest Lydia."

Her mother's agitation rose again.

Elizabeth did not wish to add to Mrs. Bennet's anguish, but it was important for her mother to consider the fault in Lydia's actions.

"Mr. Wickham spread his version of his life as the late Mr. Darcy's godson. It took me too long to recognize the deceptions the gentleman practiced. Perhaps if I were not so enthralled by my particular opinions, I might have warned Lydia against such manipulations.

"No one erred in his evaluation of Mr. Wickham except me. This madness rests upon my shoulders for when fissures of doubt touched my reasoning, I did not proclaim them as loudly and as widely as I once praised Mr. Wickham's goodness."

Elizabeth's declaration appeared to stun her mother. Mrs. Bennet frowned her disapproval.

"At least you may still claim Mr. Darcy. I am not best pleased with the man, but I could forgive him if the gentleman means to make you the Mistress of Pemberley."

Tears rushed to Elizabeth's eyes, and she blinked them away.

"Oh, Mama, I shall not know a return of Mr. Darcy's attentions. The gentleman cannot claim a wife whose family is buried in shame. Lydia's foolishness will mark all your daughters; and even if Papa can force Mr. Wickham to marry our Lydia, Mr. Darcy will not join his family with one that welcomes Mr. Wickham as its son. Mr. Darcy will cut all ties with me."

"Cowan located Mr. Sloane," his cousin announced as he entered Darcy's study.

Darcy glanced to the colonel and smiled.

"And I possess directions for Mr. Wickham."

The colonel poured himself a drink.

"You are bloody brilliant," Fitzwilliam declared after taking a large swallow of the French brandy. "How did you know where to look for the dastard?"

"I held directions for Mrs. Younge on Edward Street. The woman traded Mr. Wickham's location for a few coins."

Fitzwilliam scowled his dissatisfaction of Darcy's paying for the information.

"The old adage of honor existing among thieves is lacking in this situation."

Darcy shrugged his response.

"What might I say? The purse is mightier than honor. Now, tell me what Mr. Cowan learned of Sloane."

"The man lets a house off Edgeware Road going toward Paddington. Sloane recently inherited two copper mines: one in Cheshire and one in Wales. It is said he did not know much of mining when he inherited, but many praise his quick intelligence. I understand Sloane was originally intent upon studying the law. Cowan claims Sloane possesses a sister of twenty years, who recently withdrew from her social engagements, although it is rumored the girl remains in Town at her brother's London house."

"I suppose we know why Sloane searches fro Mr. Wickham," Darcy said with dread. "I pray Elizabeth's sister acted with better sense."

"If not, it would be to our advantage to reach Wickham before Sloane. The cad cannot marry both women. When do we track Wickham to the ground?"

Darcy glanced to the ormolu clock upon the mantel. His lips twisted into a wry smile.

"In about three hours."

Mr. Hill discovered Elizabeth, Jane, and Mary tending to the household mending in the small parlor.

"An express Miss Elizabeth," the servant said as he handed Elizabeth the letter.

She recognized the familiar slant of her name upon the paper. Setting the sewing aside, Elizabeth rose to walk to the window in a pretense of requiring better lighting before breaking the wax seal.

"Who is the letter's author?" Jane called in a tone that said her sister already knew the answer.

"Mr. Darcy," Elizabeth said. Soft longing filled her throat as she unfolded the single sheet.

"Does Mr. Darcy have word of Lydia?" Mary inquired.

Elizabeth ignored her younger sister; Mr. Darcy's salutation claimed Elizabeth's attentions.

My most beautiful Elizabeth,

Despite her best efforts, Elizabeth knew a blush claimed her cheeks, and hope crept into her heart.

> *This letter will be short, not because I possess little to speak to you, but because I have much to say, and the words must be spoken for your ears only.*
>
> *For now, know that I located Mr. Wickham, but I require a member of your family to convince your youngest sister to return to the bosom of her mother's embrace. I know Mr. Bennet is in Brighton with Colonel Forster, so I ask that you join me in London. Assuming you would agree to the sense of this request, I sent a carriage to bring you to Darcy House. Although my sister and Mrs. Annesley are with me, it would be best if one of your sisters traveled with you.*
>
> *So, my darling girl, I pray you will return to my side, where you belong, not only to aid my efforts to save Miss Lydia, but also to claim my surname. My heart aches to hear yours beating in perfect complement to mine. You are my beginning and my end, Elizabeth.*
>
> *Yours always, FD*

"Well?" Mary demanded.

Elizabeth clutched the letter to her chest.

"Mr. Darcy has word of Lydia. He requires my assistance to convince Lyddie to return to Longbourn."

She turned to her wide-eyed sisters.

"Which of you wish to journey to London?"

Chapter 13

IT TOOK HER LESS THAN AN HOUR to hustle Mary into Mr. Darcy's carriage, which arrived with a quarter hour of the gentleman's letter. Elizabeth knew she should know irritation that the man easily anticipated her response, but all she could consider was the possibility they might still claim a joining.

Jane reasoned she held the most experience with Mrs. Bennet's "nerves," and Mr. Bennet would not be happy with Kitty's absence for Kitty knew of Lydia's elopement and said nothing to her parents. Therefore, Mary became Elizabeth's traveling companion. Mary rarely held the opportunity to journey to London, and Elizabeth liked the idea of exposing Mary to a better society than found in Meryton.

At length, Mr. Darcy's coach halted before a stylish Town house in Mayfair. The gentleman's footman opened the door to set down the steps.

"This way, Miss," Murray extended his hand into the coach, and Elizabeth accepted the footman's assistance.

She glanced up to the entrance to observe Mr. Darcy and his sister coming to greet her. Elizabeth's eyes did not leave the gentleman's, but she smartly greeted Miss Darcy with a quick embrace.

As his sister moved forward to welcome Mary, Mr. Darcy caught Elizabeth's hand to place it upon his arm.

"No embrace for me, Miss Bennet?" he murmured under his breath.

Elizabeth sighed as the familiar zing of his contact claimed her skin. Why did she not previously recognize Mr. Darcy's power over her?

"Not upon the street, Sir," she chastised.

The gentleman chuckled.

"There is my adorable termagant. You hold no idea how much I missed your scoldings. But know I mean to discover a private moment designed especially to hold you in my embrace."

Elizabeth's heart raced with anticipation, as color claimed her neck and chest.

Mr. Darcy gave instructions to his servants.

"We will be going out again. Keep the coach close."

Elizabeth looked up at him in confusion.

"You mean to retrieve Lydia this evening?"

Mr. Darcy leaned close to whisper, "Another man searches for Mr. Wickham. It is rumored that my former friend ruined the man's sister."

Elizabeth could not disguise her surprise, but she permitted Mr. Darcy to escort her into his house where Colonel Fitzwilliam awaited them.

"As you can observe, my cousin is most anxious to be about our business," Mr. Darcy said in what sounded of tired amusement.

Elizabeth nodded her understanding. Although she and Mr. Darcy held other considerations, Lydia's situation took precedence.

"If Miss Darcy or your housekeeper will show us to our rooms, Mary and I will freshen our hair and remove the road dust. We will return momentarily."

Darcy watched her climb the stairs of *his* house and smiled with satisfaction. Hope spread through his chest. Elizabeth arrived in London to save her youngest sister, but a part of him prayed she meant to accept his hand again.

"I did not think Miss Elizabeth would come on such short notice," Fitzwilliam said softly from behind Darcy.

Darcy watched Elizabeth until she was from sight. The gentle sway of her hips fascinated him more than it should.

"Neither did I," Darcy admitted. "Certainly Miss Elizabeth worries for her sister's well being, but I cannot stifle the need for the lady's forgiveness."

The colonel snorted his disapproval.

"I would say it is Miss Elizabeth who should beg for forgiveness, not you. The lady did not trust you enough to seek an explanation for your absence nor did she act with prudence in her impetuous retreat. You are the one who suffered at the hands of Mr. Sloane's hirelings."

Darcy looked upon his cousin with interest.

"Odd, it is that even with your numerous conquests of some of the *ton's* most delectable beauties that you possess no knowledge of a woman's pride. Having to stand before friends and foes with a chin raised in defiance requires a special kind of woman. The questioning looks and the sniggers behind cupped hands create wounds more dangerous to the heart than any blow I suffered at the hands of my assailants. My ribs heal, and my scars and bruises disappear, but Elizabeth has yet to know that I would attempt to walk on water to prove my love for her.

"My absence, though no fault of my making, wounded not only her pride, but also Elizabeth's self confidence. She spent a lifetime with a mother who spoke of Miss Bennet's beauty and Miss Lydia's vivacious spirit. None of Elizabeth's most charming qualities are among those her mother declares as what a man desires in a wife.

"And although Elizabeth decries her mother's lack of sensibility, Mrs. Bennet's voice remains the small one in Elizabeth's head that says, 'No man will ever truly esteem you.' It is no wonder my intended ran away. How could any person not flee from the idea that he is despised?

"No, Fitzwilliam, it is I who require forgiveness for I denied my love for Elizabeth even from myself, for like her, I feared to be found wanting. While Elizabeth is under my roof, I plan to do all within my power to correct her misunderstandings."

"You ladies should wait here until we all certain Mr. Wickham is not armed," Darcy warned in a soft voice.

They stood several feet removed from the room the tavern owner claimed occupied by Mr. Wickham and a young girl.

"We understand," Elizabeth whispered as she caught Mary closer to her.

Darcy knew pride in how well Elizabeth kept control of her emotions. He realized how devastating it was for her and Miss Mary to witness how low Miss Lydia's chosen alliance to Mr. Wickham brought the girl. Some of London's most unsavory-looking residents populated the tavern's common room.

As Darcy turned to rejoin his cousin before the door, Elizabeth caught his arm to stay his steps.

"Be careful, William," she said with a bit of tremble lacing her words. "I could not bear it if…"

She did not finish her warning, but Darcy heard Elizabeth's breath catch when he caressed her cheek. He fought the urge to embrace her.

With a knowing look of promise, he said, "I possess something for which to know care."

Reluctantly, he turned to the door. Darcy wished to be finished with this business with Wickham so he might turn his thought to a contented life with Elizabeth. With a nod of approval, he motioned Fitzwilliam to use the key they acquired from the tavern owner to unlock the door.

He and the colonel and the ladies held their collective breaths as the bolt clicked its release, and then chaos erupted. Fitzwilliam shoved the door wide to send it banging into the wall. Bursting into the room, the colonel tackled Wickham as Darcy's old chum reached for a gun upon the table. Furniture exploded from the weight of the men as they wrestled upon the floor. The vehemence with which the colonel pummeled Wickham's body did not surprise Darcy. Fitzwilliam long desired to punish Wickham for Wickham's attempted seduction of Georgiana.

Meanwhile, Darcy caught a screeching Lydia Bennet and dragged her from where she attempted to pull the colonel from Wickham's back.

"Cease your protestations!" Darcy ordered as he gave the girl a good shake.

Miss Lydia swung around to clip Darcy upon the point of his chin with a half open fist. Before Darcy could react, Elizabeth rushed into the fray to jerk her youngest sister upright.

"Lydia Bennet, I shall thrash you within an inch of your life," Elizabeth declared, "if you persist in this behavior."

Darcy wished he possessed the time to congratulate her. Elizabeth knew the exact tone to take the wind from the sails of a spoiled child. Their children would pray never to rile their mother so. Somehow, the idea pleased Darcy.

Shoving his thoughts of sweet domesticity to the side for the moment, Darcy made his way to where Fitzwilliam and Wickham still struggled. Bending over the pair, Darcy cocked his Queen Anne pistol and pressed the nozzle into Wickham's temple.

"Move another muscle, and I will see your brains upon this floor," he growled.

Wickham went still, but the colonel presented his opponent another short punch to Wickham's kidneys before ceasing his assault.

Crawling off Wickham's back to stand, Fitzwilliam straightened his uniform. Other than his hair and clothing in disarray, there was not a mark upon the colonel.

"Not felt so hearty after a round of fisticuffs in many a year," Fitzwilliam proclaimed.

Mr. Wickham could not say the same. The side of Wickham's face and neck were red and bruising where the colonel rained down blows upon Wickham's head. There were numerous cuts upon his face and knuckles, likely from where Wickham attempted an escape.

"Stand," Darcy instructed.

As he stepped back, Fitzwilliam bent again to catch Wickham by the scruff of the neck to haul him to his feet before slamming Wickham into a chair.

"Such good cheer."

The colonel grinned with satisfaction.

A whimper caught Darcy's attention. He looked up to observe Elizabeth wrapping one of the blankets from the bed about her sister. It surprised Darcy to realize he did not notice the girl's state of undress when he and the colonel entered the room.

Sidestepping the broken furniture, Darcy moved to Elizabeth's side.

"Escort your sister to the room next door," he said softly as he pressed the room key into her hand. "Make certain she is dressed properly."

Elizabeth nodded her understanding.

"Mary, assist Lydia to the next room along the hall. I shall follow with her dress and brush."

As Mary Bennet placed an arm around a sobbing Lydia Bennet to lead the girl away, Darcy caught Elizabeth's arm.

"I realize this is awkward, but I must know if Mr. Wickham stole Miss Lydia's innocence. You must press your sister on this matter and then bring me the news. It is necessary to know whether to insist that Mr. Wickham marry her or to pay another to claim her," he whispered for Elizabeth's ears only.

She stared up at him, her eyes widening from the magnitude of what Darcy asked.

"I shall not fail you," Elizabeth said, at length, and then she followed her sisters from the room."

Elizabeth set her shoulders before entering the room Mr. Darcy let at an exorbitant cost for the facility in order to protect her sister. She glanced to Mary and willed her sister to silence before approaching Lydia.

As was typical, Lydia hiccupped her way through accusations against Mr. Darcy and the colonel.

"I will hear no more of your allegations," Elizabeth chastised as she shove a handkerchief into Lydia's hand.

"But, Lizzy," Lydia began; however, Elizabeth caught her sister's chin and lifted it roughly so Lydia might better view Elizabeth's determination.

"The man you defame is my intended, Lydia. If you expect sympathy from me you will speak of Mr. Darcy with a civil tongue."

"Mr. Darcy is not your betrothed," Lydia charged. "Mr. Wickham told me Mr. Darcy traveled to Brighton because your affianced thought you with Wickham."

Elizabeth schooled the shock from her expression. The fact that Mr. Wickham tossed her reputation about struck another blow to Elizabeth's pride.

"Mr. Wickham exaggerates his appeal," she bluffed. "Think upon it, Lydia. If Mr. Darcy were not meant to be my husband, why would he seek you out? Why would Mary and I accompany him? Do you think Papa would permit Mr. Darcy to act in his stead if Mr. Bennet did not consider Mr. Darcy as family?"

Lydia shot a glance to Mary, and Elizabeth prayed the third Bennet daughter would not betray the ruse Elizabeth practiced.

"Elizabeth acts with Mama's permission," Mary assured.

Elizabeth smiled at Mary. She knew it would go against Mary's strong faith to speak an untruth, so Mary chose the next best option: She told Lydia the truth and left the insinuation to

Lydia's interpretation. Mrs. Bennet encouraged Elizabeth and Mary to bring Lydia home.

Lydia's bottom lip protruded in frustration.

"Even so, what business do Mr. Darcy and his cousin have with Mr. Wickham? It is none of Mr. Darcy's concern if George and I elope."

"It is my concern," Elizabeth accused. "And Mary's. And Jane's. And Kitty's. Your foolishness marks all your sisters. Do you think Mr. Bingley will marry Jane if your wanton actions become known? And how could the entire neighborhood not learn of your shame? You did not even have the good sense to choose someone unknown to all of Meryton."

"Mr. Wickham will marry me," Lydia argued. "Then all will be forgiven."

"Has he said so?" Elizabeth demanded. "I wonder why he would. It is not as if Mr. Bennet can provide you a hefty dowry. Do you forget how Mr. Wickham abandoned us all when Miss King received her inheritance? We were nothing to him. I admit at the time I justified Mr. Wickham's desertion, presenting him credit for acting to secure his future; yet, nonetheless, the truth is Mr. Wickham requires a wife with a substantial dowry. He cannot think to marry for love."

"Perhaps you are jealous that Mr. Wickham chose me over you–that it is I that he loves."

Lydia flipped her hair across her shoulder in a gesture of dismissal.

"Has Mr. Wickham professed his love?" Elizabeth pressed.

"Has Mr. Darcy professed his?" Lydia retorted. "You possess no more dowry than do I."

Elizabeth found her youngest sister's naiveté frustratingly amusing.

"Unlike Mr. Wickham, Mr. Darcy does not require a fortune to marry, but to answer your question, Mr. Darcy has most eloquently described his affections."

The thought of Mr. Darcy's letter brought a slight blush to

Elizabeth's cheeks. The color added to the truth of her assertions.

Lydia crossed her arms over her chest and set her chin in an act of defiance, which Elizabeth recognized from previous experience with her younger sister's tantrums.

"I do not care if Mr. Wickham is not as wealthy as your precious Mr. Darcy. George owns my heart. I will have him to husband."

"But he cannot choose you," Elizabeth countered.

"And why ever not?" Lydia snarled. "If we marry, any shame I brought to Papa's name will be forgotten."

Elizabeth knelt before her sister to capture Lydia's hands.

"Even if Mr. Wickham loves you, another will be his wife. Have you not considered why Mr. Wickham avoids the calling of banns or a journey to Greta Green? It is because another woman carries his child, Lydia. The woman's brother means for Mr. Wickham to marry her."

Tears misted her sister's eyes.

"You speak an untruth," Lydia half pleaded. "You cannot know this."

"I can," Elizabeth insisted.

Although Mr. Darcy did not share the identity of the woman, it was obvious the woman's brother was the one who attacked Mr. Darcy before our wedding day.

"The reason Mr. Darcy did not appear at the Meryton church was because this woman's brother mistook Mr. Darcy for Mr. Wickham. The man's hirelings attacked my intended and left him for dead. The brother means to force Mr. Wickham to make an honest woman of his sister.'

Silent sobs shook Lydia's shoulders.

"But Wickham loves me," she said through trembling lips.

Elizabeth doubted that possibility, but she said, "Who would not love you, for you are all that is sunshine."

Elizabeth wrapped her arms about her sister to rock Lydia into soothing acceptance.

"Before this situation becomes more problematic, dearest

one, I must know one thing: Did you permit Mr. Wickham intimacies?"

Lydia shook her head violently in the negative.

"Not at all. When George consumed too much ale, he pressed me, but I hid from him under the bed until the drink lulled him to sleep," Lydia admitted. "Mama would not approve of my succumbing to the man before we spoke our vows."

Elizabeth could not help but release the breath of anxiousness she held. Thank Goodness her sister practiced a bit of sense, and thank Goodness Mrs. Bennet taught Lydia a bit of propriety.

"I am proud of you," Elizabeth whispered in Lydia's ear. "Permit Mary to assist you in dressing. You will return to Darcy House with your sisters, and between us, we will discover a spectacular future for you."

"Why are you here, Darcy?" Wickham groaned as he buried his face in his hands. "If I lost everything else, why can I not lose you?"

Darcy sat across from his former friend.

"Because you continue to make me part of your business by using the Darcy name in your dealings."

Darcy sighed heavily: How often had he "saved" Wickham from ruin? More times than Darcy cared to consider.

"What did you hope to accomplish by bringing Miss Lydia to London?"

Wickham responded only with a shrug of shoulders.

Darcy meant to wait Wickham out, but Fitzwilliam, was not so patient. The colonel jerked Wickham backwards.

"Sit straight and answer your betters," Fitzwilliam growled.

Darcy raised his hand to stay his cousin's actions.

"I understand if you were desperate," Darcy said in encouragement, "but why ruin Miss Lydia?"

Darcy prayed Wickham did not use Elizabeth's sister as a means to inflict more punishment on Darcy.

Wickham closed his eyes in what appeared to be exhaustion.

"I thought when I reached London, I could borrow enough to book passage to America, but Sloane was always one step ahead of me."

"Did you plan to take Miss Lydia with you?" Darcy pressed.

Wickham shook off the idea.

"Lydia had a few coins, enough for the hackney and this room, but I do not mean to spend a lifetime saddled to the chit."

Darcy glanced up to note Elizabeth's return to the room. A nearly imperceptible shake of her head indicated Wickham acted with the resemblance of honor. Darcy nodded his understanding.

"Then the colonel and I will leave you to your manipulations. Miss Lydia will come with me."

Unfortunately, before Darcy stood to gather Elizabeth to his side, a figure filled the still open door, and Darcy's plans for a quick retreat changed.

Chapter 14

"WHO ARE YOU? AND WHAT BUSINESS have you within?" Fitzwilliam demanded of the stranger.

Darcy's cousin held a gun pointed at the man.

Making certain Elizabeth remained from harm's way, Darcy announced, "Although our acquaintance was of short duration, I believe, Colonel, this is Mr. Sloane."

Wickham groaned his displeasure and closed his eyes again to block out the reality.

Darcy did not possess enough information on Sloane to know whether the man was dangerous or not, but he meant to protect Elizabeth at all cost, and so he shifted his weight to block Sloane from noting where she stood along the wall.

"How came you by this place?" Darcy demanded of the man.

Sloane's shoulders indicated the man was uncomfortable.

"Invention is a key component of desperation. I suspect Mr. Wickham could teach us both something of desperation, Mr. Darcy."

Sloane gestured with an open palm.

"Once I possessed a clearer head, I sent my men to return you to London, but you managed an escape. I know enough of your type to realize you would soon seek out Wickham. If the scoundrel used your family name, a previous connection existed between you. It was only a matter of time before you tracked down my soon-to-be brother in marriage."

Darcy held no use for Wickham in his life, but he was sore to permit Sloane to berate the fellow.

"As I arrived prior to you, it would seem I have first claim on Mr. Wickham's future," Darcy said with a hint of a warning in his tone.

Sloane turned to take note of Elizabeth.

"Did the dastard ruin another?" Sloane said with a snarl of disapproval.

"If Mr. Wickham dared to touch my betrothed," Darcy said boldly, "there would not be enough of him left to make a meat pie."

Darcy knew the instant Elizabeth determined Mr. Sloane's identity as the man who disrupted her wedding day. Love her heart! His lady possessed a quick mind, but she was no actress. Her emotions were on display for the world to see, and Darcy knew from experience that her temper boiled over. Mr. Sloane was in for a set down.

"Your betrothed?" Sloane's eyebrow rose in curiosity.

"Yes," Darcy hissed, adding fuel to Elizabeth's ire. "The woman for whom I purchased a ring at Rundell, Bridge, and Rundell upon the day your hirelings kidnapped me."

"Rundell, Bridge, and Rundell," Elizabeth whispered on a tearful gasp. "You were to have a ring made special for me?"

Darcy nodded his agreement.

"If I knew…" Sloane began, but the man did not anticipate the assault: not from Darcy, but from Elizabeth.

"How dare you? You call Mr. Wickham a cad!"

She stormed forward to slap Sloane's cheek before pounding upon his chest with her fists.

"Because of you I stood before a congregation to be rebuked as undesirable!"

Elizabeth punctuated each of her accusations with a punch or a jab.

"I never saw my wedding ring! A ring from His Majesty's royal jewelers! Nor did I enjoy the wedding breakfast! My wedding dress lies in rags! You ruined it all!"

Sloane ducked his head, and Darcy laughed as he moved in close to capture Elizabeth about the waist to drag her from striking distance of the man. As unladylike as were her actions, Darcy suspected it did Elizabeth well to strike out at something. Keeping her emotions under cap was not to her benefit: Elizabeth Bennet was too passionate for meekness.

"Do you possess no control of your intended?" Sloane grumbled.

Darcy turned Elizabeth into his embrace. Another woman would be in tears, but his future wife still fumed over the injustices she suffered. He was in for a life of ardor.

Darcy chuckled as he caressed Elizabeth's cheek.

"I fear not, Sloane," he pronounced. "Neither do I wish to control my lady. Why would any man wish to contain the natural instincts of God's most precious creatures when he could enjoy the beauty of their souls instead?"

Darcy caught Elizabeth's hand to kiss her knuckles.

"You will possess a bruise tomorrow," he said lovingly when he noticed the red mark upon the bone.

Ignoring all within the room, Darcy cupped her hand.

"Next time, my dear, do not tuck your thumb inside your palm. You could break it."

Darcy adjusted Elizabeth's fist so her thumb locked her fingers in place.

"In this manner," he said as he rotated her fist upright. "And use the knuckle of your pointing finger and the middle one to strike your target. They are the two strongest bones in your hand, and you are less likely to know injury."

He brought her knuckles to his cheek, and softly tapped them against his skin.

"Like so." Darcy instructed.

Elizabeth's eyes remained upon his features, and it pleased Darcy to realize she was not immune to him.

"Will you teach me?" Elizabeth challenged.

Darcy chucked her chin in a gentle caress.

"Late at night in Pemberley's ballroom, there will be no one to criticize the master and mistress. You may choose whatever new experience your heart desires."

Darcy had a few desires of his own to add to her list, but first he must win Elizabeth's trust.

Elizabeth's forehead rested against Darcy's lapel as she digested what he promised. He held her close, but Darcy spoke to Sloane.

"We possess one potential husband between us, Sir. The question is who will win the cur."

Sloane scowled.

"If not your lady, which woman of your acquaintance requires a husband?"

Darcy whispered to Elizabeth, "Would you bring your sisters in?"

She nodded shyly, which Darcy imagined was an emotion Elizabeth rarely experienced. She disappeared into the dark hallway. In less than a minute, Elizabeth reappeared with the Misses Mary and Lydia.

Sloane turned to look upon Elizabeth's younger sisters.

"What are you doing here?" Sloane stammered.

Miss Lydia appeared confused, but Miss Mary's eyes held recognition.

"Mr. Sloane," the girl said in a voice barely above a whisper.

"Miss Mary Bennet," the man pronounced with a bow. "Miss Lydia."

Elizabeth demanded of her middle sister, "By what acquaintance do you know this man?"

Mary glanced about the room to realize everyone's attention was on her. The flush of color claiming the girl's cheeks add a vibrancy not customarily found in Mary Bennet's features.

"Mr. Slo...Mr. Sloane apprenticed with Uncle Philips, perhaps a year or more removed."

"Fourteen months," Sloane confirmed.

Darcy noted an interest shared by Sloane and Mary Bennet, but the issue of a husband for Miss Lydia still hanged over their heads.

"Why did you not recognize Miss Elizabeth, Sloane," Fitzwilliam asked in suspicion.

"Mr. Sloane was only with Mr. Philips some three months before word came of his windfall. I believe Lizzy and Jane were in London with the Gardiners at the time."

Mary came to the man's defense again, a fact that did not escape Darcy's notice. He did not think he ever heard the girl say more than a dozen words prior.

Sloane glanced to Darcy.

"Might we speak privately?"

Darcy nodded his agreement.

"Colonel, I assume you are comfortable in keeping Mr. Wickham company."

"It would be my pleasure," Fitzwilliam said with a devious grin. "Do not be long. I cannot account for the itch upon my gun finger."

"As you decide my sister's future, I demand to know Lydia's options," Elizabeth insisted. "Mr. Bennet would expect me to act in the family's honor."

"Do I not have a say?" Miss Lydia began, but three voices naysayed her objections.

"You will remain in this room," Elizabeth instructed. "We shall not be long."

Accepting Darcy's proffered arm, Elizabeth moved to Darcy's side. He adored her unconquerable spirit for the trait would prove valuable in the wilds of Derbyshire.

In the second room, Darcy and Sloane sat at a small grimy table while Elizabeth lit two rush candles for light.

Sloane sighed heavily before he spoke.

"I must speak in earnest, Mr. Darcy. If Mr. Wickham does not soon marry my sister Penelope, the world will know her shame. I am persuaded that I must persist in Wickham's capitulation."

"Even so, I must protect my future family. Miss Lydia traveled with Mr. Wickham for more than a week. Wickham served in the Meryton militia, and many in the neighborhood are already privy to the tale. I cannot simply return the girl to the bosom of her family."

Elizabeth moved a straight-backed chair beside Darcy's before slipping her hand in his. Darcy tucked it into his lap.

Sloane's mouth set in a straight line.

"Both girls fell foul to a deceiver. I tell you, Mr. Darcy, it provides me no pleasure to claim Mr. Wickham to brother."

"How many know of Miss Penelope's fall?" Elizabeth asked softly.

It was hard to believe not a quarter hour earlier, she struck the man violently.

Sloane closed his eyes, battling the emotions crossing his features.

"It is only Penelope and I," he explained with what sounded of regret. "If I had my choice, I would prefer to remain Mr. Philips' apprentice, but when my uncle passed, the opportunity to provide Penelope with a bit of society could not be ignored. Unfortunately, bringing the mines up to snuff consumed more of my time than I anticipated. I left Penelope to her devices more often than I should."

Elizabeth asked with sympathy, "And your sister possesses a sizable dowry?"

Darcy studied her features: Even without Darcy's letter regarding Georgiana's shame, Elizabeth claimed a knowledge of Mr. Wickham's character. It took Elizabeth longer to arrive at the truth, but she did, nevertheless.

"Some fifteen thousand pounds."

"Significant," she remarked.

A long silence followed.

"If Mr. Darcy and I were to permit Mr. Wickham to claim Miss Sloane, we remain at a loss as to Miss Lydia's future. Mr. Wickham would use the opportunity to blackmail one of you to present him an exorbitant sum to protect your family name.

"I was considering whether you might desire a wife, Mr. Sloane. Those in Meryton would accept my sister's joining to one of Mr. Philips' former associates, and needless to say, when Miss Sloane marries, you will require a mistress for your household."

Darcy glanced to Elizabeth. She could not possibly believe that Miss Lydia would make Sloane a good wife. The man's mannerisms were antiquated at best.

Without a turn of her head, Elizabeth answered his question. She squeezed his hand and held tight to Darcy's fingertips as a warning for Darcy to hold his tongue.

Sloane's frown lines deepened.

"From what I recall of Mr. Bennet's youngest daughter, we would not suit. I am some ten years Miss Lydia's senior. Moreover, I require a woman not concerned with frills and satins. Mining communities are unique. A girl of Miss Lydia's disposition would dwindle into a hopeless soul for lack of society."

"Then support us with another who will serve the girl," Darcy insisted. "I would be willing to set a reasonable dowry upon the girl if you know of one in need of a wife."

Sloane's gaze sharpened.

"I might possess a candidate. I thought to press Penelope into accepting him, but my sister professes her love for Mr. Wickham."

"Tell us something of this man," Elizabeth encouraged. "I am certain Mr. Darcy has a like list of suitable matches for Lydia, but we welcome your insights."

Darcy created such a list only last evening, but no viable candidates surfaced.

"The man is Welsh and a former sailor. A captain in the Royal Navy."

Elizabeth shared, "Lydia fancies a man in a uniform."

"His name is Owen Vaughan. His father is the foreman for my Welsh mine, but Owen received a gentleman's education. He is five and twenty. Young for a man of his responsibilities."

"And his countenance?" Elizabeth asked.

Darcy realized Lydia would consider the man's features important.

"Fair of face," Sloane remarked. "Towheaded. Stoutly built. His father wishes the lad to marry into the gentry. Vaughan is a war hero."

Elizabeth glanced to Darcy, and he asked the question upon both their lips.

"Can the man afford to marry?"

"Vaughan earned prize money in the war," Sloane explained.

Darcy shook his head to clear his thinking.

"The man appears a better candidate than Mr. Wickham. Why would you choose to strap your sister to a man of Wickham's character?"

Sloane looked off as if he could imagine his sister.

"First, I am a highly principled man. It would bother me greatly to bind another to Miss Sloane while she carried Wickham's child. If Mr. Wickham was a casualty of war, I could more easily see my way clear, but I am a firm believer in a man claiming his children."

Darcy personally knew of two others who Wickham left with child, but he would not mention those facts before Elizabeth.

"Moreover," Sloane continued, "I am not certain Penelope would treat Captain Vaughan well. It pains me to say so, but Penny is a bit flighty in her tastes; my mother permitted Penelope much latitude in her opinions."

Darcy thought the late Mrs. Sloane and Mrs. Bennet held that characteristic in common.

"Vaughan lost part of his left arm in service to the King," Sloan explained. "Such is the reason many of the gentile class will not choose a match with Vaughan."

Darcy leaned close to speak to Elizabeth privately.

"How will Miss Lydia react to such a joining?"

Elizabeth turned to whisper in Darcy's ear. He wished he could simply enjoy the warmth of her breath on his neck, but Darcy made an effort to listen to her evaluation.

"Lydia and Mrs. Bennet will appreciate that Mr. Vaughan is an officer of renown and that he possesses a bit of a fortune. I am not certain whether Lydia will respond with more aplomb than Miss Sloane regarding the captain's injury. If we repeat the valor with which Vaughan acted during his service years and the fact Lydia will not be simply 'Mrs. Vaughan,' but rather 'Captain Mrs. Vaughan,' we possess a chance to convince my sister to accept the man."

"Might Sloane and I leave you alone with Miss Lydia? I think in this matter, your sister will respond better to you than to me."

When Elizabeth nodded her agreement, Darcy asked Sloane, "Are you certain Vaughan will accept Miss Lydia to wife if we arrange it?"

"I will speak to Vaughan's father," Sloane assured. "Having the privilege to claim a man of your status as family will go a long way to convince Mr. Vaughan of his son's future."

Elizabeth added another layer to the temptation.

"You are aware of my father's estate, but you may not realize my elder sister is soon to marry Mr. Charles Bingley. They will reside at Netherfield Park, and you may know something of Mr. Bingley's shipping lines."

"Indeed I do," Sloane acknowledged.

"And that is not to discount many of Mr. Darcy's other relatives. The colonel is Mr. Darcy's cousin and the son of the Earl of Matlock. Moreover, Mr. Darcy claims Lady Catherine de Bourgh as his aunt."

Darcy chuckled, "Miss Elizabeth is my champion. I require no other." He stood. "Come, Sloane, let us permit Miss Elizabeth time to speak to her sister. Join us, my dear, when you have Miss Lydia's decision."

When Darcy and Sloane returned to the passageway, Sloane caught Darcy's arm to stay him.

"I must extend my deepest apologies for my shortsightedness. I pray you will forgive me."

Darcy wondered how desperate he might have been if Wickham left Georgiana in the condition he did Miss Sloane.

"We each make mistakes," Darcy pronounced. "If you secure Miss Lydia's future, you will earn my benevolence. After all, it is not as if Miss Elizabeth deserted me for a life of independence after my absence from the ceremony."

"Certainly not, Mrs. Philips always spoke of the quick intelligence of her second niece," Sloane related. "Miss Elizabeth would possess enough sense to realize you are a man of honor."

Darcy wasted his attempt at humor upon Sloane. The man was quite singular in his opinions.

An awkward pause followed, but Sloane cleared his throat to speak again.

"I thank you, Mr. Darcy," Sloane said in what appeared to be a fit of nerves. "I possess another favor to ask of you, Sir, and I am not certain how best to express it except coming out with it. I am hoping you would hold no objections to my calling upon Miss Mary Bennet while she is in London. Your future sister is one of the reasons I desired to remain in Meryton."

Darcy kept the amusement from his tone.

"You wish to court Miss Mary?'

"Aye, Sir."

Darcy glanced to the room where the Bennet sisters awaited their return. Sloane would make Mary Bennet a fair husband: well educated, of modest economy, and of a protective nature. Fortune could soon see Mrs. Bennet knowing the pleasure of four daughters married.

"I expect your foreman claiming his employer as family would assist in swaying Captain Vaughan's decision," Darcy observed. "And it would do you well to claim like connections: Perhaps Bingley has a need of the captain's service or of your raw copper."

Darcy nodded toward Mr. Wickham's room.

"I hold no objections of your attentions toward Miss Mary, but you must receive the lady's agreement first. I will not tolerate your coercing Miss Mary into a situation, which would not please her."

"Mr. Darcy?"

Darcy looked up to find Elizabeth framed by the open door. It was as if his long-time dream came to life. How often did Darcy imagine Elizabeth crossing this very room to curl up in his lap? It took a good shake of his head to leave his desires behind.

He rose to cross the room to where Elizabeth waited for his permission to enter. Only then did he realize how nervous she was.

"I thought you sought your quarters," he said as he captured her hand to lead Elizabeth to a comfortable settle. "This is a pleasant surprise, but I will not have you know exhaustion."

His party returned to Darcy House some five hours prior. Sloane and Fitzwilliam agreed to detain Mr. Wickham until Sloane could arrange Wickham's marriage to Miss Sloane. Unsurprisingly, Darcy's former childhood companion readily agreed to the joining for Miss Sloane's dowry would assure payment of Wickham's other creditors, and Sloane's wealth remained an inducement for future allowances.

What Grange had yet to disclose to Wickham was the man purchased passage to India for the pair. The mine owner also negotiated a position in the East India Company military force for Wickham. Darcy admired Sloane's forethought. The man might prove an excellent influence on Mr. Wickham.

"I am all amazed with today's transactions," Elizabeth admitted. "I could not sleep."

"I always welcome your company," Darcy assured. "Do you care for claret or something a bit stronger? It might help you sleep."

Elizabeth shook off the suggestion.

"I am well tended, Sir."

Although he would prefer otherwise, Darcy sat across from her rather than beside her.

"Did you know success in convincing Miss Lydia of the necessity of her marriage to Captain Vaughan?" he asked in sympathy.

The girl was difficult with which to reason. Miss Lydia complained of the need to accept Captain Vaughan sight unseen.

"What if he possesses the countenance of an ogre?" was heard often since their return to Darcy House.

He overheard both Elizabeth and Miss Mary assure the girl that if Miss Lydia did not favor Vaughan, another marriage would be made. Mr. Wickham chose his responsibilities to Miss Sloane and his creditors over Miss Lydia.

"If you can discover something of Captain Vaughan to claim to affection," Elizabeth persuaded, "you will be married to a hero from the war, a man well renown among England's elite. Moreover, the captain will not require a large dowry from Papa. Your share of Mama's allowance, along with what Mr. Darcy is willing to provide you will settle the situation with the captain."

Elizabeth's words brought Darcy from his recollections.

"If you hold no objections, I would send for Mrs. Bennet. My mother will recognize the advantage of a captain of the Royal Navy, who won prize money for his service, over Mr. Wickham, who is embroiled in debt. Mrs. Bennet holds great sway over Lydia's opinions; she will make my sister see reason."

Darcy shared, "I wrote to your father to explain what we negotiated on your sister's behalf. I asked him to join us in London. Mr. Sloane planned to send an express to Vaughan's father this very evening. Hopefully, the captain will make an appearance by the start of next week. It would be best to permit Vaughan and

Miss Lydia an acquaintance away from the eyes of your Meryton neighbors. Mayhap we will be fortunate to disguise the truth of the matter, especially if something goes awry."

"With my parents' presence in London, we should retreat to Uncle Gardiner's house. It is too much for you to entertain the entire Bennet family." Elizabeth suggested, but Darcy noted how her eyes refused to meet his.

"I would entertain all of Hertfordshire if doing so would keep you under my roof," Darcy said in earnest as he moved to kneel before her. "Tell me you wish to remain with me, Elizabeth."

Darcy brought her hand to his lips, but instead of brushing his lips across the back of it, he turned Elizabeth's hand over to place a kiss upon the pulse point on her wrist. A hitch in her breathing served as Darcy's reward.

"We are the worst of our enemies," she whispered.

Darcy caressed her cheek before lifting her chin.

"Personally, I tire of fighting."

He leaned forward to slip his lips along the curve of Elizabeth's chin line.

"Could we not better apply our time to more pleasurable activities?"

Elizabeth's eyes drifted closed.

"Such as?" she murmured.

"I find the softness of your skin most appealing."

Darcy's fingers traced slow lines up and down Elizabeth's neck.

"As well as filling my lungs with the scent of lavender that follows you about."

He paused to lift a loose curl to his nose.

"At Netherfield I would scratch out the scent until I encountered you."

Elizabeth smiled in sadness with his ministrations, and Darcy's heart leapt with gladness. Her resistance faltered.

"I wish I knew then," she said in regret.

Darcy nibbled on her ear.

"We cannot change the past, only create a future we both appreciate," he whispered.

Her hands rested upon Darcy's chest, and he lifted Elizabeth's chin where he might look fully upon her features.

"Surely, my dearest Elizabeth, you realize how violently I admire and love you. Please say you will trust me–that you will marry me. I promise I will not fail you again."

"It is I who failed you," Elizabeth admitted. "I was so frightened you would seek revenge for my earlier rebukes that I believed the blue devils upon my shoulder."

"I mean to make you forget blame and remorse and celebrate a second chance."

Darcy claimed Elizabeth's mouth in what he thought would be a kiss of pure innocence, but which quickly transformed into one of sheer demand. A spark flared between them, taking root in Darcy's soul. The heat melded them. Elizabeth's hands encircled Darcy's neck as he rose up on his knees to drag her body deeper into his embrace.

He dreamed of this moment often, but his dreams proved faulty. Nothing in Darcy's life ever was so sweet: This kiss was not like anything he knew previously. Elizabeth lacked experience, but that particular fact did nothing to stifle the desire flaming Darcy's blood. It took all his well-honed discipline to draw back from the kiss when every instinct he possessed screamed for Darcy to carry Elizabeth to his chambers and finish what he started.

"You have yet to accept my third proposal," Darcy murmured against her skin as he showered Elizabeth's cheeks and eyelids with light kisses.

Elizabeth tightened her hold about his neck. That familiar glint acknowledging a tease brightened her eyes, and Darcy's lips turned up at the corners in preparation.

"I may require more persuasion, Mr. Darcy."

"As you wish, Miss Bennet," he said in mock sternness.

Darcy's lips returned to hers. For once, he left self-control on the shelf. He kissed Elizabeth, as he always wanted to do. Like an animal marking its trail, Darcy meant to place his stamp on her—to brand Elizabeth Bennet as the woman who owned his heart.

Chapter 15

"GOOD MORNING, WILLIAM."

Darcy chose items from those upon a serving table in the morning room. His sister and Elizabeth entered the room arm-in-arm. It was a sight he would cherish the remainder of his days.

"Good morning, my dears," he said with a smile. "May I prepare you a plate?"

Georgiana shook off his offer.

"Lige knows my preferences."

His sister assumed a chair and motioned the footman to serve her tea. Darcy suspected such was Georgiana's means to provide Darcy and Elizabeth a moment of privacy.

"And you, Miss Elizabeth," he said with a lift of an eyebrow.

Her delightful chin lifted higher.

"You have my permission, Mr. Darcy."

Darcy knew Elizabeth thought he would fail, but his intended was in for a surprise. Elizabeth held no idea how often he studied her mannerisms and choices. Darcy knew, for example, that Elizabeth preferred the butter spread thin upon her toast, but the preserves spread thick. When she ate her supper, she preferred smaller portions so the foods did not touch upon the plate. Moreover, unlike many who mixed their foods–peas with potatoes and cream sauce intermingled–Elizabeth finished her peas before touching the potatoes.

He carried the plate he filled to place it before her.

"I pray my choices meet with your approval, my dear," he whispered with a knowing look.

Elizabeth glanced to the plate, and her eyes widened.

"I took the liberty of buttering your bread the way you prefer it," Darcy said under his breath. "I asked Cook to include both blueberry and strawberry preserves upon the table."

Elizabeth's eyes misted with tears, but a smile of approval graced her lips.

"The coddled eyes," she murmured. "And the preserves and even the cut tomatoes."

Her hand brushed against Darcy's.

"You knew."

Darcy leaned closer to speak to her ears only.

"I am not yet as well acquainted with you as I wish to be, but I promise to devote my life in learning each facet of your personality."

Unable to say more, Darcy stood to give his footman instructions.

"Murray, I would prefer tea, but Miss Elizabeth indicates a desire for chocolate."

Within moments, Mary Bennet and Mrs. Annesley joined them.

"Does not Miss Lydia mean to break her fast?" he asked Elizabeth who sat upon his right.

"Lydia claims a headache, and for now, I will permit my sister her dramatics. She cried most of the night: I am certain Lyddie is frightened by the prospects of marrying a stranger."

She paused to nod her appreciation to Murray's service.

"I asked the maid you assigned us to deliver my sister a tray and to include a drop or two of laudanum in her tea. Lydia requires rest so she might make a reasonable decision. The laudanum will permit her to sleep. Mayhap Mrs. Bennet will join us soon."

Darcy wished to offer his comfort: Elizabeth worried for her younger sister's future.

Last evening, after Darcy's reason returned, he encouraged Elizabeth to sit at his desk to write her missive to Mrs. Bennet so he might add it to the express to be delivered to Mr. Bennet with the morning light.

They were both reluctant to part and so Darcy convinced Elizabeth to sit with him. They held hands and talked of childhoods. At length, Elizabeth rested her head upon Darcy's shoulder. When she fell asleep, Darcy carried her to her room and settled her upon the bed.

He was tempted to crawl into the bed with her, but it was too soon to claim more than he was entitled. Darcy would see this business with Lydia Bennet finished, not because it would prevent Darcy from making Elizabeth his wife, but because Elizabeth would more freely give herself up to him once she realized Darcy meant to protect her family.

"I am certain Mrs. Bennet will have your request by now. I will engage a coach after we break our fast. It will bring your mother to Darcy House tomorrow. I suspect it will be several more days before Mr. Bennet joins us. I assume he has not yet returned from Brighton."

"You are very kind, Sir," Elizabeth said softly.

"Like you, Miss Elizabeth, I am of a practical mind. I am certain that Mrs. Bennet will comprehend the need for her influence."

He would prefer to say more, but much of what Darcy had to say to Elizabeth required privacy.

To the table, he said, "Miss Darcy requires my escort to Bond Street. Might I convince the Misses Bennet to join us?"

Mary Bennet flushed with color.

"I fear I gave Mr. Sloane permission to call. If I held some idea…"

Elizabeth caressed the back of Mary's hand.

"You must enjoy Mr. Sloane's company. I am certain Mama

will wish to shop for cloth for new gowns while in Town. Other opportunities to partake of London's shops will occur. But please know I mean to claim a special memory of us together in London. You so rarely come to the Capital, and I mean for us to share many of the sights."

Georgiana suggested, "If you remain for more than a few days, perhaps a picnic upon Richmond's greens would meet your approval, Miss Mary. I promise a delightful day."

Mary Bennet smiled, and her features took on a softness Darcy never noticed prior. The girl would never be considered comely, but she possessed mud brown expressive eyes and enticing dimples to set off her thin lips.

"Like your brother, you are all kindness," the girl said in earnest. "Once we know more of our mother's plans, I shall be pleased to claim your company if it is within my power."

Darcy winked at Elizabeth.

"Then it is only Georgiana and Miss Elizabeth."

Elizabeth sneaked into Miss Darcy's room for a quick talk before they met Mr. Darcy for their outing.

"I thought perhaps you might require my assistance," Elizabeth offered in explanation when the girl bade her to enter.

"That is most kind of you," Miss Darcy said with a frown in her mirror. "It is moments such as these that I wish I inherited my father's thick hair rather than Lady Anne's fine locks. I find it most frustrating to pin the curls in an appropriate fashion."

Elizabeth shooed the girl's hands away.

"With four sisters, I am an expert with hair."

She removed the few pins Miss Darcy attempted and began again. Elizabeth spoke as she wrapped the girl's long blonde curls into a stylish knot upon the back of Miss Darcy's head.

"Then Mr. Darcy favors your father?" Elizabeth asked with false nonchalance.

Miss Darcy watched Elizabeth's efforts with great interest.

"William possesses our father's features and manners, but George Darcy's sternly square characteristics are softened on my brother by Lady Anne's classic lines. William is the best of our parents. There is little of Papa in my features."

Elizabeth kept her hands busy, but she listened carefully to what the girl shared.

"Do you possess any memories of Lady Anne?" Elizabeth inquired.

Georgiana started to shake her head in the negative, but then thought better of it.

"Lady Anne survived my birth for nearly a year, but my mother remained abed. My father grieved for his wife for nearly twelve years before he joined her in heaven."

"It grieves me to hear so," Elizabeth said honestly. "From my observation, a mother is a girl's staunchest defender and her greatest foe. At least, Mrs. Bennet is such."

Georgiana admitted, "I would gladly suffer any punishment Lady Anne meted out if I could spend one day with her."

A long silence followed.

"Then Mr. Darcy has held your guardianship for some years?'

"Officially only four years, but Papa was never quite what he was when I was younger: He lost his spontaneity. I sometimes feel my father only waited until William reached his majority before he gave up. He was often ill those last three years of his life."

Elizabeth finished the girl's hair by releasing several wisps to caress Miss Darcy's cheeks.

"I adore it," the girl exclaimed. "William shall be so surprised."

Miss Darcy turned one way and then the other to admire her appearance.

Elizabeth sat on the edge of the bed.

"Would you tell me about your brother? I admit I am slow coming to this agreement. It is obvious Mr. Darcy studied me over a period of time. I wasted the months at Netherfield to learn of Mr. Darcy's nature. In truth, I feel quite out of step."

Georgiana turned to look upon Elizabeth.

"What do you wish to know?"

"Anything you think significant," Elizabeth encouraged.

Miss Darcy's nose wrinkled in concentration.

"It was William who convinced our father I did not cause Lady Anne's demise. Although George Darcy recognized the dangers of a woman in childbirth, Papa's grief had him limiting his interactions with his children. Later, I thought it was because I resembled Lady Anne, but again William took it upon himself to assure me the fault did not lie with me. A thirteen-year-old Fitzwilliam refused to return to school until father agreed to call upon the Pemberley nursery daily, and when he was home on holiday, William spent long hours entertaining me with games and stories. He said he never wished for me not to know the love of family."

Elizabeth felt her throat thickening with tears, but she managed to ask, "What makes Mr. Darcy appear so severe in public?"

Georgiana laughed lightly.

"If you ask William he will tell you his actions are necessary to ward off the Society mamas. You would not believe the extent some matrons practice to trap a rich husband for their daughters."

Elizabeth smiled mischievously.

"Mrs. Bennet has five daughters. I am well acquainted with manipulating mamas."

"Perhaps." Miss Darcy returned Elizabeth's tease. "But I heard some outrageous tales at my school."

"I shall give you those," Elizabeth encouraged. "You explained Mr. Darcy's reasons. What is your estimation of your brother's unease in public?"

Georgiana's eyes twinkled in delight.

"Mrs. Reynolds, the Pemberley housekeeper, says Papa should have included a governess along with a tutor in William's education. Lady Anne's long illness isolated William from company other than when the cousins Fitzwilliam called upon the estate. Even so, William had few interactions with females beyond the estate's servants, which he always treated with respect. A comely woman makes him quite tongue-tied."

Elizabeth thought again of Mr. Darcy's letter. There was nothing deficient in the gentleman's thoughts.

"I am certain Mr. Darcy waits below. Mrs. Annesley volunteered to sit with Mary and Mr. Sloane while we are away."

"William," Georgiana said softly as she glanced over her shoulder to where Elizabeth examined gloves upon display at a modiste.

Feeling a bit uncomfortable in the shop, Darcy stood looking out the window upon a busy Bond Street. Some of the men with whom Darcy customarily did business spoke of these establishments because the shops offered intimate apparel for the men's mistresses, but Darcy never kept a woman to sate his masculine needs, and so until Georgiana left the classroom, he did not enter the female realm.

"Yes, my dear," he murmured.

Georgiana shot a second glance to Elizabeth.

"Did you notice how often Miss Elizabeth returns to the gown with the dark green and gold overlay?"

Darcy had not, but he would make it a priority.

"The gown would be exquisite upon Miss Elizabeth, but she would not hear of our interference," Georgiana observed with more maturity than Darcy expected for a girl on the short side of sixteen.

"I am certain Miss Elizabeth would refuse if I made the offer to purchase the gown," Darcy assured in quiet tones.

Georgiana bit her bottom lip, a sign of his sister's indecision.

"What if I distracted Miss Elizabeth in the fitting room, and you could order the gown delivered to Darcy House? Surely once you marry the issue would no longer exist. If you think it might be more appropriate if the gift came from me, deduct the cost from my quarterly allowance."

"The gown remains unfitted," Darcy protested, but he recalled when she attacked Sloane, Elizabeth's claimed her wedding gown in rags.

He paid no attention to her charges then, but in hindsight, Darcy suspected his feisty bride-to-be tore her original dress to shreds.

"Madame Nouri can leave the seams with a basting stitch until a seamstress can fit it to Miss Elizabeth."

Georgiana's eyes pleaded for Darcy's cooperation.

"If you believe Miss Elizabeth will appreciate the gift, I will return later to place the order," Darcy assured.

"Elizabeth will be the most beautiful bride ever," Georgiana said with a giggle.

Elizabeth noted the bookstore along a cross street.

"Would it be inconvenient for me to call upon the bookseller? I hoped to find a particular book for Mr. Bennet's upcoming birthday."

As she spent less upon her adventure than she expected, Elizabeth retained enough of her precious sums to purchase a book for her father.

Mr. Darcy nodded his agreement.

"I have an errand to which to attend. I will return for you and Miss Darcy in an half hour."

"If you are certain it is no impediment?" Elizabeth questioned.

"It is perfectly acceptable, Miss Elizabeth, for you to make a request," Darcy assured. "Miss Darcy and I welcome your presence at Darcy House and are inclined to give you sway."

Elizabeth dropped her eyes; she prayed Mr. Darcy would not think her gesture of subjugation a means to manipulate him. It was so uncharacteristic of her not to challenge every spoken word that Elizabeth felt off kilter.

"Thank you, sir. I am unaccustomed to asking for permission."

Mr. Darcy lifted her chin with his gloved fingertip.

"I imagine the same could be said of forgiveness."

Elizabeth accepted his test.

"One must err or there is no need for forgiveness."

Mr. Darcy winked at her, and Elizabeth experience a rush of pleasure in the pit of her stomach. She was not certain she liked the idea of being so susceptible to the man.

"Such is true, my dear, and you are quite fond of pronouncing my faults while I neglect to give name to yours. I suppose I will spend a lifetime pleading for forgiveness while you will be spared such piety."

"Absolutely, Sir," Elizabeth said with a gentle taunt.

She was sore to admit how much she enjoyed sparing verbally with Mr. Darcy.

"Is it not exhilarating when we agree?"

To her amusement, Mr. Darcy appeared to ignore the urge to kiss her, but Elizabeth recognized the flash in his eyes, which announced the gentleman's desire. It was comforting to her to identify the emotion. Perhaps she knew more of the gentleman than she initially thought.

"Agreement is highly overestimated," Mr. Darcy countered before offering her and Miss Darcy an easy bow of departure. Elizabeth watched him walk away. He strode along the street with his customary confidence.

Miss Darcy caught Elizabeth's arm.

"It is all amazement how you tease Darcy," the girl whispered as they walked toward the bookshop.

Elizabeth shrugged her response. Her mind remained upon the good humor found in Mr. Darcy's expression.

"Your brother enjoys a bit of bravery on my part."

Miss Darcy pulled Elizabeth to the side to permit others to

pass.

"Believe me, Miss Elizabeth, *no one* speaks as such to Darcy. Even Mrs. Reynolds is not so bold. Certainly none of my brother's business associates or his closest intimates would dare test him."

Elizabeth's frown lines puckered.

"Mr. Darcy's position in Society provides him much latitude, but I do not find Mr. Darcy unreasonable. Even when he disagrees, your brother takes what others say to heart."

Elizabeth did not exaggerate. No matter how often she and Mr. Darcy argued, the gentleman acted upon his deficiencies if he found need for change. She considered that fact admirable.

"Surely you never experienced Mr. Darcy's wrath. I cannot imagine your brother offering you anything but approval."

It surprised Elizabeth when Miss Darcy looked away.

"Speak to me, Miss Darcy," Elizabeth demanded. "Has Mr. Darcy ever raised his hand to you?"

Elizabeth did not wish to consider the possibility. She would not marry a man who struck his children or his wife when he knew anger.

Miss Darcy clutched at Elizabeth's arm.

"Never," the girl insisted. "William's heart is too kind to bring violence to my door."

"Then what brought on your dudgeon?" Elizabeth demanded.

Miss Darcy paused to permit passersby to move away.

"William knew disapproval with my foolish actions only once. I witnessed his anger, but it was not directed at me. My brother forgave what could have been my downfall. William assumed my failure and made it his. He blamed himself for not anticipating my naiveté."

Elizabeth studied the anguish in the girl's features.

"I shall not ask you to speak more of what occurred, but if you require a confidant, I am your servant," Elizabeth insisted.

Miss Darcy hid her features beneath the brim of her stylish bonnet. When she spoke again, Elizabeth had to listen with all her being to hear the softly spoken confession.

"I thought to marry a trusted friend of the family only to discover the man saw only my dowry as an inducement."

Before she could stifle the words, Elizabeth hissed, "Mr. Wickham."

Miss Darcy's eyes grew wide.

"Please do not mention this to Darcy. My brother would not approve of my speaking of this event."

Elizabeth caressed the girl's cheek.

"I shall guard your admission with my life."

She glanced about her to note the occasional look of concern upon the features of those upon the street.

"Come," she encouraged. "Mr. Darcy would be discordant if he should discover us standing about as such. Perhaps later this evening you will permit me to speak of my dealings with Mr. Wickham. In the past, my misplaced allegiance for Mr. Wickham was the source of my disagreements with your brother."

Miss Darcy placed her anguish from a few moments prior aside to assure Elizabeth of Mr. Darcy's benevolence.

"If you argued over Mr. Wickham, I am certain William meant only to protect you."

"I hold no doubt," Elizabeth said with ease. "I was at fault. It is time I asked for your brother's forgiveness."

"From the way Darcy looks upon you, I doubt William requires a confession."

Elizabeth chuckled in irony.

"Yet, despite my earlier bravado, I require Mr. Darcy's forgiveness."

"I must know it all," Mrs. Bennet demanded of Elizabeth.

Her mother arrived at Darcy House at eleven of the clock, and Elizabeth was truly gladdened by Mrs. Bennet's presence. Lydia remained recalcitrant over her situation, and Elizabeth was at her wit's end in how best to make her youngest sister know reason.

"I explained much of what occurred in my letter," Elizabeth encouraged.

Although Mrs. Bennet could read and write, her mother was not one to practice her literacy. Elizabeth always assumed Mrs. Bennet considered long letters too time consuming.

"I understand, Lizzy, but it would do me well to hear your retelling. One does not know the tone from a piece of paper."

Stifling a sigh of resignation, Elizabeth repeated how Mr. Darcy located Mr. Wickham, the deplorable conditions in which Lydia existed while in Mr. Wickham's company, how Mr. Darcy and the colonel overcame Wickham and the danger the gentlemen faced in their efforts, and how she and Mary tended Lydia.

"I am more than tolerant with my children," Mrs. Bennet admitted, "but I would have taken a strap to Lydia's legs if I discovered her in such a state of dishabille."

This statement surprised Elizabeth, but she made no comment on her mother's indignation. She could recall only a few times when Mrs. Bennet physically disciplined her children.

Elizabeth finished her tale with a recounting of Mr. Sloane's appearance and Mr. Darcy's negotiations to deliver Lydia to a better connection than Mr. Wickham.

"The captain has some twenty thousand pounds," Mrs. Bennet repeated several times. "Not ideal, but certainly very respectable.

Elizabeth added, "Mr. Darcy suggested that Captain Vaughan might prove of service in Mr. Bingley's shipping business."

"Excellent strategy," Mrs. Bennet said in deliberation. "That gentleman of yours possesses a shrewd mind."

Elizabeth's thoughts of Mr. Darcy brought a smile to her lips.

"He does indeed, Mama. I am pleased with how Mr. Darcy did all possible to protect Lydia and our family. We owe him much."

"I am certain Mr. Darcy protects his family foremost," her mother countered. "He would abandon you if Lydia's indiscretion soiled his family name."

"One would think so," Elizabeth protested, "but that evaluation is too simple. Mr. Darcy protected Lydia, not to protect the Bennet connection to the Darcy name, but because Lyddie is my sister, and I would not wish any harm to come to her. Mr. Darcy is built to protect those he affects, and I am more than pleased to admit, Mama, that I believe Mr. Darcy affects me. Even if I would choose not to accept his hand, Mr. Darcy's honor would demand that he would do all he could to see I held an easy passage in life."

Chapter 16

HOW WELL MRS. BENNET ALTERED Miss Lydia's opinions impressed Darcy. He knew real admiration for his future mother in marriage.

Mr. Bennet arrived the day after his wife, and Darcy, Elizabeth, and Mrs. Bennet spent the better part of an afternoon bringing Mr. Bennet up to snuff. Elizabeth's father wished to remove his family to Cheapside, but Elizabeth and her mother convinced Bennet to remain at Darcy House for the immediate future.

"It is essential Captain Vaughan instantly recognize the fine connections he will receive with an alliance to Lydia," Mrs. Bennet argued.

Elizabeth glanced to Darcy and smiled knowingly.

"First impressions are meant to be lasting."

Mr. Bennet's gaze followed Elizabeth's.

"I suppose, Lizzy, this charade means you chose to forgive Mr. Darcy?"

Her father's tone announced Mr. Bennet's continued antagonism. Darcy supposed it injured the man's pride to present Darcy his due.

"Mr. Darcy did not err, Papa. The fault rests on my shoulders.

If I trusted Mr. Darcy, as I should, I would have realized he would never abandon me to public declamation.

"And as to my initial assumptions of Mr. Darcy's character, they have long since been proved faulty, replaced by the knowledge that my former prejudices came about because of my desire for Mr. Darcy's approval."

It was all Darcy could do not to sweep Elizabeth into his arms and kiss her senseless. The woman never ceased to amaze him.

"It appears I am without argument," Bennet said in what sounded of exhaustion.

Darcy responded through a twist of his lips.

"I learned a hard lesson with Miss Elizabeth. In my dealings with your daughter, there are times I must lead and times I must follow."

Bennet's eyes twinkled with a taunt.

"If I know anything of Lizzy, you should also learn to remove from her way once my second daughter sets her sights upon a prize."

"I hold no doubt," Darcy said with a smirk. "I would not wish to be on the receiving end of Miss Elizabeth's fervor. Mr. Sloane can attest to your daughter's benevolence, as well as to her vehemence."

Mr. Bennet ordered Miss Lydia from her quarters, providing the girl with a blistering reprimand. Darcy held little doubt that if Captain Vaughan proved promising, the girl would accept the captain in order to escape her father's wrath.

Each evening, Darcy enjoyed the pleasure of looking upon Elizabeth's features at his table and in his drawing room. Now, if he could finalize the business of Wickham and Sloane and Vaughan, he could have her in his bed.

It was Monday before Mr. Sloane and Captain Vaughan made a combined call upon the Bennets at Darcy House. Elizabeth later assured Darcy that other than the man's missing arm, Miss Lydia found the officer equally as dashing as Mr. Wickham.

The couple, with Mr. Sloane and Miss Mary, walked in Green Park to become better acquainted. From Sloane, Darcy learned that two other gentlemen at the park recognized Vaughan, and the officer's acquaintances praised Vaughan's successes to Miss Lydia, and the girl's admiration appeared to deepen.

Elizabeth's estimation of her sister's shallowness proved true. The girl chose Captain Vaughan purely upon the man's countenance rather than his substance.

Darcy and Sloane sat in with Mr. Bennet in the man's negotiations of the marriage settlements.

"When I encountered Mr. Bennet's daughters in London," Sloane said with the ease of a man who knew something of the law of such settlements, "I thought of you, Vaughan. Your father mentioned often of late your desire to marry."

Vaughan spoke diplomatically.

"Miss Lydia is quite comely, but she is a bit younger than I hoped."

Sloane kept the floor.

"Young enough to provide you several healthy sons."

Darcy took a higher tone.

"It is true that Miss Lydia is the youngest of Mr. Bennet's daughter, but I assure you, Vaughan, the girl understands her duties of marriage equally as well as her sisters."

Darcy nodded in Sloane's direction.

"Sloane spent several months in the company of the Bennet family for his former employer was the Misses Bennet's uncle. It is my understanding that he will court Miss Mary Bennet. Your family knows Sloane would not choose from Mr. Bennet's daughters if he felt them deficient in any manner. My associate, Mr. Charles Bingley, means to make the eldest Miss Bennet his wife, and I will claim Miss Elizabeth within the next month."

Darcy meant that particular fact to be a warning to Mr. Bennet that they would soon be family.

"Although you do not know Mr. Bingley personally, you must be aware of my friend's reputation. Bingley would not choose Miss Bennet if the lady would not complement his future aspirations. Neither would Sloane or I make rash concessions.

"Miss Lydia is young, but she is exceedingly congenial. She will serve you well. Sloane says you hold aspirations to represent your neighbors in Parliament. That means you require a wife who will shine in the public eye. Without wishing to offer offense to Mr. Bennet, neither Miss Bennet nor Miss Mary would serve as well as Miss Lydia. I imagine my Elizabeth would prove worthy for she is one of the most intelligent women I know, but few men favor intelligence in their wives."

Darcy would call upon the man's honor.

"Miss Lydia possesses the right balance of society and quickness of mind, and although she is young, I would assume a man of your rank holds experience in turning dirty-necked youths into competent sailors. Most assuredly with a firm hand you could teach a girl her place in your world. Miss Lydia is of the nature to please those she affects."

Vaughan requested Sloane's opinion.

"You think what Mr. Darcy says is true?"

Although Sloane nodded eagerly, Darcy suspected Sloane was pleased to align his family with Vaughan through marriage.

"In my time before assuming control of the mines, I apprenticed with Mr. Bennet's brother Philips. As Mr. Darcy indicated earlier, I often came into the company of Bennet's daughters, not only in their aunt's parlor, but also at the local assemblies and socials. Mr. Darcy's evaluation of the Bennet sisters aligns with my own.

"Also, I would remind you that the connections you claim by taking Miss Lydia to wife crosses all social lines. You will know the gentry, the aristocracy, and the trades. Needless to say, this will feed your political ambitions."

Vaughan eyed each of them with a critical eye.

"And you believe Mr. Bingley might look kindly upon me

for a position in his shipping business?"

Darcy did not wish to speak for Bingley in the matter: He would not appreciate others making promises for him. Even if Bingley wished to look the other way, Darcy held his own connections to the various shipping lines he might call into service on Vaughan's behalf.

"I would not volunteer Mr. Bingley's support, but if you are certain you seek such a position, Bingley would welcome your expertise. With the demand for labor in the war, men knowledgeable in the shipping lanes are difficult to discover."

Vaughan nodded his understanding.

"Then Mr. Bennet, I seek permission to court Miss Lydia while the settlement papers are drawn up and a license is procured. I do wish to say if my opinions of the feasibility of the joining change, I will quietly withdraw."

Others may not think Vaughan reasonable, but Darcy silently agreed. Darcy never wished a marriage of convenience. The idea of marrying a stranger would be unnerving even for a war hero.

"Elizabeth, will you join me in the garden?"

Darcy extended his hand to support her to her feet.

"A stroll in the moonlight, Sir?" she asked in a teasing tone.

Darcy glanced about the crowded drawing room.

"I would like a word. Mr. Bennet means to withdraw to the Gardiners tomorrow, and unfinished business remains between us."

Elizabeth's eyes followed Darcy's.

"As you wish, Sir."

She slipped her hand into his to permit Darcy's assistance to stand. He led her easily about the room and out the doors leading to the steps down into the garden. No one took note of their exit except Elizabeth's father, who presented Darcy a warning glare.

Once in the early evening shadows, Darcy nudged Elizabeth

closer to him. At length, they stood beneath an ivy-draped arbor. Without prying eyes watching his every move, Darcy gathered Elizabeth into his loose embrace, celebrating the heat of her body along his front, while Elizabeth splayed her hands against his chest.

"I missed holding you," Darcy whispered close to her ear. "I never tire of having you close."

Elizabeth sighed deeply as she rested her head upon Darcy's chest.

"I do not have a name for this...this..." she began.

"I understand," Darcy assured. "It took me many weeks before I realized you were the one person who made sense in my life."

Darcy tipped Elizabeth's chin upward.

"I mean to kiss you, Elizabeth. If you do not wish it say so now."

"I wish it, William."

Darcy made himself go slow. To brush his lips across hers before claiming a gentle press. Elizabeth's lips were as satiny smooth as he recalled. She tasted of tea and the sweetness of the chocolate he procured for the ladies' pleasure, but there was a bit of hesitation, which spurred Darcy's desire for her. He wished Elizabeth's surrender, and he eased her lips apart to delve in with his tongue.

Within seconds, Elizabeth sagged against him, and Darcy tightened his embrace. It was his purpose to shove Elizabeth's defenses aside–to permit her to claim the woman of passion Darcy suspected twirled within her.

Even so, Darcy did not deepen the kiss. His tongue touched the soft tissue of Elizabeth's mouth. He nibbled on her bottom lip. Darcy wished the decision to share this moment to be hers–for Elizabeth to claim him as heartily as he claimed her. To know her trust in him.

With a soft moan, Elizabeth edged deeper into Darcy's embrace, pressing her curves tight against him.

"Please kiss me as you did before," she murmured.

Darcy was not certain Elizabeth understood this "dance" they practiced, but her words were encouragement enough.

The defenses slid from Elizabeth's shoulders as her hands encircled Darcy's neck. Her curves hugged the hard planes of Darcy's body.

"I adore you with all my heart," Darcy whispered as he claimed Elizabeth's mouth again.

"And I you," she said when their lips parted some minutes later.

Darcy held her close, his chin resting on her head as he fought for the next breath.

"Please say…you will name…another date…for our joining. I will not truly live until you are my wife. I tire of the need to prove myself to anyone but you, Elizabeth. Only you can create such deep enduring emotions in me. I tried to resist you, and although it is the worst society to admit my weakness, I hold an unconceivable need to possess you in every means possible."

Elizabeth planted a kiss against his chest, the warmth of her breath invading the fine lines of his shirt.

"And it is the worst society to acknowledge that your words of devotion bring a profound tenderness to my heart."

Darcy chuckled, "If I held an inkling, I would have professed my dearest desires earlier."

He could feel the heat of Elizabeth's blush through her day dress.

"I fear I am of a weakly feminine disposition, after all, Sir. You may wish to reconsider."

Darcy loosened his grip on her.

"As long as it is only my declarations which bring on your sentimentality, I am satisfied."

Elizabeth glanced up at him with that teasing spark Darcy now recognized as innate to her personality.

"I felt nothing when Captain Wentworth offered to show me the world."

Darcy growled as he clasped her to him.

"I will hire a frigate to send the good captain to the bottom of the ocean."

Elizabeth crept her hands up his body to lace in Darcy's hair.

"The captain thought I deserved an adventure," she countered with a lift upon her toes to kiss Darcy's chin. "The gentleman did not understand that being you wife is the most excellent adventure I could conceive."

Elizabeth's fingertip traced Darcy's lips.

"Are you certain, Elizabeth?"

Darcy's fear of never knowing her love banged against his chest.

"One week after Lydia becomes Mrs. Vaughan, I shall be at the altar in Meryton's church. I shall expect you to be prompt. The license and the banns are still in force. What say you, Mr. Darcy? Shall we attempt to right a previous wrong?"

"Absolutely," he declared with the most profound happiness he ever knew. "I must speed Vaughan's vows along. I waited long enough to know you as my wife."

"You are early, Mr. Darcy."

"Yes I am, Sir."

Vicar Williamson smiled knowingly.

"It will be another two hours before anyone will join you."

Darcy shrugged his indifference.

"But I plan to wait just the same; I am quite content with my own company in the time being."

Unable to be without Elizabeth one day longer, Darcy arrived at Netherfield some three days prior. With a special license and a speedy journey down the aisle, Wickham claimed Miss Sloane to wife. Darcy and the lady's brother stood witness to the joining before Sloane ferried the couple to a ship for the journey to India. Although Sloane freely shared his intentions with Darcy to send his sister abroad for a time, Darcy suspected that neither Wickham nor the girl knew their true destination. The couple spoke only of the kindness Sloane extended in affording them a wedding journey.

Five days later, Miss Lydia and Captain Vaughan exchanged vows. Bingley escorted Miss Bennet and Miss Kitty to London to enjoy the festivities. According to Elizabeth, Miss Lydia liked the idea of being the first of her sisters to marry.

Among the parties involved, they created a convoluted story of how Mr. Wickham escorted Miss Lydia to London so both Wickham and Lydia could claim other engagements. Thankfully, the connection to Sloane in both Wickham's and Miss Lydia's joinings gave credit to the story. As a group, they went so far as to say Mrs. Forster misunderstood Miss Lydia's hastily written note.

> *My Dear Harriet: You will laugh when you know where I am gone, and I cannot help laughing myself at your surprise tomorrow morning as soon as I am missed. I am going to Gretna Green, and if you cannot guess with whom I shall think you a simpleton, for there is but one man in the world I love, and he is an angel. I should never be happy without him, so think it no harm to be off. You need not send them word at Longbourn of my going if you do not like it, for it will make the surprise the greater when I write them of it. What a good joke it will be! I can hardly write for laughing. Pray make my excuses to Pratt for not keeping my engagement, and dancing with him tonight. Tell him I hope he will excuse me when he knows all, and tell him I will dance with him at the next ball we meet with great pleasure. I shall send for my clothes when I get to Longbourn; but I wish you would tell Sally to mend a great slit in my worked muslin gown before they are packed up. Goodbye! Give my love to Colonel Forster. I hope you will drink to my good journey.*
>
> *Your affectionate friend, "Lydia Bennet"*

The tale was the best they could do with so many in Meryton aware of Miss Lydia's flight. They each repeated it with stomach-churning seriousness when asked. With Sloane calling upon the Philipses to continue his courtship of Miss Mary, the story knew some credibility. Sloane recognized his role in quashing the rumors with a straight-faced gravity. Throughout their manipulations, it confounded Darcy to acknowledge Sloane as an ally, especially after the damage the man did to Elizabeth's self-confidence; yet, it was necessary to swallow his trepidation in order to keep peace in his future family.

Sloane, Vaughan's parents, and several of the former captain's officers attended the ceremony and the small wedding breakfast hosted by the Bennets and the Gardiners, but held at Bingley's more fashionable address. Darcy found it amusing how Mrs. Bennet claimed hostess duties at the event, which was the lady's due as the bride's mother. Nevertheless, Darcy whispered a warning to Bingley that their future mother in marriage did not do the same once Bingley claimed Miss Bennet to wife.

Darcy held a better opinion of Elizabeth's mother than previously; even so, he preferred more than three miles separating his household from the Bennets.

"Did you break your fast?" Would you care for tea, Mr. Darcy?" Williamson asked in continued amusement.

"Mr. Sheffield is likely to experience an apoplexy if I would foolishly spill something on his creation."

Darcy gestured to the ornately tied cravat.

"If my man knew I dared to bring a wrinkle to the cut of my coat by sitting, a mutiny would ensue."

He nodded to the clergyman.

"Enjoy your meal, Sir. I am content to wait for my bride."

"As you will, Mr. Darcy."

Although the church was not the proper place to reminisce over the kisses he shared last evening with Elizabeth, Darcy's thoughts naturally drifted to that exquisite moment.

Darcy presented her with the necklace he purchased for her in London.

"Oh, William, it is exquisite," she said through joyful tears. "I have never seen another like it."

"The jeweler called the darker stones chocolate diamonds. They hold hints of fire in them, very much like your hair."

They were alone in the drawing room at Longbourn as Bingley and Miss Bennet sought the dark garden for their time together.

"You noticed," Elizabeth said in wonder.

"I told you previously, there is little of importance that slips my notice when it comes to you, Elizabeth Bennet."

"I have something for you also," she said nervously. "But I fear my gift cannot compare with yours. I find I am lacking in your study of human nature." She chuckled in irony. "Needless to say this is a blow to my self importance, but I promise to be a most attentive student in the future."

"You will give me everything I desire or need tomorrow before your Meryton neighbors. I require nothing more."

Elizabeth rose to cross to a table where a large object was wrapped in brown paper.

"Then consider this a gift to both of us."

She placed the object in Darcy's lap.

"Open it," she instructed. "I asked Miss Darcy for suggestions as to something you would not purchase for yourself, and dearest Georgiana shared an idea she thought to claim as her own."

Darcy's fingers suddenly felt stiff as he loosened the string about the package. Without seeing it, he knew the object a book–a very thick book. At length, he lifted the paper to look upon a Bible.

"What is this?" he asked as he placed the paper upon the side table.

"A Bible," Elizabeth said nervously. "A family Bible."

She reached to open the front pages.

"Miss Darcy said the one at Pemberley held all the Darcy

family names, but your and Georgiana's names were the last the book would accommodate."

Elizabeth pointed to the page in the book she purchased.

"I took the liberty to begin where the Darcy family left off. See, I placed the names of your mother and father here and my parents on the opposite side. Then I placed you and Miss Darcy beneath Mr. George and Lady Anne Darcy and me and my sisters under Papa and Mrs. Bennet. If we are so blessed to have children, they will receive a proper place."

Tears filled Darcy's eyes.

"I gave you a babble, while you presented me a future. You are the most amazing woman God ever created."

Setting the book on the table, he gathered her to him, their bodies connected from chin to chest. He kissed Elizabeth with all the passion he felt for her, but it was not enough until she abandoned her defenses, shuddering in his embrace. Darcy tightened his hold as Elizabeth accepted him completely. God! He would be fortunate among the men of his class.

It was all Darcy could do not to claim his wedding night a day early. His breath abandoned him for several elongated seconds before he could reassure Elizabeth that what they shared was beyond extraordinary.

"You could tempt a man of more saintly intentions than I."

Darcy showered small kisses across Elizabeth's eyelids and cheeks. There was a time Darcy would curse his lack of control, but surrendering to Elizabeth's charms was one of his most intelligent decisions.

In the days leading up to her departure from London, they often returned to the conversation topic of their former misconstructions.

"It was most uncomfortable to acknowledge my shortcomings," she admitted as they sat together in the shadows of her Aunt Gardiner's garden. "I permitted fear to color my opinions. I should not have run away."

Darcy reached for Elizabeth's hand. He came to the opinion

of late that even the simplest of connections prevented their arguments.

"You returned to my side, that is all that matters."

Darcy kissed the back of Elizabeth's hand. He purposely permitted his breath to warm her skin.

"Elizabeth, I find I often stumble over my words when I attempt to express my feelings," he said without looking upon her questioning features.

Darcy's eyes remained upon their locked hands.

"It grieves me how often I failed to explain what I assumed was blatantly clear."

"I never provided you the opportunity. I was too quick with a saucy rebuke meant to protect my pride," Elizabeth countered.

"We are a pair, are we not, my dear?" Darcy said in earnest. "But a pair, we will always be. I cannot bear to think of my life without you."

Elizabeth caressed Darcy's cheek with her free hand.

"We are likely two of the most opinionated people God ever created, and we are not likely to change, Mr. Darcy. I recently told my mother I possessed Mr. Bennet's natural intelligence, mixed with a large dose of Mrs. Bennet's passionate emotions. I would go so far as to say you are cut from similar cloths. Nevertheless, I believe we are the perfect pair. I believe it so profoundly I mean to claim a lifelong adventure of being the Mistress of Pemberley."

Darcy stood at the front of the church and waited for Elizabeth's appearance. He pretended not to hear whether it would be who left the church alone this time; even so, Darcy knew Elizabeth would come.

At length, the sounds of whispers increased, and Darcy turned his head to see Elizabeth step into the opening from the vestibule, her hand rested upon her father's arm. She was magnificent in the gown Georgiana chose for her. Darcy enlisted Mrs. Bennet's assistance in convincing Elizabeth to accept his gift.

A shear green overdress, embroidered with gold leaves and white roses on the hem and the mid-arm sleeves covered a simple off-white gown. Darcy ordered white roses and leaves of ivy for a bouquet for her to carry, and Elizabeth added several of the flowers to her hair. She went without a bonnet so as not to crush the flowers, chosen from his conservatory. A simple pearl necklace graced her neck.

Darcy watched Elizabeth's expression, expecting a moment of panic to claim her, but no signs of "second guesses" were evident. Their gazes collided, and Darcy's heart opened to the sunshine Elizabeth brought to his life. Her chin lifted in the beautiful defiance Darcy adored. Logic and common sense went out the door the day Darcy rested his eyes upon her at the Meryton assembly. A bond existed before he could give it a name. Now, Elizabeth Bennet would be his.

She reached where he waited for her. Together they turned to face Vicar Williamson. With a clearing of his throat, the cleric began, "Dearly beloved…"

Darcy watched as Elizabeth circulated among her neighbors, accepting their congratulations. His wife was certainly not his customary type, but from their first encounter Elizabeth's bold gaze fascinated him. She was a finely crafted ornamental tracery, shaped from passion and sympathy and a quick intellect, as well as a comely countenance and a playful seduction. The new Mrs. Darcy held no idea the feminine powers she wielded.

At length, she reached the place where Darcy waited for her. Without his reaching for her hand, Elizabeth laced her arm through his. He leaned down to whisper for her ears only.

"You are quite beautiful, my dear."

Ducking her chin, Elizabeth glanced up at him; a twinkling of impish humor crossed her features.

"What woman would not he beautiful with such a delicate necklace gracing her neck. I received multiple compliments upon it."

His wife's delight was all that Darcy hoped.

"*Mr. Sloane's men did not think to steal it?*" she asked as she cuddled into Darcy's embrace.

"*As foolish as it may sound, I made certain that I protected the necklace and your ring from theft,*" Darcy explained as he tightened his hold on her.

"*Oh, William,*" she gasped. "*What I ever did to deserve your regard, I shall never know, but I am most grateful you chose me when I had so little to offer. But you must promise me you will never place yourself in danger again. The jewels are of little significance, but our future family is.*"

"The only compliment necessary is the one from your luscious lips," Darcy murmured.

"Mr. Darcy," Elizabeth breathed in a voice that said his boldness affected her.

"Yes, Mrs. Darcy," he teased as his eyes traced the links holding the diamonds and topaz in an intricate embrace.

"We should speak our farewells, Sir."

It did Darcy well to hear the hitch in her breathing. He permitted the teasing tone to remain as he lifted the back of Elizabeth's free hand to his lips.

"See how well matrimony suits us. We agree at last."

Chapter 17

FROM THE OVERHANG, DARCY LOOKED DOWN upon his wife of some three months. Elizabeth crossed the open field, her skirt hiked high enough for Darcy to have a peek at her shapely calves and ankles. He returned to Pemberley after spending time examining the new forge with his steward to discover that Elizabeth meant to call upon the Burrells' cottage to take Mrs. Burrell a basket of welcome for the woman's new daughter. Immediately Darcy set out to find her, not because he did not trust Elizabeth to exercise her duties properly, but because he missed her with an ache never quenched.

It was the oddest realization that he frequently abandoned his work to seek out Elizabeth in his manor house. One would think as often as they enjoyed intimacies that Darcy would tire of her closeness, but all it took was the sweet scent of lavender to set his groin afire and have him on the move through Pemberley House.

Their first night together remained the most spectacular of Darcy's life. Certainly they shared more passion on other evenings since, as Darcy taught Elizabeth how to please him, and he learned something of his new wife's preferences, but their wedding night came after months of longing.

From Longbourn, Darcy escorted Elizabeth to Brighton where they spent their first evening together at the same inn Fitzwilliam claimed a month prior. The following day, they boarded the yacht bearing his wife's name to spend three leisurely days enjoying the calm seas, the excellent food prepared especially for them, and many moments in undress.

"You are magnificent," Darcy whispered in Elizabeth's ear when the innkeeper closed the door behind him, and they were alone in a room with a large bed for the first time.

He took her in a loose embrace.

"I will treat you kindly," he assured.

"I do not fear you," she admitted. "Only disappointing you."

"That would be impossible."

Darcy kissed her forehead.

"We will enjoy some champagne and permit things to happen naturally. There are no expectations other than the pleasure of looking upon you wearing my ring."

Elizabeth held her hand up to admire the band.

"It is beyond exquisite. There is none to compare to it."

"And none to compare to you."

Darcy lifted her chin to brush his lips across Elizabeth's. He heard her breathing turn ragged, and on impulse Darcy swayed to a tune demanded by their hearts. At Netherfield, he wondered what it would be to hold Elizabeth close and to dance a waltz with her. Expertly, he turned his wife in a tight circle, his left hand pressing against Elizabeth's lower back to edge her closer to his center.

They gazed into each other's eyes. A sizzling bolt of heat warmed Darcy's desires, and he knew the exact instant Elizabeth knew a shock to her control. It still bothered Darcy that his absence from their first wedding ceremony injured Elizabeth so deeply. His heart reached out to her; somehow, he would wipe those memories clean.

Darcy sucked in a breath to reclaim his senses, but the

scent of woodsy lavender filled his lungs. It was a scent that held promises of wildflowers and sensual delights. Its essence declared this particular woman Darcy's heart. Elizabeth's eyes reflected Darcy's passion, and he kissed her fully as they swayed to a halt.

He threaded his fingers into Elizabeth's hair, sending pins and rose petals drifting to the floor.

"You are trembling," he whispered, his mouth hovering above hers.

"I never dreamed of this..." Elizabeth said in what sounded of confusion. "Until your letter, I never permitted myself to consider love as a possibility. I did not know it would be like this. So overpowering."

Pressed closely to him, Darcy felt her heart beat with his. His mouth returned to hers for only that gesture erased a remnant of Darcy's fierce need for her. For a moment, he thought to savor Elizabeth's acquiescence, but her lips parted, and his wife yielded to the rising heat between them.

Darcy swept Elizabeth into his arms to carry her to the bed. Unable not to touch her, he followed her down. Darcy's world melded into a swirling mix of past, present, and future. For more months than he cared to consider, he desired Elizabeth beneath him.

"I love you," he murmured, his lips skimming her skin.

"And I love you," she whispered.

What ensued played out before Darcy's eyes, mixed with the image of the woman, who haunted all his dreams, crossing the field. Despite reliving every second of their first coming together, his conscious mind registered when his wife stopped to turn in playful circles, her arms spread wide.

Darcy eased his desire for Elizabeth to begin his descent to the field below. As he crossed the rock ledge, he watched Elizabeth remove her bonnet to toss it in the air in pure abandon. Setting his steps along the path, Darcy recognized how often his wife likely experienced such pleasure. Miss Bingley's remark of Elizabeth's petticoat being six inches in mud brought a smile to Darcy's lips as he approached.

"There is my darling girl," he called as Elizabeth stumbled to a halt.

She glanced up to Darcy and smiled.

"You searched for me, Sir?" Elizabeth teased.

"Always," Darcy said as he swept her into his arms. "Searched until I found the one."

He kissed her gently.

"I was just considering our makeshift waltz on our wedding night. Would you care to attempt it again with a bit more room? A field of flowers to soften our steps?"

"We have a ballroom at Pemberley House," she taunted as she set her hand upon Darcy's shoulder.

He chuckled easily.

"That room is for sword lessons and a bit of wrestling."

Elizabeth kissed his chin line.

"Heaven forbid if we decide to host a ball at Pemberley. We will scandalize our guests," she murmured.

"I care not."

Darcy stroked her back and hips before he set their steps in motion, sweeping Elizabeth through the twists of yellow, blue, red, and purple. Her laughter filled the air with a tinkling sound to which Darcy accepted his addiction.

"You are scandalous, Mr. Darcy," she chastised as he reached to loosen the pins holding her hair in a loose chignon.

"I am the Master of Pemberley. If I wish to dance with my wife among the wildflowers, it is no one's concern, but mine."

Elizabeth tightened her grip upon Darcy's shoulder, sliding her hand to the back of his neck.

"What if the Mistress of Pemberley wishes to kiss the Master while standing in said field?"

A catch in Elizabeth's breath told Darcy his wife's heat climbed as quickly as his.

"Your wish is my command," he murmured as he lowered his head.

He kissed her with all the hopes he held those long months they were apart, and Elizabeth responded with a like yearning. The fact his wife expressed her open affection did Darcy well.

Without thinking, Darcy released her to sweep off his long coat, the one he regularly wore when he examined the fields and structures of the estate. He bent to spread it upon the ground before lifting Elizabeth to his arms to place his wife upon the coat.

Kneeling beside her, Darcy looked upon her seductive appeal. Elizabeth's hair rested in rolling waves about her shoulders, and she closed her eyes to drink in the sweetness of an early autumn day. The sleeves of her gown slipped from her shoulders, and Darcy's eyes drank his fill of the creamy expanse of skin.

He stretched out beside her, holding Elizabeth's hand to enjoy the moment.

"I who have everything," she whispered, and Darcy recognized the source of the words she recited as being from his letter, "still have nothing of value if you are not at my side to share my wealth. You rejected my adoration, proving me unworthy of tempting you with either the luxury of my fortune or the deep affection with which I hold you."

"That was long ago, Elizabeth."

"But it was the moment I knew how foolish I acted," she countered.

His wife rolled to her side to snuggle against Darcy's arm.

"I realized how lost I would feel if I never were to encounter you again and the misery I would know when watching you offer your attentions to another. A heart that breaks cannot mend unless it joins to another. I cursed myself for never saying the words that I wished you to know. I so feared that your affection would fade away."

Her hip caressed Darcy's thigh, and they remained as such in silence for several elongated moments, each lost in his recollections.

Life would never be perfect, but Elizabeth's presence in his life made Darcy a finer man; he felt it so with his entire being. His wife softened Darcy's edges, made him wish to achieve all he could for her and their future family, and Darcy loved Elizabeth with all his heart.

"You are lost in your thoughts again," Elizabeth teased. "You do that often, Mr. Darcy."

Darcy rolled upon his side to face her.

"My thoughts are always of you."

"Why ever for?"

Elizabeth placed her hand over Darcy's heart, and he cupped it to press her palm to his chest.

"Because in both countenance and soul, you are the most beautiful woman of my acquaintance."

"Your wife and someday the mother of your children," she said on a tremble.

Darcy leaned over her to roll Elizabeth to her back as he covered her mouth with a kiss of promise of infinite love. A warmth awakened in Darcy's chest as his wife wrapped her fingers about his nape to hold him to her. Darcy pronounced a silent prayer of thanksgiving as Elizabeth's sweet breath whispered his name. Later, he would claim the joyful sound of his children's laughter filling the halls of Pemberley the sweetest sound he would ever know, but until then, Darcy found comfort in his wife's gasp of "William, we cannot. Not here," which Darcy skillfully proved her in error.

Other Novels by Regina Jeffers

Jane Austen-Inspired Novels:

Darcy's Passions: Pride and Prejudice Retold Through His Eyes
Darcy's Temptation: A Pride and Prejudice Sequel
Captain Wentworth's Persuasion: Jane Austen's Classic Retold Through His Eyes
Vampire Darcy's Desire: A Pride and Prejudice Paranormal Adventure
The Phantom of Pemberley: A Pride and Prejudice Mystery
Christmas at Pemberley: A Pride and Prejudice Holiday Sequel
The Disappearance of Georgiana Darcy: A Pride and Prejudice Mystery
The Mysterious Death of Mr. Darcy: A Pride and Prejudice Mystery
"The Pemberley Ball" (a short story in *The Road to Pemberley* anthology)
Honor and Hope: A Contemporary Pride and Prejudice
Mr. Darcy's Fault: A Pride and Prejudice Vagary
Elizabeth Bennet's Deception: A Pride and Prejudice Vagary
The Prosecution of Mr. Darcy's Cousin: A Pride and Prejudice Mystery

Regency and Contemporary Romances:

The Scandal of Lady Eleanor: Book 1 of the Realm Series (aka A Touch of Scandal)
A Touch of Velvet: Book 2 of the Realm Series
A Touch of Cashémere: Book 3 of the Realm Series
A Touch of Grace: Book 4 of the Realm Series
A Touch of Mercy: Book 5 of the Realm Series
A Touch of Love: Book 6 of the Realm Series
A Touch of Honor: Book 7 of the Realm Series
A Touch of Emerald: The Conclusion of the Realm Series
His American Heartsong: A Companion Novel to the Realm Series
His Irish Eve
The First Wives' Club: Book 1 of the First Wives' Trilogy
Second Chances: The Courtship Wars

Coming Soon...

Angel Comes to the Devil's Keep
The Earl Finds His Comfort
"One Minute Past Christmas"
Mr. Darcy's Bargain: A Pride and Prejudice Vagary

Meet the Author

Writing passionately comes easily to Regina Jeffers. A master teacher, for thirty-nine years, she passionately taught thousands of students English in the public schools of West Virginia, Ohio, and North Carolina. Yet, "teacher" does not define her as a person. Ask any of her students or her family, and they will tell you Regina is passionate about so many things: her son, her grandchildren, truth, children in need, our country's veterans, responsibility, the value of a good education, words, music, dance, the theatre, pro football, classic movies, the BBC, track and field, books, books, and more books. Holding multiple degrees, Jeffers often serves as a Language Arts or Media Literacy consultant to school districts and has served on several state and national educational commissions.

Regina's writing career began when a former student challenged her to do what she so "righteously" told her class should be accomplished in writing. On a whim, she self-published her first book *Darcy's Passions*. "I never thought anything would happen with it. Then one day, a publishing company contacted me. They watched the sales of the book on Amazon, and they offered to print it."

Since that time, Jeffers continues to write. "Writing is just my latest release of the creative side of my brain. I taught theatre, even participated in professional and community-based productions when I was younger. I trained dance teams, flag lines, majorettes, and field commanders. My dancers were both state and national champions. I simply require time each day to let the possibilities flow. When I write, I write as I used to choreograph routines for my dance teams; I write the scenes in my head as if they are a movie. Usually, it plays there for several days being tweaked and *rewritten*, but, eventually, I put it to paper. From that point, things do not change much because I completed several mental rewrites."

Every Woman Dreams https://reginajeffers.wordpress.com

Website www.rjeffers.com

Austen Authors http://austenauthors.net

Join Regina on Twitter, Facebook, Pinterest, Google+, and LinkedIn.

Excerpt from *Elizabeth Bennet's Deception: A Pride and Prejudice Vagary*

Chapter 1

DARCY FROZE IN HIS STEPS.

"It could not be," he whispered to his foolish heart. He returned to Pemberley a day early to make the final arrangements for the surprise he meant for his sister. He left Georgiana in the care of his friend, Charles Bingley, and Bingley's sisters. Darcy experienced a twinge of guilt at his expecting Georgiana to contend with Caroline Bingley and Louisa Hurst, but Miss Bingley's effusions sorely wore Darcy's patience away, and so he made his excuses.

Upon arriving at his family's home, he cut across Pemberley's parkland to come forward from the road, which led behind it to the stables. Upon his approach, Darcy noted the unmarked carriage before the estate. Recognizing the possibility of visitors in the common rooms, he remained in the shadows, meaning to enter the private quarters through the back entrance; yet, the appearance of a young woman upon the rise leading to the river brought Darcy to a stumbling halt. From a distance, the woman had the look of Elizabeth Bennet, but he did not approach. Darcy acted the fool previously and refused to be found wanting again.

Perhaps a month after his disastrous proposal to Miss

Elizabeth at Hunsford Cottage, Darcy spotted a young lady entering Hatchard's Books, and without thinking, he followed her.

"Miss Elizabeth," Darcy said as he came up behind her, but when the woman spun around to greet him, the lady was not the woman whose being haunted Darcy's thoughts for almost a year.

The girl's forehead furrowed in confusion.

"Pardon me, Sir. Do we hold an acquaintance?"

Darcy bowed stiffly.

"It is I, miss, who begs your pardon. From behind, I thought you a long-standing acquaintance." He stepped back to widen the distance between them. "I apologize for the inconvenience."

The girl's frown line deepened.

"Yet, you called me by my Christian name."

The tone of the girl's voice spoke of her suspicions.

Darcy swallowed the blush of embarrassment rushing to his cheeks.

"If you are also an *Elizabeth*, it is purely a coincidence," he insisted.

"I am."

Darcy rushed his apologies when he spied a matron marching to the young woman's rescue.

"Then I am doubly apologetic. My actions placed you in an awkward position. Please forgive me."

He held enough experience with Society mamas to know when to make a speedy exit.

During his return to Darcy House, Darcy silently cursed his inanity for stumbling into what was a most humiliating situation. Later, in his study, he admitted to the empty room, if not to himself, that he missed looking upon Elizabeth Bennet's animated countenance.

"If it were she," Darcy warned his conscience, "Miss Elizabeth would have, in all probability, presented me the direct cut. The lady spoke quite elegantly upon her disdain, and you are imprudent to think your letter would change Miss Elizabeth's mind. Accept the fact the woman is not for you."

And so when Darcy noted another lady possessing Elizabeth's likeness upon the streets in the warehouse district of Cheapside a fortnight later, he turned away with the knowledge that as a gentleman's daughter, Miss Elizabeth would not be found in Cheapside.

He strove to convince himself that he would soon replace Elizabeth Bennet's charms with that of another.

Belatedly, realizing he studied the woman standing upon the rise longer than was proper, Darcy slipped through an open patio door to escape the vision of Elizabeth Bennet at Pemberley, which so often followed him about. It was deuced frustrating to look for the woman wherever his steps took him.

"Leave it be," Darcy chastised as he crossed the drawing room only to be brought up short a second time by the appearance of his housekeeper.

Mrs. Reynolds caught at her chest in evident surprise.

"Mr. Darcy," she gasped. "I did not realize you returned, Sir."

Darcy caught her elbow to steady the stance of his long-time servant. Mrs. Reynolds came to Pemberley when he was but three. She, Mr. Nathan, his butler, and Mr. Sheffield, his valet, all knew the Darcy family's employ for over twenty years.

"I noted visitors, and as I was not dressed properly, I thought to avoid the necessary greetings," he explained.

"I just this minute turned them over to the gardener," Mrs. Reynolds assured.

Darcy swallowed the question rushing to his lips.

"Very well. Then I am free to seek the privacy of my quarters."

"Yes, Sir." Mrs. Reynolds glanced toward the entrance hall. "Should I ask a footman to bring up bath water, Sir?"

Darcy nodded his agreement. Again, he fought the urge to ask of the estate's visitors, but Darcy chose not to punish his pride with false hopes.

"Has Miss Darcy's gift arrived?"

"Yes, Sir. As you instructed I placed the instrument in Miss Darcy's sitting room. It fits perfectly. Miss Georgiana will know such joy."

He smiled with the woman's kindness.

"My sister deserves a bit of happiness. After my ablutions, I mean to view the arrangement personally."

"Very good, Sir." Mrs. Reynolds started away to do his bidding. Yet, despite his best efforts, Darcy called out to her.

"Yes, Master William. Is there something more?"

Darcy's eyes searched the staircase where he often imagined Elizabeth Bennet standing. Such yearning swelled his chest that he experienced difficulty breathing. *It is best not to know*, he cautioned his wayward thoughts.

"Would you tell the footman I will require his assistance in dressing. Mr. Sheffield and my coach will arrive later this evening."

"Certainly, Sir."

"And you and I should speak before Mr. Bingley's family arrives. Miss Bingley did not enjoy the vista from her guest room when last the Bingleys were here."

A scowl of disapproval crossed his housekeeper's features. Darcy knew many of his servants prayed he would not take up with Caroline Bingley. He expected if he were to act so foolish, he would receive a large number of resignations from his staff.

"Perhaps before supper, Sir," Mrs. Reynolds said stiffly.

Darcy nodded his approval, and the lady strode away; yet, he whispered to her retreating form.

"Have no fear. Only one woman knows my approval as the Mistress of Pemberley." Darcy chuckled in irony. "And it remains unfortunate that even Pemberley's grandeur could not entice the lady to overlook its master's shortcomings."

Mr. Darcy's housekeeper consigned Elizabeth and her aunt

Excerpt from *Elizabeth Bennet's Deception: A Pride and Prejudice Vagary*

and uncle over to the gardener, who met them at the hall door. As they followed the man toward the river, Elizabeth turned to look upon the gentleman's home. For very selfish reasons, she opposed her aunt's suggestion of the tour of Mr. Darcy's estate, but Elizabeth was glad she came. In her future daydreams, she would picture him on the grand staircase.

If Elizabeth, when Mr. Darcy gave her the letter he wrote in *clarification* of his actions, did not expect it to contain a renewal of his offers, she formed no expectation at all of its contents. But such as they were, it might well be supposed how eagerly she went through them and what a contrariety of emotions they excited. No one observing her progress could give voice to her feelings. With amazement did she first understand that Mr. Darcy believed any apology to be in his power; and she steadfastly denied that he could possess an explanation, which a just sense of shame would not conceal.

With a strong prejudice against everything he might say, she examined his account of what occurred at Netherfield. She read with an eagerness, which hardly left her power of comprehension, as well as from an impatience of knowing what the next sentence might bring, so much so she could not attend to the sense of the written lines before her eyes. Mr. Darcy's belief of Jane's insensibility Elizabeth instantly resolved to be false, and his account of his real objections to the match brought such anger that she could not declare his actions just. The gentleman expressed no regret for acting upon his beliefs, at least none, which satisfied her. Elizabeth declared his style lacking in penitence, instead of naming it haughty and prideful and insolence.

But Mr. Darcy's account of his relationship with Mr. Wickham bore so alarming an affinity to Mr. Wickham's own narration of the events that astonishment, apprehension, and even horror, oppressed her. Elizabeth wished to discredit it, but every line proved that the affair, which she believed beyond the pale, could name the gentleman entirely blameless throughout the whole.

In hindsight, Elizabeth grew absolutely ashamed of her accusations. Of neither Darcy nor Wickham could she think without feeling she was blind, partial, prejudiced, and absurd.

"I acted the harpy," Elizabeth whispered as she implanted the image of Pemberley upon her mind.

When her relatives insisted upon touring the estate, Elizabeth convinced herself that viewing Mr. Darcy's property would prove just punishment for the pain she caused the gentleman.

"Of all this, I might be mistress," she reminded herself with each new discovery of how easily she and Mr. Darcy could suit. They held similar tastes in architecture and décor. "So different from his aunt's ornate presentation at Rosings."

And so, although Pemberley's gallery sported many fine portraits of the Darcy family, Elizabeth searched for the one face whose features she wished to look upon again. At last, it arrested her, and Elizabeth beheld a striking resemblance to Mr. Darcy, with such a smile upon his lips as she remembered to sometimes see when he looked upon her. The viewing brought Elizabeth instant regret for she recognized the honor of Mr. Darcy, which led her to consider his regard for her with a deeper sentiment of gratitude than she ever admitted, even to herself.

Elizabeth wished she could tell Mr. Darcy that she found Pemberley "delightful" and "charming," but she quickly deduced the gentleman would assume her opinions mischievously construed: Mr. Darcy would think her praise of Pemberley a device to elicit a renewal of his proposal.

"Better this way," Elizabeth whispered as she turned to follow her aunt and uncle further into the woods. "I have memories of Pemberley, and no one is the wiser of my presence under Mr. Darcy's roof."

Unable to quash his curiosity any longer, after supper, Darcy sent for Mrs. Reynolds.

"Yes, Sir?"

The lady curtsied from her position inside the open door to his study.

Darcy motioned her forward.

"Would you see there is a vase of yellow roses placed upon the new instrument in Miss Darcy's quarters."

Mrs. Reynolds' countenance relaxed.

"I asked Mr. Brownley for fresh cuttings previously, Sir."

Darcy nodded his approval.

"I should not think to instruct you on providing for Georgiana's pleasure. You have been an exemplary member of Pemberley's staff for longer than I can remember."

The woman blushed at Darcy's kindness, but she kept a business-like tone.

"I also aired out the green bedchamber for Miss Bingley's use. I pray that will serve the lady's purpose."

Darcy understood Mrs. Reynolds' poorly disguised question.

"You may inform the staff I hold no intention of seeing Miss Bingley in the family quarters. The green chamber is close enough."

Mrs. Reynolds closed her eyes in what appeared to be a silent prayer of thanksgiving.

"Will that be all, Sir?"

Darcy's heart raced, but he managed to pronounce the necessary words.

"Did we have more than one set of visitors today? Thanks to your efficiency, I so rarely encounter the estate guests, but I would not have you beset upon. Your first duty is to the running of Pemberley."

"No, Sir. Mr. and Mrs. Gardiner were the only ones we accepted in well over a week. It is no bother: I am proud of Pemberley."

"Mrs. Gardiner," Darcy's mind caught the name and rolled it through his body like a tidal wave striking a ship. *If the lady he observed was Elizabeth, had she married? Had she thought to compare what she earned to what she lost?*

Darcy's mind retreated from the possibilities, but he could not quite quash his fears.

"A young couple then? Perhaps on a holiday?"

Mrs. Reynolds shook her head in denial.

"Mr. and Mrs. Gardiner would be the age of your late parents. I overheard Mrs. Gardiner tell her niece a tale of the village oak. It sounded as if the lady spent part of her childhood on the London side of Lambton."

"Her niece?" Darcy's mind latched onto the one word in his housekeeper's tale that rang with hope.

"Yes, Sir. A fine young lady. Very kind to her aunt, offering her arm to Mrs. Gardiner's support. I believe the lady held an acquaintance with you. She and her aunt held a private conversation when they spotted the miniature of Mr. Wickham on your father's mantelpiece." Mrs. Reynolds' shoulders stiffened. "I am sorry to report, Sir, I could not give Mrs. Gardiner a civil account when she asked her niece how the young lady liked it. In truth, I quickly turned the conversation to your miniature."

"I appreciate your loyalty," Darcy said with a wry smile.

"My respect for the girl increased when she admitted she knew you 'a little' and that she found you 'very handsome,'" Mrs. Reynolds continued.

Darcy's eyebrow rose with curiosity. He hoped perhaps Mrs. Reynolds described Elizabeth Bennet, but he could not imagine Miss Elizabeth's declaring him handsome: The woman abhorred him.

"And how did this conversation come about?"

Mrs. Reynolds blushed, but she did not avoid his unspoken accusation, a sign of her long-standing position in his household.

"Do not look to place blame, Master William. I respect the late master's kind heart and his benevolence toward his godson, but I see no reason to display George Wickham's image in this house. Even the late Mr. Darcy could peer down from Heaven and see Mr. Wickham turned out very wild."

"We will discuss the future of Mr. Wickham's likeness upon another occasion. Speak to me of your conversation with the young lady."

It was Mrs. Reynolds' turn to raise an eyebrow in interest; however, as a well-trained upper servant, the lady swallowed her questions.

"Mrs. Gardiner remarked of your fine countenance when she looked upon the miniature, and then the lady asked her niece whether it was an accurate likeness. I then inquired if the young lady held an acquaintance with you. When she admitted as such, I asked if she found you a handsome man."

"Then, it was Mrs. Gardiner and you who placed words in the lady's mouth," he reasoned.

Darcy felt the female in question likely agreed only to be rid of the conversation.

Mrs. Reynolds blustered.

"The girl's aunt and I stated the obvious," she declared with a tone commonly found among established servants. "But neither Mrs. Gardiner nor I instructed the young lady to search out your portrait in the gallery nor did we lead her to it again and again."

Darcy's heart hitched higher.

"I count no one named Gardiner among my acquaintances. Did you overhear the young lady's name?"

"Her aunt called her 'Lizzy' several times so I would assume it is Miss Elizabeth or Lady Elizabeth."

"Miss Elizabeth Bennet," Darcy corrected.

Remorse at not meeting her today filled his chest. A glance to his housekeeper said Mrs. Reynolds wished an explanation.

"The young lady's parents are neighbors of Mr. Bingley's estate in Hertfordshire. If it is truly Miss Elizabeth, we met upon several occasions. I believe I stood up with her at the Netherfield's ball."

"Then perhaps you might renew the acquaintance," Mrs. Reynolds suggested. "Mrs. Gardiner was to dine with friends before the family moved on to Matlock. I am certain Mr. Bingley would wish to behold Miss Elizabeth again."

An invisible hand squeezed Darcy's heart. Should he risk an encounter with Elizabeth Bennet? Had his letter softened the lady's disdain for him?

"Miss Bingley took a dislike for the Bennets," Darcy offered in explanation. "Mr. Bingley developed a regard for Miss Bennet. His leaving Netherfield was poorly done."

"I am sad to hear it, Sir, but your confidence explains the halfhearted air, which follows Mr. Bingley about these last few months."

Darcy nodded his acceptance: His housekeeper gave voice to what Darcy's pride denied. Darcy sorely wounded his friend by acting in partnership with Miss Bingley in separating Bingley from Miss Bennet. With a second nod, he excused his servant. For several long minutes, Darcy stared off into the emptiness, which marked his life.

"I cannot seek out Miss Elizabeth," he told the rise of expectation climbing up his chest. "Even if the lady might offer her forgiveness, Miss Elizabeth holds no interest in renewing our acquaintance. Furthermore, I do not deserve happiness when I robbed my friend of an opportunity to know it."

"You are very quiet this evening, Lizzy."

Her aunt's friends invited them to dine in the evening, but once they returned to their let rooms, Elizabeth preferred to spend time alone with her thoughts of Mr. Darcy.

"Just a bit tired."

Elizabeth made herself smile at her dearest aunt.

"Then you should retire early," her Uncle Edward declared.

Her aunt ignored her husband's lack of intuitiveness.

"Are you certain what the Pemberley housekeeper said of Mr. Wickham did not upset you? I would venture the woman's loyalty to the Master of Pemberley colored the woman's opinions."

Elizabeth expected her aunt to ask of Mr. Darcy, not of Mr.

Wickham.

"Not in the least," Elizabeth assured. "While in Kent, I learned more of what occurred between Mr. Darcy and Mr. Wickham, enough so to acquit the former of any ill doing."

Aunt Gardiner's interest piqued.

"Would you care to elaborate?"

"I promised my source secrecy."

Elizabeth would like to confide in her aunt and uncle for she wished someone would provide her permission to beg Mr. Darcy's forgiveness, but she dug the pit of regret in which she wallowed.

"As I explained in my letter before I departed for Kent, Mr. Wickham bestowed his affections upon Miss King, and I held no loyalty for the man when I arrived on Charlotte's threshold; therefore, I was free to accept other versions of the events."

Hers was an exaggeration of what occurred, but it held some truth.

"Although I still believe handsome young men must have something to live on, I pity whoever accepts Mr. Wickham's hand."

If only I did not previously express my opinions to the contrary, Elizabeth thought.

"That is quite a transformation," her uncle observed.

"I am only aggrieved that I behaved with foolish disregard for Mr. Darcy. I treated the gentleman poorly."

Her aunt's question came quickly.

"Is this revelation the source of your reluctance in viewing Mr. Darcy's home?"

Elizabeth swallowed the bile rushing to her throat.

"I rejoiced today when Mr. Darcy's housekeeper informed us that we missed his return to Derbyshire by a day. I would not wish to encounter the gentleman. Our last exchange of words was far from pleasant."

"If I knew..." her uncle began.

Elizabeth shook off his regrets.

"I asked the inn's staff of Mr. Darcy's presence at Pemberley before we came to the place."

"We should be on to Matlock the day after tomorrow," her aunt declared. "Even with Mr. Darcy's attendance at Pemberley we are not likely to encounter him. My friends do not travel in the same circles as Mr. Darcy. We shall be gone soon, and the gentleman will know nothing of our coming into his part of the shire.

Made in the USA
San Bernardino, CA
30 October 2015